The Angel with One Hundred Wings

THE
ANGEL
WITH
ONE HUNDRED
WINGS

~

A Tale from the
Arabian Nights

Daniel Horch

THOMAS DUNNE BOOKS

ST. MARTIN'S PRESS ≋ NEW YORK

THOMAS DUNNE BOOKS.
An imprint of St. Martin's Press.

www.stmartins.com

The quote on p. vii is from *The Conference of the Birds* by Farid ud-Din Attar,
translated by C. S. Nott, copyright 1954 by C. S. Nott, and is reprinted by
permission of the publisher, Pir Publications, Inc., Accord, New York.

The poem on p. 199 is from *Harun al-Rashid and the Age of the Thousand and
One Nights* by André Clot, copyright 1986 by Librairie Arthème Fayard,
translation copyright 1989 by Saqi Books, London, and New Amsterdam
Books, by permission of the publisher, Ivan R. Dee.

Library of Congress Cataloging-in-Publication Data

Horch, Daniel.
    The angel with one hundred wings : a tale from the Arabian nights /
Daniel Horch.
      p. cm.
    ISBN 0-312-28418-7
    1. Baghdad (Iraq)—Fiction. 2. Pharmacists—Fiction. 3. Alchemists—
Fiction. 4. Mistresses—Fiction. 5. Princes—Fiction. I. Title.

PS3608.O49445 A38 2002
813'.6—dc21

                                                                2002075915

First Edition: December 2002

10   9   8   7   6   5   4   3   2   1

FOR MY PARENTS

ACKNOWLEDGMENTS

I am deeply indebted to the friends abroad who opened up their homes to me. Among many others, I am grateful to Hicham Rashid, and to Jamaa, Omar, and Fatima Oulachguara. For their kindness in different ways, I'm also grateful to Elijah Aron, Winsome Brown, Christopher Caines, Richard Derus, Jori Finkel, Ethan Gold, John Hodgman, Dianna Ilk, Elizabeth Johnson, Paul LaFarge, Dara Mayers, Richard Nash, Joe Regal, Jennifer Rich, Simon Romero, Frances Sackett, Rachel Samuels, and Raymond Scheindlin.

Last but not least, I'd like to thank my agent, Michele Rubin, and my editor, Pete Wolverton.

A man who loved God saw Majnun sifting the earth of the road and said: "Majnun, what are you looking for?" "I am looking for Laila," he said. "But Laila is a woman," the man said. "How can you hope to find her there?" "I look for her everywhere," said Majnun, "in the hope of finding her somewhere."

Sheik Yusuf of Hamadan said that all that which is seen, in the heights or in the depths—each atom, in fact, is another Jacob asking for news of his beloved Joseph, whom he has lost.

—Farid ud-Din Attar

THE ANGEL WITH ONE HUNDRED WINGS

After death, we are told, after Resurrection and the Last Day, we must all try to cross a bridge. Darkness extends above and on all sides, so that the world is a black vault; smoke rises from below. There is nothing to be seen, not a star and not a cloud, nothing except the bridge, the smoke, and a point of light that glitters in the distance—and that point is Paradise.

The good will fly over the bridge like lightning, led by the Prophet who shines like the sun. Yet when a sinful man steps forward, his feet will open and bleed, for the bridge is finer than a hair and sharp as an assassin's wire. As the sinner stands and sways upon the road to Paradise, heat sears his skin, smoke chokes his lungs, and the bridge itself cuts deeper and deeper into the soles of his feet. He cries out in agony and finally falls into the darkness, where he will cry forever.

They say too that between Heaven and Hell is a wall, meant for certain believers who have done evil and unbelievers who have done good. Able to see both the pits of Hell and the gardens of light, these reprieved ones will wait on top of this wall for centuries, until God releases them. Where does this wall lie, I wonder? It must be on the far side of the bridge, I think, just before the gates of Heaven. From what other place could one see both the light and the darkness? But how will this man, neither good nor evil, cross over the bridge? Being impure, surely he cannot travel with the Prophet, and so his passage will be neither easy nor swift; but since the Most Merciful God still considers him worthy of salvation, surely too this man must approach Heaven.

There are merchants who have traveled the world, sons of the earth who have sailed to China and India, the Greek empire and the Western kingdoms. When they return to the City of Peace, they bring not only furs and spices, swords and silk; they also bring stories. The Franks, one story goes, wear black to mourn their dead. For them black is the color of evil, and they believe that death is evil.

At first, I thought that my informants must have misunderstood. I know Christians here, and I know that their religion also tells them that death is no evil. Yet traveler after traveler has given the same report: the Christians of the West wear black to mourn. It is a beautiful custom, I think, one that could speak to my own heart that has so often feared death, but I still know that the old song speaks truth: "White is the true color of mourning. What mourning is sadder than the whiteness of hair?"

I am an old man. My friends have all left me except for one, and that one, the truest one that I had and the one whom I loved the most, I have risked my life in order to betray.

My beard is not as white as it once was. When I was younger, trying to win the dignity due a wise man rather than the envy due a shrewd one, I dyed it the color of snow. I kept my reputation for wisdom for many years; when I walked in the street, men bowed to me. "The ink of the scholar," said the Prophet, "is worth more than the blood of martyrs." All knew that the sultan had showered me with honor; all knew that I was the one man in the empire with whom he still played chess.

"What is this life," says another song, "but loving and surrender, to the drunkenness of wine and pretty eyes?" Those verses never pleased me. My own life has been free of wine, and I have known but one woman. "What is this life but surrender," I thought instead, "surrender to drunkenness and

eyes?" For years and years, I have submitted to the eyes of
others. In the last few weeks, though I still have not tasted
wine, I have given myself up to a drunkenness that at moments has felt holy. Death could come at any instant, but I am
no longer full of fear. I am eager to live.

Tonight I sit in my library. The gates of my villa are
barred, my servants are in their quarters, and my wife is in
hers. The room is luxurious, with tapestries, sofas and soft
cushions, silk carpets from Persia and Armenia; but I am still
most comfortable sitting on the floor, on a worn wool carpet
that my wife wove, half a century ago. A gold lamp lights my
paper, brought from Samarkand in dainty bundles of twelve
sheets; a yellow ribbon holds the sheets together. When I am
done writing a bundle, I shall roll it up and place it in a leather
sheath, where it will await the eyes of a man who may choose
never to look at it. I am lucky, so lucky that men now stare
rather than bow when I walk in the street, but from this day
on, I shall always wear white.

It is now forty-five years since the previous sultan decreed
a new capital for his new empire and I bundled my terrified
family onto a caravan bound for it. My fortune went to buy
a stretch of mud in the new "city": a sea of tents encircling
mounds of bricks, swarms of donkeys and camels and men, a
few half-finished mud houses with timbers reaching up to the
sky. Workers deepened irrigation ditches into canals; baskets
hoisted men and bricks high up into scaffolding, behind which
the Great Mosque and the Palace of the Green Dome took
shape before my dazzled eyes. I had never seen a house with
more than two stories; I had never lived in a land where water
was so plentiful that men let it flow freely, day and night.

I soon had servants who scattered beyond the ever-
growing city to gather herbs and flowers. Others roasted powders, boiled syrups, distilled aromatic baths, and mixed lotions.

One assistant ran my shop inside the inner city; others ran my booths in more distant markets, in the bazaars of medicine and the bazaars of perfume. I became the most famous pharmacist in the city, and I made even more money from perfumes; everyone, man and woman, had to wear scents that came from my shop. The fragrance hardly mattered, so long as the ingredients came from distant lands: ambergris from whales, my lady, gathered at great expense and danger by fishermen in China; this frankincense is from the Holy Land, my lord, who knows if the Prophet Himself did not step upon the ground in which it grew; and of course, my lady, I use only dried rose petals from India, where the flowers are more fragrant. . . . I often doubted that the rose petals and fragrant clumps that my agent bought in Basorah had originated anywhere other than Basorah, but if my customers did not ask questions, why should I?

Once established, I was more merchant than pharmacist, and for the past fifteen years I have done no real work; until recent events my time went to that fantastic ambition, turning lesser metals to gold. Yet every few days I still walked into my storeroom, where I picked out a few simple plants. One day I might take sebesten, cassia, and raisins to my laboratory, where I then brewed cough syrup in a furnace meant to melt lead. When longer occupation was desired, I could instead take flaxseed, vetch and almonds, pine cone, lily root, and gum arabic. The advantage of those ingredients was that besides boiling and crushing, which I did regularly for alchemy's sake, I had also to peel the root and crack the almonds.

When I retreated from pharmacy to alchemy, I retreated too from the company of men. No longer did I buy and sell, diagnose and consult; no longer did I go to the baths and to banquets, hoping to ingratiate myself with customers; no longer did I host dinners where servants hurled rose petals into the air, red slivers that then drifted down from the night, falling upon my nose and mouth, my eager eyes and wise white beard. For the past fifteen years I have spent my days alone, amidst furnaces and stills, mercury and sulfur, coal and ashes. I do not know if solitude was what I wanted, but I certainly did not want any more buying and selling, flattery and stratagems, insinuations and outright lies. I had no time for rose petals. I had grown tired.

There were two exceptions to my solitude, both remarkable for a pharmacist son of a rope maker, born to a humble tribe in a small village. One was the sultan himself, the Commander of the Faithful, the shadow of God upon this middle world. The other was Prince Abulhassan Ali of Persia, son of Abu Bakr, descendent of the men who had once called themselves kings of kings. Ironically, I met the prince through one of my submissions to the eyes of others.

Even after I had abandoned pharmacy, I continued to go to my shop every day, after afternoon prayer. There I greeted and sometimes served prestigious customers, but most of my visitors were young men from the empire's best families. "Seek ye knowledge, though it be in China," said the Prophet, and our young men are told to seek the conversation of older, wiser ones. More than any real knowledge, the sultan's favor proved my wisdom. My simple life and cautious words also gave me an aura of strict, old-fashioned village morality.

We sat on the thick carpets and soft cushions that I had bought for customers, and I explained Aristotle and Democritus, the humors that make up a man's body and the elements that make up the world. Sometimes too the conversation drifted to more general topics. What is virtue? Does free will exist? Was the Holy Book created by God, or is it coeternal with Him? Virtue I would happily discourse on, but religious controversy could be dangerous; almost every month there was some brawl in the street, or even a riot. Obey God, the sultan, and your father, I told my pupils; believe the word of God and leave foolish questions for the foolish. Be generous; live moderately; let your parents choose a wife for you, and have no more than one.

I should have enjoyed these discussions, but I soon realized that most of the young men cared nothing for my thoughts. They were there out of obligation, and after a few months, I was too; it would be awkward to turn away such powerful lords.

When the Prince of Persia first came to my shop, he had just the beginnings of a beard. He sat down with the others, but after a few moments, I felt his gaze upon me. When he spoke, his questions and comments were clearly chosen to win my approval. His father had died when he was an infant, I knew; his sudden affection was flattering, but it made me nervous.

One evening, the prince begged me for the honor of a private conversation. I assumed that his question was medical; over the years other young men had come to me in secret, seeking cures for shameful diseases.

The prince's dilemma was different. A few days before, he had asked the sultan to let him join the war against the Greeks. The sultan had refused.

"Why, my lord?" he asked me. "Why did his majesty refuse?"

Although Persia was ruled by a governor, and the prince had no real power, his name was still sacred to the empire's many Persian subjects. If he ever attained a position of influence, he could inspire a revolt as no other man could. I also knew, though this I did not tell the prince, that if his father and grandfather had not served the sultan so loyally, he surely would have died of a "mysterious disease" when he was a child.

The prince frowned, then began to pace about my library; he swung his arms about with a frantic air. "I can understand," he said. "I suppose I can't even blame him." He stopped pacing and turned to me. "But if the sultan will never permit me any real responsibility, then what am I supposed to do with my life? Please, my lord, advise me."

It was quite a question, I felt, to ask an old pharmacist. I could have responded as I did in my shop—run your estates with care, marry, and raise brave sons—but I sensed that he wanted more than that from life in this world. I shook my head.

"My lord prince, I don't know."

He looked at me a moment. "And you, my lord," he said softly. "You and your family have suffered greatly from war, have you not?"

I stared. "Yes. How did you know?"

He broke into a boyish grin; he was pleased that he had guessed right. "From what you said over the last few days, when we talked about war. I just knew it." Then, although he barely knew me, the Prince of Persia took my hand, gnarled and withered from years in the laboratory. "You are a man who has suffered much, my lord, and because of that you are wise."

Soon after, he again came to me. I hastily washed the coal and ashes off my hands, doused my beard in perfume to hide the stench of sulfur, and changed into a fresh robe, but it was still evident that he had brought me out of my laboratory. "Forgive me, my lord," he said, "for disturbing you in your important work. I beg your mercy to forgive me, when my own merits do not deserve it. I did not know that you were occupied, but a less foolish man than I would have guessed it. Please pardon a callow youth his thoughtlessness, and permit me to leave immediately. Let my foolishness serve as my excuse, and let my shame be proof of my respect for your lordship."

"Stay, my lord prince, I beg of you. An interruption such as yours is like sudden shade during the midday sun, and I only regret that my idle pastime kept me from greeting your lordship more quickly. I hope that my lord will honor my home by taking some refreshment, and I pray that he will grant me the boon of his company for the rest of the morning."

"No, my lord, I am too shamefaced to remain in your presence any longer. Your kindness only increases my awareness of my lack of merit. Please permit me to depart, my lord, leaving with you only my esteem, my apologies, and my readiness to be of service to your lordship."

So it went, back and forth, the game of manners which had long ago tired me—except that the prince seemed genuinely to regret having interrupted me, and I was truly eager for him to stay, so curious was I to know the reason for his visit.

He finally gave in, and agreed at least to stay long enough to explain what had motivated his visit. He wanted my advice. The previous day he had disguised himself and gone wandering about the poorer parts of the city, as the sultan himself had once done. "But, my lord, people look at me and are suspicious. When I try to talk to them, they become frightened." He bowed his head. "I am deeply ashamed that I have interrupted your work for such a trifle, but I had thought that you, with your wisdom and experience, might be able to explain to me my errors."

It was an unusual request, but I found that I was both

flattered and intrigued. "How are you disguising yourself, my lord prince?"

"As a porter, my lord."

I nodded. "Sit down, my lord prince, I beg of you this honor."

"My lord . . ."

"Not another word, my lord prince. I shall be offended if you refuse my hospitality."

We sat down. My salon for guests had rich carpets and embroidered sofas; the wooden grates on the windows were carved into floral patterns that let in light and air but maintained privacy. "My lord prince," I told him, "perhaps you would do better as a merchant. A silk merchant, or a dealer in carpets or some other merchandise of value. Your hands are too soft for a porter's, your speech too refined for a man unused to frequenting the houses of the great."

He lifted up his hands and stared at them. "Yes. Of course."

We gradually abandoned our formal tone. We talked about how men who are neither princes nor rich merchants live, and I remembered my own humble youth. How had the prince guessed that I really did know how poor people lived? We talked about discretion and feigned indifference, the indirect ways in which men communicate. It was his idea to complete his disguise with a Persian accent, so that he could pretend to be newly arrived, ignorant of our customs. As evening fell, my wife brought in cups of her famous sorbet: she made it with ice brought in from the caves outside the city and a mix of fruits whose recipe was more complicated than many of my medicines. "Prince Abulhassan," I said, "my wife, Fatima." For a moment the prince was too surprised even to stand up—my own wife and not a servant was bringing in refreshment?—but then he quickly bowed and tried to kiss her hand; she nimbly withdrew it from his grasp and waved him away.

And then, to the prince's utter bewilderment, she stayed. Calm in her plain cotton robe, she watched the Prince of Persia and me, who were both dressed in rich silk; gold thread embroidered our turbans and spelled out verses from the Holy Book upon the sleeves of our robes. My wife was unveiled, since it was her own house and she was too old to fear for her modesty. She looked at the prince and at me with a smile in her eyes that only I could see. I smiled back. "Would you like to sit with us, Fatima?"

The prince stared at me. Still silent, my wife shook her head. I turned back to the prince. I was happy at her presence, which had become rare in my life, but he was shocked at her presence in a conversation of men. "Fatima is my wife," I said simply.

He stood up and bowed again; she again waved to him to sit. "My lord prince," I said. "What part of the city do you next plan to visit?" He eyed my wife quickly, then turned to me. "Perhaps the street of the carpet weavers." He smiled. "I ought to learn my new profession." We talked about how a carpet merchant might approach the weavers, and as the conversation progressed the prince forgot my wife, who remained silent. A moment later I sensed that she had gone. She had not said a word and now had returned to her own occupations, but her sorbet tasted even sweeter than usual.

Disguised as a carpet merchant, the prince went to boxing matches and cock fights; he visited taverns and wandered along the docks on the river, bargaining over newly arrived merchandise. He wandered through the central bazaars, with their brick streets and iron gates, and he saw the outer bazaars too, where poor merchants just spread out their goods on a carpet, beneath the open sky. He visited the bazaar of men, where laborers gather in the hope of a day's employment, and he visited the street of women, where fallen souls offer their services for the night. He left the city to see the fields that peasants had abandoned to flee the tax farmer, and on his way home he met a band of "flesh eaters," as such gangs are called: the groups of idle, landless men who extort money from merchants. He gave them his purse and his horse and had to walk back to the city. After each adventure, he came to me. He described what he had seen, and he asked my help in understanding. I sometimes felt as if I were traveling with him, having adventures in parts of the city that I too did not know.

While we talked my wife often came in to bring us some refreshment, then stayed to listen. She never said a word, but I could tell, from a look in her eyes or the way she shifted from one foot to another, whether or not she approved of what I was saying to the Prince of Persia. She approved more often than not. The prince grew used to her presence; he smiled and bowed gallantly when she entered, but she always refused to let him kiss her hand. Fatima has never liked such etiquette.

The prince took a bundle of carpets and spent a month sailing down the river, buying and selling alongside his shipmates. "But I think," he said with a shrug, "that I lost money on every sale." Yet the journey had whetted his appetite; he spoke about leaving his estates for years, perhaps forever, in order to travel. "I want to see the Holy City and the Pyramids," he explained, "the cities of the fire-worshipers and the caravans through the Great Desert. I want to see the ways of the Greeks and the Indians, the nomads and the mountain peoples. I want to see everything."

One night, the day's last prayer was called when the prince was in a tavern in the outer city; he could not make it home before curfew. He told the man next to him that his caravansary was far away. Could he recommend some shelter for the night? The man brought him home. He was a glass-blower who lived with his wife and four children in a single room. The prince shared their humble meal, then slept on a straw mattress beside them on the dirt floor; during the night, in her sleep, one of the little girls curled up against his side for warmth. The prince had never seen such a home, never guessed how, among the poor, husband, wife, and children live side by side, without a harem to divide them. When the next morning he told me of his adventure, I was disturbed: that life of poverty had once been my own. The prince asked about it. It only increased his esteem that I had raised myself up from such poverty, and I found myself telling him memories that I did not even know that I had.

He also looked at my wife in a new way. "My lord," he said, "your noble wife and you . . ."

"Yes," I said. "We used to live in a single room, where she and I, together, prepared our medicines and perfumes. We worked side by side, just like that glassblower and his wife. For many years, we hardly ever spent more than an hour apart."

Yet those years had passed long ago. I now could go days, weeks even, without exchanging more than a few words with my wife. My children too had left home many years before, and now I saw them only on feast days. The prince listened to me talk about my past and seemed to understand; he told me about his present and sought my advice. For years I had taken dinner by myself, amidst my crucibles and stills and ever-hot furnaces. The only exceptions came when the prince sometimes stayed after the others had left, and my wife brought us dinner. It was a gift that, for reasons I did not yet understand, the Most Merciful God had sent me in my old age.

It is true that I never suspected that the danger might come from a woman, but I often worried about the prince. Matters inside the palace are so complicated, so devious, and so deadly that I have never even hoped to understand them, but everyone knew that certain Persians were trying to increase their influence. Aside from the usual governorships and appointments, the throne itself was at stake: the queen's son was heir, but the sultan's first born was the son of a Persian concubine, and everyone knew that the sultan preferred him.

The prince kept aloof from this debate, as did many of his compatriots, who were no more and no less than loyal subjects, but he was still a symbol of Persia. Hostile elements might want to disgrace him, so as to damage the Persian cause. On the other side, many Persians at court did not like the prince's public support of the sultan. The prince's father had also been a grand ally of the throne, and rumor had it that the arrow that killed him had come not from the Greeks, but from our own lines. Our bowmen, of course, are almost all Persian.

When he had first come to my shop, the prince had been fourteen years old, naïve and impetuous. Three years later, he was still impetuous, but he was also thoughtful and compassionate. I had seen him grow from a boy into a man, and I knew that he had grown listening to my words. He and I were both named Abulhassan.

II

Three weeks ago, the prince and I were in my shop, talking after the other young men had left, when we heard a bustle in the courtyard. My servants jumped to stand and then bow; one beckoned me to come to the door, quickly; and then I too bowed deeply.

Shemselnehar had come with ten of her prettiest servants and no eunuch, but as she stepped out of her palanquin, mounted between two donkeys, her words were modest: "Please rise, my dear Abulhassan, you embarrass me."

She stepped into my shop, leaving her servants in the courtyard. I bowed again. "I am deeply honored at your lady's deigning to grace the poor shop of a humble old man. How may I be of service to your ladyship?"

She had come in person, with her whole train of attendants, just to pick up a flask of perfume. While my servants hurried to fetch her perfume, I invited her to go sit in a private room, where my wife would bring her some refreshment.

"Please, Abulhassan, do not insult me by thinking that I have so little respect for your gracious wife as to ask her to serve a foolish girl. It is I who would happily serve her, out of respect for her virtue and her husband, but I have no need of refreshment."

I bowed again at the compliment, and was about to retrieve the flask from my servants, when I decided I had better not move.

The prince had stood up to vacate the seat of honor. He brushed and fluffed the cushion, refusing to let the servant do his job, then bowed so low that his head touched the ground. As Shemselnehar sat he stayed bowed until she bid him rise; he continued to stand at her side, ready for whatever service she might ask.

The prince treated most women with playful familiarity. It was unusual in so young a man, but he was a prince, and he was also handsome, with strong features, a muscular build, and a full black beard. His large mouth grinned easily, his eyes twinkled with mischief, and he generally held himself like a man who sees the world as his toy. A stranger, unaware that he was a great lord, might still guess it from that supreme self-confidence, and yet his playful eyes and ready smile invited you to approach him. Even now, standing chivalrously beside Shemselnehar, his eyes shone and his lips looked ready to burst into a smile.

Shemselnehar's gold-embroidered silk, careless diamonds, and ten servants indicated a woman of rank. Even without knowing her beauty, hidden behind one of her more modest veils, the prince must have deemed her worthy of his most respectful manner. Ignorant of her identity, he did not know his rashness: with Shemselnehar, one bowed deeply and begged permission to leave. Adultery, of course, is punishable by death, and so it was dangerous even to talk to Shemselnehar, who had unprecedented liberties. I have sometimes thought that the real reason why the sultan, wise as he is, does not permit his women to go about without eunuchs is not to protect them. Who would dare seduce the sultan's mistress? With his eunuchs, the sultan is protecting his subjects from rumors that might oblige him, for the sake of imperial honor, to have them banished or killed. But Shemselnehar, his beloved, he shielded only with his subjects' fear, and she walked through this world as if she had the plague: men and women alike kept their distance. Though she was not yet sixteen years old, even powerful lords approached only with the protection of exquisite formality. Never before, I was certain, had a handsome young man stood beside her with playful eyes and the hint of a smile.

Sometimes she played with her power, and refused men permission to leave. She might ask them to recite an obscene poem by Abu Nuwas, or for help adjusting her veil; and she mimed anger when they refused, trembling with fear. Yet never before had I seen her do what she did that afternoon: under the pretense of adjusting her veil, she let it drop from her face. She cried out in mock surprise, but then took a long, calm moment to fix it.

In the moment that her veil was down, I saw wavy, coal black hair, white skin, and a small, red mouth. Amidst delicate bones, her eyes were large and dark.

Veil reattached, she walked over to me. "Is my perfume ready yet, Abulhassan?"

"Yes, my lady." I signaled the waiting servant, who bowed as he approached and thrust the vial into my hand, not daring to give it to her himself. I gave it to her.

She leaned closer, pretending to examine the flask, and spoke into my ear. "Abulhassan. Who is that man?"

I blinked but did not think fast enough, and so I answered truthfully. "My lady, that young lord is the Prince Abulhassan Ali of Persia, son of Abu Bakr."

"The Prince Abulhassan," she said slowly. "I have heard of him. He is the descendant of the former kings of Persia, is he not?"

"Yes, my lady. Since the conquest of that kingdom by the faithful, he and his family have been loyal servants of our lord and master."

She stood still. Hidden behind her veil, her face showed nothing of her thoughts. After a long moment she again whispered in my ear, this time with a tone of decision.

"My lord," she said, "you have given me great pleasure by introducing me to the young prince." My face remained expressionless, but I was afraid. I had not introduced her to anyone.

She turned from me and beckoned to the prince. He approached and bowed. "Rise, my lord prince."

He rose, and Shemselnehar spoke. Her voice was clear but soft, so that my servants could not hear.

"When I return to my palace," she said, "I shall send Mona here, to Abulhassan's shop. My lord prince, she shall bring you and my lord Abulhassan to me. I shall be honored to show you the hospitality of which I am capable."

I was so surprised that I did not even bow. Shemselnehar stood back and looked at me, then leaned forward again, and whispered into my ear.

"Don't fail me, Abulhassan. If you do, I shall be angry with you until the end of my days."

I bowed to the ground. "Queen among women, may God forbid that you ever have the least cause of dissatisfaction with your servant. Your wishes are and always will be my commands."

She placed the vial of perfume into her sleeve. "Thank you, my lord. That will be sufficient." She turned and departed, with her women in train. For a moment we just stood there, silent. I should have been frightened for the prince, perhaps angry at Shemselnehar, but all I could feel was sadness.

"My lord prince," I finally said. "May I invite you into my library?"

He blinked as if waking from a dream.

My villa has three courtyards, each with rooms surrounding a garden. The first courtyard is for my shop, servants, and stable. The second is for my library, laboratory, and storerooms, and I had rooms there for entertaining guests too. The third courtyard is for my wife; it had also been for children, before they grew up and married. I now took the prince through the gate into my second garden, then pushed aside the leather straps that hung in my library's doorway. It had threatened rain in the morning, so my windows too were covered with dark leather. Though it was still bright outside, inside my library I had to light the lamp that hung from the ceiling. Only then, when the lamp swayed gently, casting shadows on my dim walls and carpets, did I turn to face the prince.

Over the years I had hollowed out niches in the mud walls to hold my manuscripts. The prince now stood in front of such a wall, full of rolls of old paper in dusty leather sheaths. He glowed. "Abulhassan . . ."

I held up my hand for silence. In the three years since I had known the prince, he had never let danger give him pause, but this invitation was more than just dangerous.

"Prince, the woman you saw is Shemselnehar, the sultan's favorite. I do not know what game she is trying to play, but I do know that if you accept her invitation, you will likely face death. At the very least, you will be banished. It even seems possible to me that that is her plan, that Nuraddin or someone else in the palace wants a scandal." Nuraddin was the grand vizier, a bitter enemy of the Persian lord chamberlain. It was true that, unlike the sultan's other mistresses, Shemselnehar had never been involved in any intrigue, but how else could I explain this invitation?

The prince sat down. The sofa had been a present from the sultan and was black, the color of the royal family; it looked as if it might swallow up the pale young man.

I bent my head. It was wrong to carry one's heart in one's cheeks as the prince did; it made it hard to look him in the

eyes. At my feet was the carpet that my wife had woven in
our home town, over fifty years before. Its original, heart-red
background had faded to dark pink, but the pattern that Fatima had sewn in black and orange was still clear: palm trees
and the Pyramids, which neither she nor I would ever see.
Like all carpets the women from our town make, it was sturdy
and warm, meant to be slept in as well as trod on. She had
finished it just before our first son was born.

"Abulhassan," he said finally, "I am still going to accept
her invitation. I know that she is not treacherous—that much
I am sure of."

I looked up. His face had regained its confidence, but his
eyes were serious.

I bit my lip. "Whether she is or whether she isn't, what
do you hope to gain? You know that you will never be with
her."

He smiled. "Perhaps. But it was she who invited us—she
must know something that we do not. And I have never, ever
seen a woman like her before. I didn't know that such a
woman could even exist." He smiled wider and shook his
head, surprised at his own feelings. "I know that this is not
love, because you and I have talked about love." He paused,
and his forehead furrowed. He was choosing his words with
care. "I still believe what you once told me, Abulhassan. I
believe that love only comes with time, so this is certainly not
love. But dearest Abulhassan, my whole body is trembling."
He shook his head again. "Because maybe it is love, after all."

I took a breath. "Prince, she is a beautiful woman, but
there are many beautiful women. It's not love that beauty
attracts, but something, something else." I had been about to
say "something lower," but I stopped myself in time; telling
a man that his feelings are not serious only makes him cling
to them. After all, other than emotions what do we have, aside

from things and, for believers, God? I started to say that in a few months he would forget her, but I stopped there too. Who wants to hear that sentiments die?

"Abulhassan," the prince said, "I know that you are the wisest of men and also the kindest, I the most foolish in the whole world, but I have known beautiful women. None has been so beautiful as she, of course, but I also saw something in her eyes, something more than teasing or temptation. There was something hard, but also something sweet and even appealing in her eyes, as if she were asking for help. It was terrible, Abulhassan, that mix of hard and soft—it frightens me even now, as I think of it—but it certainly has nothing to do with Nuraddin or any other kind of treachery." He looked up. "Abulhassan, I've never seen such a look before. Right now, as I try to look at you, as I should be seeing your face, I'm not—I just see the look in her eyes." He closed his hands into fists and banged them together. "I must see her again. Perhaps the sultan is tiring of her."

"No," I said. "And even if he were, you know that she could still never marry another."

His eyes widened. "Yes. She will just be locked up in his harem until he dies. Abulhassan, how many other women are in there now?"

I stared at him. "As far as I know, the sultan is devoted to her, and she to him. And should the sultan tire of her, she will still have wealth and leisure for the rest of her life, even if she can never marry. Most women would envy her."

"No, Abulhassan, you know you don't believe that. I know better, just from the look in her eyes. It's a horrible fate. Doesn't the Holy Book forbid it?"

I shook my head. "Prince, whatever the Holy Book says, and whatever her fate may be, you cannot go see her. You really could die if you enter her palace. You would have your head impaled upon a stake, left on the city walls for the vultures to feed on."

He looked at me. "I suppose I could die." Then he stood up and smiled. "But I won't."

I looked down at my wife's red carpet. Did the prince understand that death was real? When I was a boy, poor as a lizard and hungry each night, I knew that if there was one thing I did not want to risk, it was my life. At fifteen I had abandoned my mother, my shop, and my honor to flee the civil war then raging. The prince was going to risk his life for a woman with whom he'd never spoken. "Only drunkards," Abu Nuwas once said, "understand the language of the rose." The last time I had seen Abu Nuwas was at a royal banquet, shortly before his death. He had put a leather cushion on my seat that made an obscene sound when I sat on it. I had blushed, and everyone's eyes had turned to me.

"Abulhassan, I know it is your duty to try to dissuade me, but I tell you now that you won't succeed." He grinned. "Much as I respect your words, have you ever talked me out of anything that I really wished for?"

It was true. I had often convinced him of a safer way to do something, but never not to do it.

"Besides," he continued, "don't you think that she must have a safe way for us to enter? And even if I were caught, would the sultan really have me killed? So long as she and I were never alone together, and witnesses could attest to it? The sultan may be jealous, but my family is powerful. You know him, Abulhassan. He will not execute me just for this visit."

The prince was right. Despite my talk of heads on stakes, the sultan would have to be lenient. Persia had been restless, and many there thought the prince's family divine. Not even Nuraddin could want the prince executed under such circumstances. The sultan might banish the prince from the capital, but if Shemselnehar's honor remained intact, he would not behead him. Yet what could Shemselnehar be planning?

The thought came to me suddenly: since the prince insisted on going, I would have to accompany him, just as Shemselnehar had ordered. I could make sure that nothing dangerous happened, and for the sultan, I would be the most trustworthy of witnesses. If needed, my presence and then my word would surely ward off banishment. What else could I do? The sultan was traveling just then, I knew, and there was no one besides him to whom I could confide news about Shemselnehar.

Before I could think further, a servant announced that Mona had arrived.

III

When Mona entered, the prince bowed low and remained bowed, waiting for permission to rise as if she were a great lady. Mona giggled. "Your highness can please rise, I'm only a servant girl," she said, but she then bowed prettily herself as the prince rose. When she stood up the prince tried to speak, but it is hard to talk faster than Mona, and she had turned to me. "How are you, Abulhassan? Are you two ready? My mistress is very eager to see you in the palace. As am I."

Originally the queen's servant, Mona had been too silly for Zubaidah. The sultan had guessed that Shemselnehar needed a companion close to her own age, and the two women had become inseparable. Mona wore veils so transparent that they were more provocative than bare skin, but unlike her mistress, she talked to people just because she liked to. She thought Shemselnehar the paragon of all beauty and wisdom; she delighted in her triumphs and encouraged her silliest fancies. I thought that Mona misplaced her admiration, that her warmth and liveliness were more appealing than Shemselnehar's show of cold perfection, but Mona was always happiest when talking about her mistress.

"We are ready, Mona. How are we going to enter the palace?"

"Why, we're going to walk right in the main entrance. How else?"

I closed my eyes. It was certain, then: Shemselnehar had no real interest in the prince; she was allied with Nuraddin or some other faction that I, in my blessed ignorance, did not even know of. In a sense it was a relief, since my presence would keep the prince from any compromising act.

Even though I would tell the sultan everything, I still did not want us to enter the palace openly. The sultan would not want the whole city to know that the prince of Persia had visited his mistress. It might force his hand, which was certainly what Shemselnehar and her ally were planning.

"What's wrong, Abulhassan? Everyone knows that the sultan trusts you completely, the eunuchs won't think to question. Besides, you've been in our palace before."

"With the sultan," I said.

"Exactly!"

"Mona, what reason could I possibly have to visit your mistress in her palace?"

"The truth—that she invited you."

I shook my head. "No. We will come to the palace, but only in secret. I know that that is what his majesty would prefer."

"But . . ."

"Mona, if we do not come in secret, we shall not come. Isn't there a back entrance, onto a canal?"

I insisted, the prince deferred to my judgement, and Mona finally had to yield. She would come for us by boat and hide us inside it. If we were discovered, I was sure the sultan would spare us. He trusted me; I would be able to explain. Together we would invent a story to explain all of this to the public eye, since the sultan too would not want the Prince of Persia involved in scandal. I tried not to think of Jafar, the sultan's friend since birth and then his trusted grand vizier. On a rumor of treason that everyone had considered absurd, the sultan had beheaded him and banished his family.

An hour or so later Mona returned to say that the boat was waiting. We left on foot, since the canal is only a short walk from my villa. In the street, high windowless walls of villas like my own blocked the late afternoon sun, leaving us in twilight; arches crossed over our heads and dangled down lanterns, still unlit. Veiled women rode by on donkeys, and young nobles in shining robes cantered past on horseback. Sweaty porters balanced baskets on their heads, carrying sweet-smelling bread and ripe fruit, fabrics and carpets, or clothes that had been washed in the river and now smelled of soap. Poor merchants in dark, hooded cloaks called out the goods that piled up on the backs of their mules or donkeys: "Aubergines! Almonds! Melons! Freshly picked! Sweeter than honey! A bargain for my lord! A steal for my lady!" A fan merchant, blind so that he could enter the harem, walked by, ringing the bell that only the blind may use. "Fans of silk and fans of feathers," he called out, "the finest fans in the city, from humble and modest Buzurg, the poor blind man."

Mona had come in a wide-bottomed boat, complete with a tent meant to shield Shemselnehar, and now us, from the sun and the eyes of others. The eunuch bowed without comment; the prince took my arm and helped me step into the swaying boat. Although I had no need of such assistance, I also permitted him to help me lie down on the cushions inside. A breeze had picked up, and he asked if I wanted a rug for warmth, but I waved him away. I was strangely calm. The prince had told me many of his adventures, and now I was accompanying him on one. I began to think that it would prove a harmless prank, that when I told the sultan, he and I would laugh about my brief spell as an infiltrator.

The boat drifted slowly down the canal; its sway lulled me. Evening was falling on the City of Peace, and through the tent's flaps I could see the waterfront villas of the rich, among whom I was numbered. Inside those villas, I knew, were gardens, flower beds, fountains, pebble paths, and pools of exotic fish. On the hills above, the capital's innumerable houses flowed into each other in smooth waves, their shimmer broken only by the towers that would soon issue the call to prayer. The white city was turning gold under the setting sun; black banners flapped in loyalty to the sultan. I thought of how I had seen the City of Peace at birth, how it had grown and how my life had grown with it. It belonged to me, and for all my weariness, I knew that I was even fond of the noise in its streets.

Sunset is the busiest time on the canals. The wealthy hurry back to dinner from markets in the outer city; peddlers and poor tradesmen leave the inner city's walls for their homes outside; and barges try to deliver their cargo before curfew. Yet our progress was smooth: barges and gondolas alike made way for the royal boat with the black banner. I drew back from the tent flaps as we approached the palace canal, but remained strangely calm as the boat stopped. Mona and the guards were talking; her voice rose in mock indignation; the guard laughed, and we resumed our journey. We drifted down the canal to the dock, where I heard her dismiss the eunuch, and then the flaps flew open to show her grinning face.

"Land ho, Sinbad. Your highness can come ashore now, if he pleases. I sent Nestor away."

"My lady," the prince replied, trying to stand up in the low tent, "I am not anyone's highness."

"Well, I'm not a lady, so that makes us even. And I can't call you Abulhassan because we've already got one. Come on, climb on up, right here."

I rather regretted having to leave the gently swaying boat, the warm, dark tent out of which I could choose to see nothing. With a sigh, I permitted the prince to help me ashore. The dock was solid teak except for the rails, which were silver. After looking the prince up and down smugly, Mona led the way through a cloakroom and corridor to a small piece of paradise.

Only fifteen feet high at its peak, the dome made the room feel warm and intimate; against a black background, gold calligraphy spelled out the names of God, the Prophet, and the royal family. Rugs, cushions, sofas, and tapestries were all silk and down, gold, black, and scarlet, soft and sensual in the sultan's innermost sanctum. Perhaps still lulled by the boat ride, I only shook my head at Shemselnehar's boldness. I sat down, letting the deep cushions envelop my thin body.

The prince placed his hand on my arm. He was smiling, but I thought that his smile was forced.

"Forgive me, Abulhassan, because I know it is late to ask such questions, but the sultan could walk through the door at any moment, couldn't he?"

I shook my head. "The sultan has gone down the river, inspecting the troops that have returned from Khorasan. He might return this evening, but he only visits Shemselnehar after sending Mesrour to prepare her. It would be best to leave before then, but for the moment, until Mesrour comes, we are safe." I looked to the side. "And I say that we enjoy our dinner." Because the doors had opened on two servant girls, carrying a gold table laden with food.

The prince nodded.

We ate, waited upon by servants as if we had each been the sultan. When we finished they brought a cup of wine for the prince—Shemselnehar knew that I did not drink—followed by two gold basins for us to wash our hands in. Next came a censer of aloe smoke that the servants passed around our robes, then they sprinkled rose water on our hands so that we could perfume our beards. It had been decades since I had used such ceremony. I thought back on the hours I used to spend preening at home and even in the street, where on my way to banquets I proudly tossed money to the men who kept man-tall mirrors under cloth, ready to rent a reflection.

Mona returned, unveiled, elegant, and solemn except for her sparkling eyes. "Follow your humble servant, my lords, if you please." She pulled open a small door I had not noticed; we entered the grand hall.

A hundred feet high, the dome was all blue and white, gold and silver; it made one think of sky and sun, ocean and sails. The room was big enough for jousting, and the carpet was all one piece; gold threads woven with white and red silk as if a gold sea grew lilies and roses. Small clutches of couches around gold, silver, jade or agate tables sprouted up like so many islands, apparently random yet pleasing in their placement. Between each pair of marble pillars a window opened onto the garden, where alleys of differently colored pebbles imitated the carpet's pattern exactly: inside and outside appeared one space. Thick groves of orange trees separated the alleys, and at the end a canal circled the garden, topped by flowers and then cypresses that hid all but the green dome of the sultan's own palace.

I had been in that hall several times before, but never had I enjoyed it so much.

"Won't you please sit down, my lords," Mona said. "The musicians are ready."

We turned to see a dozen singing girls with lutes. We sat, and they began to sing—about love. These were not the obscene poems of Abu Nuwas that Shemselnehar pretended to like; these were the beautiful old songs, the ones old men like the sultan and I had heard when we too were young—I with my wife in my village bazaar, amidst storytellers and rhymers, snake charmers and sword swallowers, as the sun set over the date trees that stood between us and the desert; the sultan in a palace like this one, after a banquet, surrounded by men who pretended to be his friends and women who claimed to love his every gesture. These songs spoke of stars and of night, of fate and of love that conquered all, even pride, even honor; and they woke me out of my lazy pleasure. "Shemselnehar," I thought, "cruelest of the foolish, this is past the limit."

The prince was listening happily but calmly—as if he had expected nothing else. When the musicians finished he stood and bowed, so grave and formal that several of the singing girls smiled. Mona came forward again. As she approached, her solemnity gave way to excitement. "She's coming," she said. "Stand up."

Ten women carried out a solid silver throne that belonged to the sultan. Large doors swung open: unveiled, Shemselnehar entered like a Persian queen in blue and gold silk, diamonds and pearls. She strode slowly, majestically, followed by ten women dressed as royal ladies in waiting. Impressed by her beauty, I was even more scared by her pretension. "This woman," I thought, "is mad enough to get us all killed."

Shemselnehar glittered; the prince went pale. She was not yet sixteen, and her father was a humble wheat merchant, but now she looked a queen; and for the first time since I had known him, the prince lost his courage: he blushed like a child and turned, showing his back to her, which was an insult. I put my hands on his shoulders.

"Prince," I said, "it would have been far better if we had not come, and best of all if you had never seen her. If I could do it all again, I'd do it differently, but now you must show the respect that you owe her. Later on there will be time to turn and leave."

The prince blinked at me, then turned to face her.

She ascended the silver throne and sat down. We bowed. I wondered how often Shemselnehar had prostrated herself where we now stood, proclaiming her submission to the old man to whom the throne belonged.

"My lords, please rise. Your grace in my modest home is a boon for which I can only thank you as my humble means of hospitality allow."

I chose my words with care. "Powerful mistress, respectable, modest, and virtuous woman, more than the welcome you have given us, worthy of the sultan, our lord and yours, your beauty and kind heart are more recompense than any man's service could deserve for its own merits."

Shemselnehar did not respond; her eyes were fixed on the prince. He tried to speak but his mouth would not form the words. He finally bowed again, and when he rose, he smiled: sweetly, sadly, and apologetically. "I wish . . ." he said, and shook his head. "I wish, my lady, that I could be of some service to you." He looked down, miserable. "I am incapable. I am unworthy."

I turned my gaze back to Shemselnehar, and I saw what I had least expected: her dark eyes had become soft; her expression showed compassion.

"My lord prince, why so unhappy? But no, such questions should not be asked." Before my disbelieving eyes she stepped down from the throne, strode forward, and took the prince by the hands. "My lord," she said, "please forgive a poor, silly girl her folly. Do me the honor of sitting with me on this couch, if you so condescend, for am I but a slave, with nothing I can call my own, and you are one of the greatest lords of this land. Sit, I beg of you this grace."

"My lady . . ."

"Sit," she repeated. "I beg of you, my lord. Please."

The prince sat. She sat down next to him.

"Music," she called out, "but without words. And Abulhassan . . ." She turned to me and paused. Her dark eyes were apologetic, her cheeks and brow unhappy. A moment before she had seemed a queen, but now she appeared the fifteen-year-old girl that she was.

"Abulhassan," she said, "my lord. I have never had the honor truly to know you, but you have always seemed to be one of the few kind men in the sultan's court. Perhaps you are even the only one. I am sorry to have involved you in this. I thought . . ." She shook her head. "I really hadn't thought enough, about anything, but I had wanted you to enter openly, with nothing to hide from the sultan. It had to do with the sultan, not with you and not even with the prince. But now . . ." Her eyes dropped. "Now I don't know, but I am grateful that you came in secret. Please, stay here beside us, but let the prince and me talk for a few moments away from your ear."

As I looked at her, I remembered how she had been a year and a half before, when the sultan had first brought me to see her.

We had entered her chambers without warning; she had been only partially dressed. It was just a day or two after the sultan had acquired her, and at the sight of him and another, unknown man she had colored with shame and reached for something with which to cover herself. The sultan had laughed at her shyness. "No need, my love," he said, "no need at all. You can drop that sheet." He clapped his hands. "Drop it, I said. And look up at us. Come on, look up, I said." She dropped the sheet. After a moment, she looked up, her eyes burning with shame and fear. I turned away, but I realized that my refusal to look would anger the sultan. I forced myself to turn back, but my gaze was full of pity that I think she understood. What was it like to be deflowered by an old man whom she had to call "your majesty"?

"She is beautiful, Abulhassan, is she not?"

"Yes, sire. Very beautiful. Let us go."

"Oh, come, you've barely seen her. Turn around, Shemselnehar, let's show my friend just how beautiful you are." He made her turn so that I could see all of her, but I really had to look away, no matter what the sultan thought.

"Sire . . ."

"She is beautiful, isn't she? Look over there, where she's just beginning to take form. Think how she'll be in another year or two, when she is fully a woman."

"Yes."

He stepped forward, took her in his arms, and kissed her in front of me. "Ah," he said, "I can barely tear myself away. I've half a mind to just ask you to leave so that I can stay here with her."

The sultan was not himself. Even without a thought for the girl, he knew me well, and normally would not embarrass me so.

"But no," he said with a sigh. "I must meet Nuraddin and the other counselors. Let us go, Abulhassan. Good-bye, Shemselnehar."

"Good-bye, your majesty. Thank you for the honor of your visit."

We left, and he turned to me. "Well, Abulhassan?"

Of all the men in the empire, I was the only one who might criticize his private life, but even I was wary—he was in such a state of passion. "She is very beautiful, sire. But you know that I am not accustomed to seeing other men's wives unveiled."

The sultan frowned. "Forgive me," he said. "Forgive me, my friend. It was most inconsiderate of me. I am so enamored of her that I think of nothing else. But I am still glad that you have seen her, and that she has met you. I believe that she is going to be an important part of my life, and I wish you to know her. But I am truly sorry that I have shocked you."

His concern was all for me, not for her. To be afraid of your husband at first is the fate of many young wives, but this display to another man was an unprecedented humiliation. Over the months that followed, as I saw real tenderness grow to replace the sultan's initial desire, I had forgotten that first meeting; but as I looked at Shemselnehar sitting next to the prince, inside the palace that the sultan had given her, I knew that she had not. All the pity I had felt on that first day flowed back into my heart. I bowed and accepted her request: I stood back from the couch so that I could still see her and the prince, but could not hear the words that they spoke.

From their gestures and expressions, I could see that she was apologizing; he was reassuring her. The prince spoke earnestly, she smiled and responded, and then they both smiled. They talked rapidly, asked and answered questions, and finally he made some sort of declaration. She blinked and paused, looking at him; then she closed her eyes and, ever so slightly, with the hint of a tremble, leaned forward. The prince did not hesitate: in front of me and all her servants, he took her hand and kissed her on her mouth. I turned away, but I could not pretend that I had not seen it. When I turned back, their hands were clasped and their gazes entwined.

At the kiss the musicians had stopped, but now a few started playing again. The rest soon joined in, but some had turned away to avoid looking at the pair, and many lost the melody, found it, then lost it again; from note to note the whole ensemble verged on collapse. They all stopped with evident relief at the sound of a different music: the call to the day's last prayer.

Shemselnehar and the prince looked up. I stepped forward. "My lady, time is passing. With your leave, the prince and I shall go—now."

She looked at me with confusion, as if she did not know where she was. "A few more moments, my lord."

I had never imagined such a kiss possible. It was perhaps the prince's death sentence. "Shemselnehar, curfew is about to fall. The prince and I will leave this instant."

She blinked, then bent her head. "You are right, Abulhassan, of course. Forgive me. Forgive me please. I don't know what I am doing tonight." She looked around, suddenly remembering where she was. She saw the great palace that belonged to the sultan, with its dome and its walls, its garden and the additional set of walls and gates on the far side of the trees. She saw all the servants who surrounded her and who, like her, belonged to the sultan. "Mona . . ." she began, but she did not finish her thought; another servant had rushed into the room.

"Mistress, Mesrour is at the gate with two other eunuchs!"

Shemselnehar stood up. For a moment she looked bewildered and miserable, as if she had given up all hope in this world; but then decision took over her face, and when she spoke her voice was firm. "I'll meet him outside. Pull the shades down over the windows and tell the servants in the garden to get ready. Mona, take the prince and Abulhassan upstairs to my dressing room and lock the door. Leave them the key and get the small gondola ready." She turned to me. "It will be better if you wait inside the palace until the sultan has left or is asleep. He always arrives with tens of torches. It would be hard to leave undetected." She turned to the prince and took his hands. He pulled her to him and for a dizzy moment I thought they would kiss again, but they just exchanged quick whispers. She turned and hurried away without looking back. Mona beckoned; the prince and I followed.

We left the hall for a corridor, climbed carpeted stairs, sailed down another corridor draped with silk tapestries, and passed through a small wood door hidden behind one of those tapestries. Mona gave the prince the key and slammed the door; he locked it. I sat down and closed my eyes while I caught my breath. Aside from back and joint pain, caused more by alchemical exertions than age, I was in excellent health, but I was not used to moving as fast as I just had. All was blissfully quiet for a moment.

"Abulhassan," the prince whispered. "Have you ever been in love?"

My eyes still closed, I shook my head. "No."

He remained silent; I opened my eyes. He was looking at me intently, but his lips carried a hint of a smile. At a moment like this, how could he smile? "Forgive me, my lord," he said softly, "but I don't believe you."

I stared, and his smile broadened; it was gentle and strangely wise, as if he were the old man and had to take care of me, the younger. "I know, Abulhassan, that now is not the time to talk about love, that we have weightier affairs. But you will admit that for the moment, our fate is not in our hands—we can talk and think as we wish." He gazed at me a moment longer, then stood up and began to pace around the room, swinging his arms with boyish exuberance. "Love," I thought, "love and madness. And me." I shivered. I tried to think of when my wife and I were young, but just then the memories wouldn't come. I watched the prince pace and think, smile and frown until I shook my head, blinked, and noticed the room.

Quilted, too-shiny pink silk covered walls and ceiling. The lantern was stunning, even if made of brass rather than gold, but the tapestries were mismatched: fine calligraphies brushed crude children's hangings. I reached out to feel one naïve pattern, of daisies on a green background; it was wool, and not even good wool. Several mirrors were simple and elegant, but one looked as if the jeweler had been told to fit as many prize diamonds, emeralds, and rubies as he could onto a gold frame. One chest was similarly excessive, but another had sea shells sloppily glued to its surface. I stood up to touch it: beneath the shells it was made of copper, battered and scratched. Above was a cheap piece of parchment inside a magnificent gold frame; in a child's hand, the letters spelled "Marida"—the name of my mother.

There were worn furry red pillows, like those my youngest granddaughter still slept with, and ones with gems layered in a rainbow pattern that made them impossible to lie on. The rug beneath my feet had heavy gold woven through it—uncomfortable and impractical—but another, in black and red wool, was in a peasant style similar to that of my home town; a third was one of the finest samples I had ever seen from Isfahan. The cushion I sat on was regal and elegant, but others were made of rough camel hair. The variety and cost of makeup and perfumes astonished me even though I had sold her most of them; yet amidst the rare dyes and paints were several good luck charms, the kind you buy for half a dirham in dirty old shops, and there was an amulet that I recognized as a "love magnet." I knew those good luck charms well. Religion and reason condemn them as superstition, but before I stopped trying, the most I could ever get my wife to do was hide them from me.

Music started. Surprised at how well we heard it, we both looked around for its source. The prince must have examined the room while I was catching my breath; he stepped over to a curtain, then beckoned for me to join him. Behind the curtain was a small window that looked down onto the grand hall. We pulled back the curtain slightly, knelt, and watched.

Mesrour and Wasif, the chief eunuch and his second, stood to the sides of the gate that led into the grand hall; a dozen other eunuchs spread out along the walls. After a moment, he entered. He was the absolute ruler of the largest empire in the history of man, Commander of the Faithful, wherever they might be, God's shadow upon earth—and he smiled as Shemselnehar prostrated herself before him.

He bent down and took her hands; he helped her to her feet. "Rise, dearest lady. My happiness at seeing you only increases my anger at myself. Affairs of state are affairs of state, but I never should have gone so long without seeing you." He kissed her hand, and then kissed her left hand, which I had never seen anyone do before. She looked at her feet with what the sultan probably took to be shy submission.

"Ruler of my every moment, I am as honored by your presence as I am miserable in your absence."

The sultan laughed and stroked her cheek with his hand. "Enough of that. One day you'll actually convince me that you like me."

"My lord and master, I . . ."

"Enough, I said. Mesrour, take your men outside; I'll spend the night here. Can we have a cup of wine, Shemselnehar? And do you have a concert prepared? But why are the shades all drawn?"

With her head still bowed, she took his hand and led him to the throne. It had been moved to face the garden, or rather the curtains that now hid it.

At fifty-nine, the sultan was a large, powerful man. He wore sumptuous fabrics—that night a burgundy robe with gold patterns, a midnight-blue vest with silver ones, and a white turban—but he wore jewelry only when he sat in state. I had first played chess with him some twelve years before; ironically, that had been several years after I had chosen to withdraw from society in favor of alchemy. I realized with a shudder what thought was going through my mind: aside from the prince, all my other friends were dead. The sultan, the Commander of the Faithful, was my friend.

After motioning to one of her servants, Shemselnehar sat at the sultan's feet. Her face was blank, but did it tremble? It was hard to tell. A girl poured out wine that Shemselnehar refused; the music became louder and faster. As the sultan's smile grew, the music rose and rose, whirled, whipped and spun incomprehensible, frenetic rhythms . . . and then stopped. The curtains flew open. Strung with lanterns, sprinkled with torches and candles, the garden looked as if a magic sky of soft stars and glowing planets had descended and scattered amidst the orange trees; startled birds erupted in song and streaked across the new heaven. The music resumed, soft and melodious.

Smiling from ear to ear, the sultan stood up to watch; then he looked down at the woman who still sat at his feet. The sultan is a man burdened by his responsibilities; I had never before seen such childlike joy on his face. "Shemselnehar, each time I see you, you find a new way to delight me. My worries have always vanished at your sight, and I have tasted paradise in your arms; but never before have you shown it to me. Come, stand up, my love, and let me thank you as I can, if not as you deserve."

Still looking down, Shemselnehar put both hands on the ground and clumsily moved up to a crouch; with a wobble she placed one hand on the throne, pushed herself up a little more, and then fell into the sultan's arms, apparently unconscious.

As we watched through our tiny round window, the music fell to cacophony and then silence, women screamed, and the sultan boomed out for a doctor, for all the doctors in his empire. Servants and eunuchs ran here and there, bringing wine, smelling salts, and hot cloths. There was a knock on our door.

I made a move to stand but the prince stopped me with a hand on my shoulder. He put his finger to his lips. I nodded.

The knock repeated. "It's me, Mona," Mona whispered. "Open up, quick."

The prince opened the door. Mona grabbed his hand, scared and serious. "Come quick, the boat's ready now."

"Are you sure . . ." the prince began.

"It's now or never, prince. Hurry."

"Is she . . . ?"

"She's fine, she's just pretending. I'll come to Abulhassan's shop tomorrow and tell you everything. If God pleases. But now come with me, quick!"

In a moment we were back at the dock, but instead of Shemselnehar's boat an unmarked gondola awaited us. "Get in, and Nestor will cover you up. Pole slowly, Nestor! Or no, pole fast, say you're getting medicine from Abulhassan!"

Mona disappeared. We stepped into the gondola and lay down on our backs. Blackness fell as a damp canvas dropped down to cover us; it pressed against our skin, forcing warm breath back into our faces. The boat began to sway as Nestor's pole entered and left the water, entered and left it with strong strokes. We would be at the palace canal's guardhouse in a moment.

"Ho, Nestor! Where to at this time of night?"

"If you're getting wine, don't tell us, we're on duty."

"Not wine, medicine! Open the gate, quick! Shemsel-nehar's fallen sick in the sultan's arms and everyone's in a panic. I'm off to Abulhassan the pharmacist's!" But they had already started to pull back the gates. The gears cranked, pulling the bars through the water. The boat swayed; water slopped onto my face and I nearly coughed.

We were lying side by side, our inside shoulders touching each other and our outside shoulders pushing against the boat's sides. The black canvas covered us like a shroud, suffocating and increasingly hot from our breath and bodies. The sultan's guards stood only a few feet away, and it seemed to me as if our breathing were impossibly loud, that the guards had to hear it; I could certainly hear them breathing, panting as they turned their pulleys. Nestor was talking loudly about the chaos inside, how they probably didn't need any extra medicine but the sultan was in a frenzy. The thin boat swayed and swayed; water trickled over the sides onto our arms and legs.

I heard Nestor's pole strike the canal's bottom; with a shudder, we started moving. "God speed, Nestor!" "God speed!" After a moment, I pulled down the canvas to let in a little fresh air, and listened.

I expected to hear only Nestor's soothing stroke; after curfew the City of Peace is silent. There were times when I missed the old days, the late-night peddlers, the parties in the streets and canals; but the sultan's decree had its advantages, among which was quiet. That night I heard music, faint but unmistakable, and a woman's shriek that soon blended back into the hum. The music was getting louder: new songs, fast, tricky dance rhythms . . . strange accompaniment for an old man in a floating, swaying coffin, escaped from what the sultan had named the Palace of Unending Pleasure.

"Ho, Boatman! Identify yourself and to shore! In the name of His Majesty the Sultan!"

I heard no reply from Nestor, only his pole strokes, still regular but faster than before. The boat rocked from side to side with each of Nestor's strokes; the prince and I rolled with the boat. I felt as if I were hammered into a barrel, and increasingly queasy. The canvas dripped my condensed breath back onto my face as if it sweated; it mixed with my own perspiration and drenched my beard.

"Boatman! This is the royal watch! Stop or be fired upon!"

Nestor's strokes quickened again, and now he gasped. As the watchman called out "Renegade boat on the New Canal!" I pushed away the canvas—just in time to feel an arrow whistle past. I pulled the canvas back over us for a moment, then pushed it off again. Carefully, ever so slightly, I lifted my head and turned it around. On the canal's left bank, fortunately far behind us, a watchman shot arrows while his comrade held a torch; even further behind, another torch-lit boat was being launched; and ahead, I saw what Nestor was aiming for: a cluster of boats and gondolas, all strung with lanterns covered with blue, green, red, or yellow silk; in the center was a barge with more colored lanterns and torches. It was a canal party, which meant a host well-connected enough to flout curfew, which meant that he would know both me and the prince. I pulled my head down; the most recent arrow had come from the watchmen's boat.

The music became louder. It drowned out the alarm bell and the watchmen's shouts, but not the occasional arrow's breeze.

Our gondola rammed into another much larger boat, a yacht from the looks of it. "Off!" Nestor croaked, but the prince had already stood up. His movement was too sudden: the narrow gondola rocked and he and Nestor both almost fell over until Nestor managed to grab the rim of the neighboring boat. The prince pulled himself onto the boat, reached down to help me up, then collapsed and retched over the side. I knelt beside him. Nestor broke his pole in half and drove the halves through the gondola's bottom; it sank beneath his feet as his hands grasped the boat's side and pulled his body up. "Stay," I said to him as he clambered on board. "You are my servant, and the prince and I are sick."

He grunted and knelt on the other side of the prince. I stared into the water. The joyful music shrieked at me; the water reflected green, red, yellow, and blue lanterns that danced amidst the sinking gondola's bubbles. Those hypnotic lights, I thought vaguely . . . the angels that they say will question me in my grave. The guard boat's prow dispersed the colored bubbles; harsh white lanterns glared. "Don't move! Royal guard!" I raised my head to see sword-wielding watchmen; my annoyance and bewilderment was only part feigned.

"What is this?" I asked.

"Who are you? What are you doing? Speak!"

"I," I said slowly, "am Abulhassan son of Taher, pharmacist to His Majesty the Sultan, and this is His Worship the Prince Abulhassan Ali, of Persia. Oh, and that," I nodded at Nestor, "is my servant Younes. As to what we are doing, we have been at this party where the prince has, perhaps, overindulged himself, and I am rather queasy myself from the water."

The watchmen had bowed before I finished the prince's name. Their captain spoke. "A thousand pardons, my lords, but we have been pursuing renegades who boarded this very ship. My lord, you must have seen them."

"Well," I said, "I don't know about renegades, but I did see two young gentlemen and a young woman of, well, perhaps not the best of families. They climbed aboard scarcely a moment ago, quite rudely splashing the prince and myself. Our clothes, as you can see, are thoroughly drenched. I did not see their faces, but the men were richly dressed and could hardly climb aboard, they were laughing so. I believe they were drunk, especially since they sank their gondola before climbing on."

The captain bowed again. "I am deeply indebted to your lordship for his observations. With your permission, my lieutenant and I shall board briefly, to make sure there is no disturbance in your lordships' festivity."

"As your duty commands. Younes, give these gentlemen a hand on board."

Nestor reached down to help them up; I put my hand on the prince's shoulder. "How are you feeling, my friend?"

He managed a smile. "I don't know if I can give you a short answer to that, but I am no longer sick. It was a moment of weakness."

I smiled back. "We'll wait another moment. There's no hurry."

I closed my eyes but despite my exhaustion could find no peace; the lutes, flutes and shrill voices of what sounded like hundreds of musicians throbbed inside my head. Of all that I had faced that evening, nothing seemed as terrifying as a giant party where none would suspect me of anything but many would want to shake my hand, to express pleased surprise at my presence after so much reclusion. I would have to explain myself. Any explanation would do; I just didn't feel like talking that much.

Nestor knelt down beside me. "The guardsmen have gone into the party, my lord. I saw an invitation lying on the deck. Qasim, the son of General Harthama, is the host."

I smiled at him. "You are as wise as your namesake. But if you are to be Younes, my servant, then you must call me master, not my lord, although you may speak without my asking you to—I am not harsh."

He nodded and smiled back, his round face mottled like a jester's from the lanterns' colored lights. "Thank you, master."

The musicians burst into a fanfare of cymbals and trumpets; I noticed that the prince was watching me. "Are you rested, my lord?" he asked.

"I suppose I am."

All my joints complained as the prince helped me to my feet, but once I was up my body quieted. I was tired, that was all. I turned to face the party.

The lights on the barge blinded me a moment, but I nonetheless walked towards them, across the boat. As my eyes adjusted I saw that my ears had exaggerated. Perhaps twenty musicians played on a stage before which several women danced, but most of the guests sat on cushions under lanterns that colored them red or yellow or green; they drank wine and talked to each other or to paid women, dressed as if they were ladies. Perhaps some of the other boats were not as empty as the one we had boarded, but decorum was maintained; the groups along the barge's sides were of men only, talking, taking in the night breeze, enjoying the reflections on the water.

We stepped onto the main barge and walked along its edge. Snippets of conversation emerged through the music:

"Why, if Isa isn't put in charge of the Post . . ." (a young man) ". . . Burd's poetry cannot be compared to . . ." (a young woman) ". . . half a million dirhams, at the least, my friend . . ." (an old man) ". . . never been in a monastery, why, you haven't lived! The wine, my dear, those Christians haven't even any debate about it, though a girl like you would have to watch herself with the monks. . . ." The last was from an even older man to an even younger woman, and I paused because I knew him—Yacub, a cotton merchant—but I then went on. I knew him only because my oldest son had business with him; we didn't like each other.

Many men looked up at us, with recognition and then with interest, but none approached us. I had not frequented a party such as this in decades; the prince too only went if the festivities were in honor of the sultan or one of his sons. Our presence was surprising, and out of the corner of my eye I saw men whispering to each other and pointing our way. Qasim, the host, was a grand ally of Nuraddin, the enemy of the Persians.

Cymbals crashed; scattered applause became full as distracted men like myself realized that the musicians had finished a song. I shook my head and clapped a few times. We had been approaching the stage, and the sudden pause in what had been increasing noise surprised me.

"May God be praised! It really is! Abulhassan son of Taher and why, that's . . . that's Prince Abulhassan! Why, bless my eyes and may God shower down his bounties upon the both of you! Abulhassan and the Prince of Persia at a party!" Jibril, a doctor at the royal hospital, took my hand. "What, in the name of the Most Merciful, are you doing here?" He was red and reeked of wine. I imagined his delight was more from novelty than affection; I had only met him two or three times.

After a night of ingenious lying, I found myself unable to

speak, to come up with a laugh, say something about living it up before I died or, no, that wasn't right . . . All I could do was stammer and blush as I looked at the prince, who had evidently expected me to do the explaining, for he now stared at me in alarm.

I heard Jibril draw his breath in suddenly; he had stepped back and was staring at the prince and me as if he had just understood a shocking truth. It took me a moment before I understood what he thought he had understood. Perhaps it was his own inclination? Well, if rumor got about, fathers might forbid their sons my shop, but more likely no one would believe him. I was also beginning not to care what happened the morrow, so long as I slept.

I smiled weakly, a man caught in the act and trying for sympathy. "Jibril, can I count on you? The prince and I will be eternally grateful, and we know how to thank our friends. We hadn't planned to be out so late." I smiled wider and shrugged. The prince suddenly understood too; it was all he could do to hold back a chuckle.

Jibril nodded, too surprised to return my smile. "Of course, Abulhassan. However I can be of service."

"Our transportation, well, it's complicated. I am tired, and the prince ate a little too much, and I'd rather not stay on this barge till morning. Excuse my imposing on your kindness, Jibril, but if you had a gondola, just to get us to shore."

"But of course, Abulhassan. It will be an honor to serve a man of your . . ." He smiled. ". . . of your reputation."

I smiled back.

"Follow me, my lords. My boat is over here."

We followed him past more tables and a group of men, one of whom stared at me, then spoke my name uncertainly: "Abulhassan?" I ignored him, but out of the corner of my eye

I saw another man grab the first one's shoulder and whisper hastily in his ear; several pairs of eyes turned to us. It no longer mattered, I realized, whether Shemselnehar had planned from the start to entrap the prince, or whether her kiss was simply foolishness. Tens of servants had seen that kiss.

The music had started again. We were behind the stage, and though the music was just as loud as before, now it felt more distant. When we came to the group of servants and slaves on the edge of the barge, I felt at peace. The men were drinking wine, rolling dice, and laughing around a small lamp; the lanterns above bathed them in swaying blue and red light which danced onto the water, floated and disappeared in the dark waves. Instead of thinking about the journey that re-mained, or about all the dangers that the prince and I had incurred and the implications for the sultan, I wondered dreamily if those servants needed the extra lamp to read the dice, or if there was just some basic human need to gather round a fire. I remembered how in my village I too had sat by the fire at night. I had had neither wine nor dice, and I hadn't laughed much back then; I mostly just stared at the flames. When I was a young child I thought of nothing; when older, I thought of the future; and as an adult, I stopped staring at fires except, of course, for pharmaceutical and then alchem-ical ones. Was it gold that I really wanted, or fire?

"My lord? The prince and your servant are waiting for you to board."

I shook my head. "Forgive me, Jibril," I said simply, too tired to explain myself. As I stepped down into his boat, and as the prince grasped my hands and guided me to a cushion, I noticed how harsh and drunken were the laughs and voices of the gamblers. Their lamp was surely just to read the dice.

I watched dumbly as the prince and Nestor sat facing me.

Jibril leaned down into the boat. "My servant will bring you and the prince to shore, Abulhassan. May God keep you both."

The next instant we were at the shore; strong hands pulled me to my feet, brought me from the boat to the dusty street. I blinked at the row of smooth white houses; we were in one of the few more modest neighborhoods left in the inner city. One task remained. "Nestor, can you see what street we're on?"

"Street of the Two Black Dogs, my lord."

I smiled. I liked the name, and I knew the street. "Don't call me 'my lord' any more, Nestor. And not 'master' either. I don't feel up to the responsibility. Tomorrow, or whenever we see each other again, you may go back to it as custom requires, but not tonight. Here, I think I live only a few hundred feet away, to the left at that intersection, no? If we meet the watch, we invite them in for some wine, or rather we send them out for it, I don't have any in my house."

"My . . . I believe it's to the right."

"Well, lead on."

He did.

When we arrived, I produced a vial of "dragon's blood" for Nestor to bring back, though it was really black currant syrup; I didn't want to waste a rare elixir on a feigned illness. A servant ran to tell my wife that I was well; others prepared a room for the prince. I visited my laboratory and then went to my library to sleep, but when I arrived I had to blink my exhausted eyes: the prince was there. As I shook my head to clear it, he stepped through the yellow lamplight. After a pause, he took my hand.

"Abulhassan," he said. "I want to apologize for the danger I put you through."

I removed my hand. "I put myself through it, really."

He looked at the floor and shook his head. "No." He was quiet a moment, then looked up. "But I also want to thank you. I want to thank you because I have now met the most extraordinary woman in the world."

His face was adult and earnest. I looked away, at my mud walls filled with holes that overflowed with books. Some of the manuscripts I had not bothered to put into leather sheaths; their rolls of paper looked gold in the lamplight. I looked down at the mat that I only wanted to unroll and sleep on. "Extraordinary how?"

"Extraordinary because she is intelligent and bold, tender, kind, and very, very unhappy."

Still looking at my mat, I nodded. "So what happens now?"

"I don't know." I looked up. His gaze was sad. "I know only that I promised to see her again, and I will."

I bowed my head. My wife's old, formerly red carpet was at my feet; I closed my eyes so as not to see it. "Don't do anything rash," I said. "You know that your life is at risk. Even if she is sincere, her palace is surely full of spies."

"I know, my lord. I know that your life may be at risk as well. I shall do nothing that would put your life in danger, my lord. You may be sure of that." He took my hand again, and again I removed it. I felt even older than my many years.

"Good night, prince."

He looked at me a long moment. His gaze was tender, and I could not meet it.

He bowed. "Good night, my lord. You will forgive me if tomorrow I leave before dawn. I am afraid that my mother will send out servants to look for me, and there is no need for the whole city to know that I was not at home last night."

I nodded. He bowed again and left. I went to sleep.

V

The next morning, just as I had fallen back asleep after the call to morning prayer, a messenger arrived from the sultan; I had to greet him. Had he been Nestor or Musa or some other servant I knew, it would have taken but a moment. This slave was new; ceremony had to be performed. We bowed and exchanged compliments: "Your gracious reception embarrasses me, my lord, I am but a slave." "My noble friend, we are all slaves of his majesty." He handed me the letter, I kissed the sultan's seal before breaking it. "Abulhassan: Come this evening, after sunset prayer. Harun." When I finished reading I bowed again, loudly proclaiming my submission to his majesty's will as I placed my hand upon my head, thus indicating that I would rather lose my head than disobey his majesty.

As soon as the messenger left, I felt exhausted. I wanted to sleep through the whole day, forgetting all about the sultan, the prince, Shemselnehar, and even my own danger, but I did not go back to bed. Instead, I went to another place where I could forget the world around me.

Alchemy, I have often thought, is something like love: in practice it is immensely difficult, perhaps even impossible, but the theory is simple. For alchemy, the theory comes from Aristotle. He tells us that matter is made of four elements: earth, air, water, and fire; their different proportions and combinations create the variety we know of as this world. Take an object, change the amounts and pattern of these four elements within it, and you have a different object; such is transmutation. For example, if (says Zosima) you remove some earth, add a little air and a good deal of fire, your piece of lead becomes purest gold, purer even than that found in nature.

From other authorities we learn that the process is even easier. The four elements make up all simple matter; complex matter is a combination of the simple. Sulfur and mercury are the simple metals from which all others are made. The alchemist need not go all the way back to the four elements; sulfur and mercury are his building blocks.

Theory mastered, I approached alchemy with confidence. History had records of men who had succeeded; these men had written books. Certainly, these books were difficult; the last successful alchemist, Jabir son of Hayyam, had died before I was born. I did not expect instant success, but I was not yet sixty, at the height of my powers. I had built a fortune from nothing, invented potent medicines that bore my name; I felt up to the challenge. I already had plenty of gold, but success would crown my career and make my name immortal, like Jabir's.

My name was not all that wanted immortality; the elixir has other properties. Gold, as all know, is indestructible, impervious to decay or corrosion. As lead is the basest of metals, gold is perfect and eternal, the end of metal's evolution as Judgment Day will be the end of man's. The elixir can perfect man as it perfects metal; he who consumes it shall live until the end of time. Most say that Jabir abstained, preferring to sleep in good faith until Judgment Day; others believe that at this very moment he breathes, thinks, and studies. When the time is ripe he will emerge from hiding to lead us out of darkness, replacing superstition with the light of philosophy and alchemy. Men who believe this story keep silent; the sultan cuts off the heads of those who urge atheism in public.

I set to work. Twelve manuscripts are attributed to Jabir.

Some are apocryphal, and most refer only in passing to al-chemy, but tens of recipes remained. Jabir is not the only al-chemist: Jafar al-Siddaq also wrote a book, and then there are Persians, Africans, Franks, Greeks, Jews, Magi, infidels. One of Jabir's recipes called for blood, hair, bones, marrow, urine, the sperm of a lion, antimony, saltpeter, vine ashes, morning dew, and the blood of a giant roc. It came from a volume unanimously considered authentic; I spent vast sums on the sultan's zookeepers. In my presence, they interrupted a pair of lions at the climactic moment; I acquired what I needed. The stars seemed to shine favorably upon me; Sinbad was visiting the capital at that time. He claimed he would never sail again, but everyone knew better, and I spoke to him. When he duly sailed and returned again, it was with a few drops of roc blood. I followed Jabir's directions to the letter, poured half the elixir onto molten lead and the other half down my gullet; I ended with molten lead and a most unhappy stomach. Perhaps the lion's sperm had gone bad, and I needed a fresh sample, but I was out of roc blood. Other recipes remained.

I have always tried to be an orderly man, and for phar-macy, my laboratory simply had two furnaces, several vats near the windows, a chimney, and half a dozen stills. I soon ac-quired or built over a dozen furnaces, one no wider than the palm of my hand, another taller than I. The smaller ones I kept near the windows, but I had to build three additional chimneys; for space I knocked down a wall and took over the adjacent storeroom. My once tidy laboratory became a maze of hot furnaces, some spewing smoke and flames into the air, others sending mud chimneys up to the ceiling as if they were elephant trunks. I carved out niches in the walls to hold jars and vases, bars of lead and iron, flasks of shining mercury, scales, mortars, hammers, and filters.

Depending on the quality of heat that I needed, in my

furnaces I burned charcoal, wood, peat, oil, or even dried dung. The air filled with smoke into which tongues of flames reached up; between the furnaces stills bubbled and steamed. Their joints could never be sealed perfectly, so damp scents of vinegar, camphor, and ammonia mixed with the foul air, but the strongest smell was always sweet, sickly sulfur. Amidst the smoke and fire I mixed arsenic and mercury on low tables; I pulverized lead and dung. I cut out three more windows, hung lamps from the ceiling, and put mirrors above the lamps, but with all the furnaces and smoke, the four chimneys and the high piles of clay vessels, my laboratory was eternally dark, as if it were some cave deep under the earth. When I came out into my garden, I blinked in the sunlight. Smoke had blackened my face and hands; my clothes and beard reeked of sulfur, charcoal, and dung.

I tried hundreds of recipes and developed new ones based on hints and allegory; many books were painfully allusive. "Know that this science is easier than any other," said one, "but the names and recipes make it obscure, for the ignorant take our words without understanding." Yet what was I to do with a recipe that instructed me to "remove half of the spirit from lead, torture it slowly, then replace it gradually, evenly, with a half part soul"? Others one could interpret as one pleased: "You shall separate earth from fire, thin from thick, gently, with great care. It rises from the earth to the sky, then immediately falls back to the earth, and it receives the force of superior and inferior things." I melted and steamed, bleached and vaporized, burnt and smelt and sublimed, roasted and filtered, washed, cooked, and decomposed. I turned a great deal of gold into clay and iron pots, glass and copper instruments, antimony and lead.

Jafar al-Siddaq's preferred method requires forty days. You start with calcination which, writes Jafar, purifies the gold so that it can accept the necessary infusion of soul; only then can it become elixir and reproduce.

Day One: Beat together forty mitqals of gold and a hundred and twenty mitqals of crude mercury. Heat in a pot over a coal fire. Stop when it is exactly as hot as a piece of iron left out in the midday desert sun; place in cold water. Pulverize with a clay pestle. Pour out the water, pulverize again; stop when it is as soft as camel marrow. The mercury has now "swallowed" the gold.

Distill green vitriol. Pour an exactly equal weight of distillate on the "swallowed" gold; heat in a covered pot over a fire of horse manure, the fire maintaining a constant temperature. Upon absorption, remove from heat. Pulverize. Add ten istars of sal ammoniac. Pulverize again; put in two glass beakers on a stove. Heat at the exact temperature at which water boils until all moisture evaporates; continue to heat from morning to midday prayer. Let it cool until the next morning.

The thirty-nine subsequent days require camel dung and pigeon droppings, glass and lead, earthen, wooden, and golden containers, mirrors to catch the starlight, morning dew, evening rain, verdigris, egg yolks, ocean water, and sand from the Holy City. Everything, al-Siddaq writes, must be done exactly: if the stove's temperature is at all above that at which water boils, the process will fail. When the recipe states, "Heat from morning to midday prayer," it does not mean any equivalent period; spiritual elements are at work. Hence, on day one, you must time the process so that all moisture has evaporated at the exact moment when the crier calls out the morning prayer. One error means that the whole process must be begun anew. "Calcination," wrote Jabir, "is the treasure of a thing; be you not weary of calcination."

I have spent years of my life on formulas such as al-Siddaq's. Always I make some error, am compelled to start again until I give up and move onto another. I have mentioned formulas with impossible ingredients and ones with incomprehensible instructions; al-Siddaq's belongs to my third category, which eventually became my favorite: that of instructions so complex as to be impossible—impossible to execute, impossible to disprove. They are endless. I was near seventy when I reached this enlightenment. For ten years I had done little else but search for the elixir. What would I do if I found it? What would I do with endless wealth, how would I fill a life that had become eternity? It may seem strange, since my dark, smoky laboratory perhaps resembled Hell more than Heaven, but I found that I was happy there, spiritually at peace. In a way that I cannot explain, the process, formulas like al-Siddaq's, my search—they all reminded me of God.

I decided that God did not destroy the Tower of Babel with wind and an earthquake. Instead He sent down the devil, handsomest of angels, with instructions on how to build it. The builders read them, discussed them, thought they understood, tried to build the tower, and failed. Clearly, they had misunderstood the instructions. So they argued, broke into sects, and finally went to war over interpretations; and this was the confusion of tongues. Yet there were still some who spent their evenings at home, rereading those instructions after a hard day's work. These ones built small towers, knee height at most, meant only as models; and they, I believed, were happy.

Some alchemists spoke of this spiritual side, though not quite in the way that I understood it. Many recipes, including al-Siddaq's, required prayers and fasts. "Know, my dearest son," wrote a Christian, "that this science is none other than the love of God." Creating gold, he writes, is but the outward manifestation of the real transmutation: the old, inner man must die, replaced by one spiritually pure. Only then will the alchemist succeed, and with the simplest of methods: a beaker of mercury and sulfur is buried in warm, constantly renewed ashes; when the alchemist is pure, gold will "hatch in the mercury as an egg hatches from a hen." The immortality thus acquired is not of this world, but the hereafter.

I was skeptical, but skepticism had long before ceased to be a barrier to any experiment. In addition to my other projects, each morning and each evening I renewed the ashes; I diligently checked the beaker of mercury and sulfur for signs of gold. I did so after returning home with the prince and then again that morning, as soon as I entered my laboratory.

As I was finishing, my wife called through the beads in the doorway. "Husband!"

"Yes, Fatima. Come in, please."

As she pushed through the beads I turned around on my stool; a young woman in Shemselnehar's livery accompanied her. I stood up. Shemselnehar had sent the servant to thank me for the dragon's blood; she was not yet entirely well, but much better than the day before. She hoped that I and all my loved ones were safe and sound.

"Tell her that everyone is fine, and that I am gratified that my poor science could do her some little good." I neglected to add that she should always consider me at her service. I hadn't decided that she should.

The servant left. My wife remained by the door.

We stood facing each other, which was unusual. In recent years our conversations have generally occurred with her standing and me sitting: in my laboratory, after the meals which I ate alone. It was not that I was the master; it was simply that if we were in the same room, it was usually because she had walked in while I was sitting at work, and I felt that we were enough past ceremony that I needn't stand up. Often

I didn't even turn around, and so we talked without looking at each other. She did the same on the rare occasions when I walked in on her, in the kitchen, or weaving, or reading the Holy Book.

"Another messenger came too," she said, "while you were sleeping. He was from Nuraddin." Her face was expressionless, but everyone in the city knew that Nuraddin, the grand vizier, was not a man who had friends. He had never before sent me a message.

"What did the messenger say?"

"That Nuraddin was concerned for your health. He heard that you had an unusually late night."

I nodded. My wife and I looked at each other. She was old like me, but her eyes had lost none of their luster.

"It was a strange night, Fatima. I'd like to talk to you about it, but nothing is urgent."

She looked at me a moment longer, then left. My wife has always listened more than she talks, and with the years she has grown even quieter.

For the last forty-seven years, my wife has not called me by name: I am "husband." Our mothers arranged the marriage, as tradition and wisdom instruct. I was a young merchant, just starting to find my feet. I needed a wife who could assist me and who would not expect a life of comfort. Fatima's father, a judge and doctor, would be a useful father-in-law; she had a reputation for hard work, if not for beauty or intelligence; and old Osama's third daughter was already eighteen. In those chaotic days following the civil war, many men had died, and few had the means to marry; Fatima's oldest sister was already condemned as a spinster. Both she and I knew, or thought we knew, that the passions, the adventures in song and legend were not for us. We were not looking for love.

I taught my new wife to read less for her benefit than for my profit and vanity: as a merchant in need of assistance, as a man of science, I wanted a literate wife. Few men in our village could read, and no woman that I had ever heard of. Fatima had always been thought slow; her mother had not even taught her to play any kind of music. When she read the opening verses of the Holy Book, recognizing the words she had so often uttered in prayer, pronouncing each syllable as if it were a discovery, she burst into tears and kissed my hand—a gesture that I was vain enough to accept. Yet Fatima and I were partners as only simple people can be: I hadn't the money to keep her locked away in a harem; we worked side by side. My wife, called stupid by her mother, knows more of pharmacy than half the scholars in the sultan's House of Wisdom.

Five years passed; we were prosperous and happy. I call my home town a village because it seems one compared to the City of Peace, but even then Three Springs had over five thousand inhabitants. The surrounding land was mediocre for crops but good for grazing; more importantly, caravans and pilgrims from the empire's center all had to pass through on their way to the Holy City. My wife and I made a good living; I was a man of standing; we had two small children. Then word came of the new capital.

Back then my wife did not have the sharp tongue that she has since developed. She did not mock me; she just said no. We were happy, we had friends, family, enough of everything. In the capital we would be far from everything we knew; even the dialect in the center was different; she was afraid. I cajoled and soothed and got nowhere. So I did what it had never even occurred to me to do in our first five years together: "Wife," I said, "I am your husband. I am the one who makes the decisions, and it is your duty to obey me." I then appealed to what she believed in and what she knew I did not: "Religion commands you to obey me."

She looked at me. She was so young then—as was I. "Abulhassan," she said. "I don't want to go." I said nothing. She bit her lip; tears swelled in the corners of her eyes but went no further. She continued to look at me. I turned red but said nothing. I wanted to back down, I wanted to make her happy, but I knew that I couldn't. The rest of my life in Three Springs, plodding and mediocre . . . I was so ambitious then, and despite my affection, I would leave without her if I had to. Fatima, my wife and my friend, saw that in my eyes. She blinked, wiped her eyes with the corner of her shawl, and when she looked up again her eyes were hard. "Very well, husband. As you command." She left the room. A month later, we left for the newborn City of Peace.

Today, Fatima still dresses in the deep blue or dark gray cotton cloaks that she wore in our village; she never wears jewels, and she never wears silk. She has a few friends, all from the area around Three Springs: a butcher's wife, a soothsayer, the wet nurse for our last four children. When we first arrived in the city, she refused even to meet my new friends' wives, and she has chosen to retain her provincial accent. As soon as I could afford to hire a servant, I asked her to stay out of my shop, and when I built my villa it included a harem for her and the children, as befitted a man of my stature. Yet the bond between us proved stronger than my vanity and her resentment. Timidly, I began again to ask her advice: on pharmacy, trade, our children, and all the new people that I met. I was still "husband," but soon she spent every evening sitting by my side, knitting while I worked into the night; we had four more children. Once more we fought about religion and magic, she fearful that I would go to Hell, I indignant that my wife should believe in astrological almanacs, in magic potions and knots of hair.

In recent years, that argument has stilled; perhaps she has even won it. In order to fulfill certain formulas, I put a prayer rug in my laboratory and marked the wall in the direction of the Holy City. I use the rug only for the formulas, and sometimes not even then, but its presence is precisely the sort of gesture that I had formerly refused, on principle, even to make her happy. I no longer object to the occasional snake skin I find outside my door, the complicated knots of white, red, or black hair under my pillow, the surprisingly bitter taste my sorbet has at times. These magic charms come when I have some difficulty; even if I have not mentioned my problems to her, she always guesses. Her sorcery has yet to do me any harm, and the money wasted is trivial compared to what I have thrown into furnaces and roc blood. What can I say? When, the day after my adventure in the Palace of Unending Pleasure, she brought in my lunch, I surreptitiously smelled the sweetened lemon juice that she had made for me; it had a distinctly unlemonlike smell, rather like mustard. Fatima kept a straight face, but I smiled as I drank it down. Who knew? Perhaps it would turn me into gold.

VI

Religion claims that two angels are with each of us at all times; that afternoon I dreamt of them. In the dream I saw myself as if from afar. I was sitting rigidly in a gondola, floating down one canal and then another; the maze seemed unending, but I knew it led to Shemselnehar's palace. No boatman poled, no other traffic creased the smooth water; I was alone except for the two angels about my head. They say that the angel on the right records our good deeds, she on the left our bad, but in my dream one of the two angels did all the writing, and she flew round and round my head, left to right and right to left. She wrote without pause while the other laughed. I stared straight ahead, ignorant of my Heavenly companions. I looked lonely.

My scribe had the happy dimples, the sudden pout, the glancing eyes of . . . my daughter Zaynab? No, the laughing one was my youngest and favorite daughter; the scribe was Mona, Shemselnehar's servant. I opened my eyes suddenly. I was not confused, I knew that I had been dreaming and was now awake, but the thought rushed into my head like a vision: if each of us has two guardian angels, then millions of angels are floating above the City of Peace. If only I could see them, the air I breathe would be cluttered with glittering wings.

I stretched and looked out at the sun. I had nearly over-slept. If my vision continued to haunt me, I could tell it to the sultan, who liked to talk about angels and God. Still half asleep, and in a state of numbness that covered up my fear, I set out for the Palace of the Golden Gate.

I had first received a royal invitation some twelve years before: His Royal Majesty Harun the Righteous, Commander of the Faithful, Conqueror of the Greeks, Son of . . . Son of . . . Son of . . . Cousin of the Prophet, requests your loyal opposition in a game of chess. A game of chess? Hadn't he any more infidels to conquer? I had retired from the world several years before. I had no wish for his favor, no talent or inclination for the game.

Earlier that day I had strained my back bending over a furnace; the requisite prostrations and bows completed my ill humor. After a brief exchange of compliments—such an honor would overwhelm even those with far more than my feeble share of merit; he had long desired to meet a man numbered amongst the wisest of his subjects—we sat down to play. Brilliant on the attack, the sultan left his pieces defenseless. Three times I let go prize opportunities, thinking they must be traps; no player capable of such stunning offense could be so foolish. Then he left his queen open. I looked carefully. My sultan was fully protected; I could not imagine a gambit short of mate that required sacrificing the queen. I took it. He blinked, looked from the board to me and back to the board, and then he smiled.

"I was careless, was I not?"

"Perhaps his majesty has laid a trap for me."

He smiled wider. "No," he said. "You have won my queen, that's all. Elephant to horse four."

We played on. Twice more he staged a stunning attack, brought my sultan two moves away from mate. Each time he left his flank unguarded; I took an elephant and then both his camels. At this point he should have resigned, but he showed no signs of distress. Was it a feint beyond my capabilities? I was not much of a chess player. The sultan's favor for the game was well known; he should have been an expert from so much practice. We played to the end. I won. Bowing, I called myself the most fortunate of players, both for having an opponent so much greater than my humble worth, and for the blind luck that had enabled me to gain an unjust victory over one so clearly my superior. Indeed, I suspected that he had lost on purpose in order to humor, in his kindness and wisdom, his unworthy slave.

"Nonsense," the sultan said, "and stand up, please." He clapped his hands and the doors opened; he called for Mesrour and even Jafar, the grand vizier, who surely had better things to do.

"What is your name again?"

"Abulhassan, son of Taher, sire." Bewildered, I began to worry that I had committed a fatal error.

Jafar, Mesrour, Majnun the lord chamberlain, and several other lords arrived. "Do you see this board?" the sultan asked.

They bowed.

"This pharmacist, Abulhassan son of Taher, has beaten me. He is the only man in the empire worthy to be my opponent. Have you any desires, Abulhassan, any wishes that I may fulfill? An estate, a musician, a concubine? A thousand gold dinars?"

It took me a moment even to remember to bow. "His highness is too kind. I fail to understand what honor I have won through my blind luck, and I cannot even imagine any act within my powers that has not already been more than rewarded by the honor of his majesty's presence."

"Come, then. Ten thousand dinars and . . . have you a wife?"

"I have, your majesty."

"Then a necklace of finest pearls for your lady. I expect your presence here a week from this time."

I was still bowed so could not see if he was laughing; I

had to assume that he was serious. "His majesty's kindness confuses me, but I beseech him to allow me to treat the honor of his invitation as a more than ample reward for my insignificant service—whatever it may have been. His vizier's kindness in allowing me to loyally supply his majesty's hospital has removed me from want, and my wife, who is honored beyond belief at his majesty's thought, never wears jewelry."

"Rise, pharmacist."

I rose.

"Look at me."

I looked. The sultan, even now warm and expansive, back then was still playful and impulsive. His smile broadened. "Well, my friend, you look in earnest to me, so it's your loss if you're not. The gold I'll give to the poor in your name, but I insist you take the pearls to your wife, with my best wishes for her health and children. If I know women, my guess is that it is you who don't like jewelry; but even if she chooses not to keep it, then surely you have a daughter or a niece who will enjoy it." He clapped his hands. "Begone, Abulhassan, son of Taher. I am well pleased with you, and I look forward to our next game. Majnun, find him a prize necklace."

The servant who brought me out of the palace explained. In my earlier attempts to rise in status, I had indeed risen, but only within limits. I had never entered the first circles of the realm; far from meeting the sultan, I had not even frequented those lords who make up his court. How could I have known that no one had ever dared beat the sultan at chess? Jafar, the only man who would have played to win, had hated the game ever since his son had choked to death on a piece.

I saw him every week. His playing improved rapidly, as did mine; we were evenly matched. Once, when he was crushing a heretical rebellion, he sent me his moves by letter. I responded in kind, and so we played during the six months he was away in Khorasan. After a year or two he asked me to call him Harun. I refused. My back was happy to skip the bows and prostrations, but I would not pretend an equality that could not exist. Abu Nuwas called him Harun, pinched his cheek and spilled wine on his lap; it reminded me of a little boy allowed to take liberties with his father. I preferred to bow briefly and to call him "sire," as did his other honored servants; it was more dignified. Years passed. We talked of love and of God, of the old traditions and the new customs, of alchemy, of growing old. "Abulhassan," he said, "my friend." "Sire," I said, "my lord."

Now the guards bowed to me as I passed into the outer garden and walked down its marble alleys. Lotus floated in crescent-shaped pools; roses spelled out the names of God, the Prophet, and the sultan; cypresses, their trunks plated with silver, gleamed in the last of the evening sun. The silver was no good for the trees, and no good for the animals either: peacocks stared at metal reflections, fought and strutted before them.

Before the gates of the palace proper, Yazid son of Mazyad, lord chamberlain since Majnun had been poisoned, awaited me.

He bowed with a fond smile on his face. "My lord Abulhassan! What a pleasure!"

The lord chamberlain was responsible for the sultan's household, including Shemselnehar's palace; he also decided who entered the sultan's presence. The sultan's personal spies presumably had their own entrance, but otherwise the only road to the throne led through this short, fat, and apparently cheerful Persian. He wore robes and turbans of gold silk, embroidered with silver, and he had dyed his beard bright red; he would have looked like a soft and shiny toy, were it not for his black eyes. I returned his bow.

"How are you, my lord Yazid? Peace be upon you."

"Peace be upon you too, dear Abulhassan, my noble lord. I am very well, thank you. And yourself? You were up late last night, were you not?"

I looked at him. "A little, yes." I hoped that I hid a tremble, but Yazid's jet black eyes were sharp. What could I tell him? I had only one asset at court, I realized, but it was tremendous: I was the only man in the empire whom the sultan called friend. I looked at Yazid. "I am on my way to his majesty, to speak to him about that very subject."

"Are you?" Yazid smiled slightly. In truth, I had not decided what I was going to tell the sultan. My instinct had been to tell him everything, to let the two of us together decide upon a solution, but as Yazid's black eyes gleamed, two coals in a soft mass of gold silk, flabby cheeks, and red hair, I became afraid. How could the prince avoid banishment? And Shemselnehar's honor was no longer intact. Not only could the sultan have the prince killed, but many men would say that he had to. It would be a foolish act, with repercussions throughout the empire, but who knew what the sultan might not do in the heat of jealousy?

I permitted Yazid to take my arm; we began to walk. "Abulhassan," he said, "when it comes to religion, philosophy, alchemy, all the truly important things in this world, no one could deny that you are a wise man."

"Thank you, my lord."

He smiled humbly. "Your thanks are unwarranted, my lord, for I only speak a truth known to all men. For, my dear Abulhassan, as a wise, thoughtful man, you have justly earned the respect of our sovereign, of my lord Prince Abulhassan, and of course . . ." Without either slowing his pace or letting go of my arm, he bowed slightly. "Of course you also have the respect of my humble self. I am your servant, my lord."

I eyed him. "Thank you, my lord Yazid. You may be sure that I too have nothing but respect for the loyal, capable way in which you serve the Commander of the Faithful."

Yazid shrugged. Underneath his beautiful silk robe, I could see rolls of fat shifting. "I do my best," he said. "His majesty is so wise, so thoughtful, and so perceptive, that perhaps a small part of his wisdom is reflected in a humble, foolish servant such as myself, just as an imperfect mirror may still shine, should the sun be strong enough. Every success I have, you know, is because of his majesty's guidance, and every error that I commit comes from not listening closely enough to his words, and not studying his every action more carefully."

We walked past the reflecting pool. A swan was paddling through the green dome's reflection, and so the whole palace trembled in the water.

"In addition to our devotion to his majesty," Yazid continued, "you and I have another thing in common, dear Abulhassan—our affection for the young Prince Abulhassan, heir to the House of Persia, the symbol of my people's utter loyalty and submission to his majesty and to the Faith. He is such a noble, loyal soul, that if he were to be dragged into some sort of disgrace, it could only be because evil men had entrapped him."

"My lord Yazid, your fears reflect your true and generous heart, and so it gives me pleasure to tell you that you have no need for worry."

As his smile widened, Yazid's hand tightened about my arm. It was surprising that such a flabby man had such a strong hand; his grasp was beginning to hurt. "I hope so, dear Abulhassan."

"I understand, Lord Yazid, but I assure you that your fears are groundless."

"No, my dear Abulhassan, for all your wisdom, I don't believe that you do understand." As we walked his grip on my arm suddenly moved down to my elbow and tightened further; pain shot from my elbow up to my shoulder and neck.

I stopped walking and gasped. Still smiling, he spoke softly.

"I don't know what game you're playing, Abulhassan, but I do know that you're not meant for it." He let go of my arm, and for a moment we looked at each other. From afar, boatmen cried out on the river. At this distance I could not make out their words, but from the shrill tones of their cries, I guessed that two boats had bumped into each other. Yazid's smile broadened; he clapped me on the shoulder. "Come speak to me, Abulhassan. At home, of course, after evening prayer. I believe that the prince was planning to leave on a journey in the next day or two, and I'd like to be of service in planning it. He's going on pilgrimage to the Holy City, if I understand it right, which is indeed a worthy desire in so young a man—but of course you and I have never doubted the prince's extraordinary virtue and piety. Besides, the capital's a dangerous place. Poor Majnun, dear old man, he never quite understood that." His smile turned into a pout. "You know, I still miss Majnun now and then. It seems that his sudden death, that awful poisoning, was a surprise to many people. Like you, he was interested in philosophy, and like you he was proud of his majesty's faith in him. May peace be upon his soul." He turned abruptly and began to walk again; he spoke without turning his head to look back at me, where I stood with my aching arm. "You're a good man, Abulhassan," he said. "And a good man has no place near a man like Nuraddin."

After a moment, I walked after him. "I am on my way to see his majesty," I said, so loudly that the guards turned to stare, "not Nuraddin or anyone else."

Yazid slowed his pace so that we were again walking side by side.

"You know the confidence that his majesty has in me," I said softly. "You know too the affection that I have for the prince. You see many things, Yazid, but perhaps you do not understand everything that you see." I shook out my arm. "You too ought to be careful, Lord Yazid. If you interfere with matters that the sultan, in his wisdom, has chosen not to share with you, you may bring harm not only to his majesty, but also to the prince, and, if I dare say it, to yourself."

I was bluffing, of course, but Yazid knew well that I was a friend to both the sultan and the prince. He might just believe me; he certainly would want to.

He eyed me. "I shall remember what you said, Abulhassan, for I always treasure the words of a wise man. In return, my dear friend, known throughout the city for his prudence and for his prudent guidance of young men, remember what I have said. I am always greatly concerned for the prince, which means that my affection, and my attention, extends to you too. I cannot tell you how I would be saddened if I had any reason to lessen the love and honor in which I have always held you. In the meantime, I shall be honored if you choose to visit me, and I hope that you too honor me sufficiently to accept my invitation."

We walked another minute in silence, along a marble path through a stately row of palm trees. Then he stopped and stood up straight; his gold robe and turban shone dully in the evening light. He stepped forward, bowed until his head touched the ground, then motioned for me too to step forward. We had entered the small garden where the sultan was waiting.

Babylonian willow trees, that some men say are weeping for the loss of that city, swayed in the breeze; pomegranate trees' ripe fruit glowed fiery in the twilight; goldfish glittered in small, scattered pools. The tree trunks were unadorned, the pools plain black stone. As in Shemselnehar's palace, the garden's arrangement appeared random but pleased immensely. Beyond were peaceful waters and then thick forest; all traffic halted on that stretch of river when the sultan was in his garden, and all houses on the riverbank had been bought and then razed to make room for those woods, imported tree by tree from the mountains in the north. The sultan sat at a plain stone table in which a chessboard had been carved; just to his side, wide steps led down to the river. Several musicians played the lute; a eunuch waved a fan.

"Your majesty, Abulhassan son of Taher has arrived."

"Abulhassan!" The sultan stood up with a smile, but his forehead remained wrinkled, his eyes elsewhere. "Thank you, Yazid, you may go. Abulhassan, for goodness' sake, do not bow. And you too may go." He waved his hand at the musicians and eunuch, who vanished. Yazid backed out slowly, bowing again before he disappeared behind the corner of the palace. "Soldier to sultan four, Abulhassan, but how are you? Still waiting for that egg to hatch?" I had told him of the recipe that involved nothing but sulfur, mercury, spiritual perfection, and ashes. He came forward through the trees and took my hand. I forced myself to smile back, and hoped that the trembling of my hand would be attributed to age. Nuraddin knew what had happened the night before, as did Yazid and tens of servants; the question was whether any of them had told the sultan. As master of both the harem and the sultan's audiences, Yazid had great power to muffle the news;

and I knew that the sultan, who had spies everywhere, had ordered that none follow Shemselnehar. Yet if Nuraddin wished to inform the sultan, he would find a way; but then why had he sent a messenger to inquire about my health that morning?

"I am well, sire, even without the egg. Thank you."

"Glad to hear it. But you weren't ill this afternoon? I heard that you weren't in your shop as usual."

I might have gone a little pale at this reminder that the sultan seemed to know everything, but the attentiveness on his features was likely solicitude.

"I was asleep. I was up late with the Prince of Persia."

"Yes, I heard that you both were at a party, which surprised me. I thought that Abulhassan Ali had the same temperate habits as yourself."

I managed to smile again. "I did, too. But . . ."

"And of course," the sultan interrupted, "one of Shemselnehar's eunuchs woke you in the middle of the night. My apologies."

I shook my head. "I was awake—I had just returned home. I hope that my medicine helped her some. One of her servants came this morning to tell me that she was better."

The sultan frowned. "Better, yes."

"But not well?"

Perplexed, he looked at his feet for an instant before shaking his head. "Come, Abulhassan, sit down and look at the board. Forgive me for keeping you standing so long. Do you want anything to eat?"

I shook my head. We made our way through the willows and sat down.

It was a warm summer evening, but the breeze off the river was cool and moist; the willow trees rustled. Above the forest, a nearly full moon gleamed in the dark blue sky. It was hard to remember that the previous night I had committed a crime, and that now I had to deceive the sultan. Sadness filled me: I did not want to lie to my friend, but I could not tell the truth just then. If I got the prince to leave the city, as Yazid had suggested; if tempers and passions cooled; if I had a little time . . . In the end, the sultan would understand and even thank me. If he executed the Prince of Persia in a fit of jealousy, riots and even rebellion would be likely.

Except for the sultan's own apartments, every room in his palace had at least one entrance hidden by a tapestry, so the sultan or one of his spies could listen to any conversation. The garden, I realized, was full of shadows, groves of trees, steps below which a man could lie and listen unseen.

I forced myself to examine the board. Soldier to sultan four? Why, I could check him with my camel, then take his horse with mine when he moved his sultan away. He must indeed be distracted; not even during the Zoroastrian revolts had he made such a reckless move. I had to think back to our first few games to find an equivalent.

I looked up—and was scared to see him staring at me, hard. "Sire." He blinked.

"Yes."

"What happened last night?"

"Oh." He looked away and waved his hand vaguely. "Well, she fainted a few minutes after I came. She recovered with smelling salts, but she still felt weak, though your blood apparently helped her some. The doctors can't find anything wrong with her, but she insists that she feels queasy when she stands, and refuses to eat anything." He paused, expectant. I put on a thoughtful expression.

"You told me once that the doctors said her nature was hot and moist, easily disturbed. Perhaps it was something she ate?"

"Perhaps. Abulhassan, take a look at her on your way out. I've told the eunuchs to expect you, and let you come and go as you please, though of course they already know that my trust in you is complete. You don't have any more dragon's blood with you, do you?"

"I can send for it."

"All right. Aside from some mysterious blind doctor, it was the only thing that seemed to help. But also talk to her. I think she trusts you, like a father."

"More like a grandfather."

He closed his eyes for a moment. The breeze from the river picked up. Day was falling rapidly, but the sultan did not call for light; dusk deepened around us, filling the gaps among the rustling willow trees. Quiet and dark peace were descending about us like a warm bath. He opened his eyes suddenly. In their green irises, frightening to most, I saw anguish.

"Abulhassan, do you remember the theologians I put to death a few years ago?"

"Which ones, sire?"

"The ones who tried to worship me."

I nodded. Several theologians had declared that the sultan was the Prophet's equal, that he could do no wrong, and that all mortals could learn wisdom from the simplest of his actions. He had put them to death as blasphemers.

"I think Shemselnehar is unhappy, Abulhassan." I tried, but I could not meet his gaze. Instead I looked out on the darkening trees, now still; the breeze had died down. A year and a half before, the sultan had surprised me when he announced that he would call Shemselnehar's palace Unending Pleasure. Deeply religious, he had seen much death; he knew that no pleasure on this earth is without end. I had wondered too what he thought in the arms of a girl one-fourth his age. They say that old men frequent youth to fight against aging, but I suspected that what the sultan enjoyed was the reminder of his mortality. I had suggested it; he had laughed, well pleased. "You are too subtle for me, Abulhassan. You forget that she is beautiful and utterly delightful." Yet it was the sultan's nature to pretend that he was less philosophical than he really was.

For a long time, the sultan had chosen his women very young; he moved on to a new mistress when a girl turned sixteen or seventeen. Surrounded by ruthless manipulation, he had to seek solace in innocence. To have the sultan's ear meant estates, titles, positions of power for your brothers and allies. Sooner or later, he had found, the women that he loved began to use him. Power is seductive; only a woman too timid to care for it might care for him. Zubaidah, his queen, had giant estates, servants in her own livery, and a circle of nobles who owed allegiance only to her. He had not spoken to her for over a decade; not even I knew why. Shemselnehar he permitted great personal freedom, but he did not even let her give alms to the poor; he was afraid that she too would develop a taste for power. He had told me his hope that she would be different, that she would remain with him, that he would never have to search for a new love. She had never asked him for anything except his person.

He had also kept me apart from his court. I had no interest in such matters, but I knew that he had forbidden his courtiers, even Nuraddin and Yazid, to speak to me unless ceremony required it. "I have many servants," he told me once. "A few of them are even loyal. I do not need any more."

"Abulhassan."

I woke from my reflections and saw his gaze. It was full of pain. "Sire."

"Do you think she's unhappy?"

I looked away, at the willow trees drooping in the fading

light. "She seemed fine when she came to my shop yesterday."

"But from what you know of women, what would you think?"

"You know that I have only known one woman in my life."

"Don't give me excuses, Abulhassan, we've known each other too long for that. You have daughters and you have seen and heard as much as any man. And the mystics claim that since God is in every atom, you can learn His entire truth by studying a pebble."

I turned from the dark willow trees to his face, sad and serious. Behind him, the river lapped against the stone steps. There were no bridges over the river, I knew, or at least none near the capital. When men wished to cross into the City of Peace, they had to go by boat. Sometimes, when large groups arrived, a dozen barges were lashed together, creating a swaying, uneven bridge over which men could cross.

"Sire," I said, "She is very young. You have raised her from poverty to a palace, treated her like a queen and given her great liberties, which are also responsibilities. It cannot be easy."

"You think I give her too much liberty?"

I shrugged.

"I don't think I give her enough."

He turned away; I followed his gaze to the pond where goldfish darted across the black pool. The fish seemed not to know how to curve; they swam straight forward in one direction, then straight to the left or to the right, but always in a straight line so that instead of circles they turned in irregular polygons.

"You know," he said, "if someone else were the sultan, he might have to put me to death as an idolater, I worship her so. I cannot help treating her like a queen. And when all women fear not to love me, it's hard to tell, but I think she really does."

"You should know best."

The sultan knew that she had been afraid of him at first. He knew too that he had been unkind, blinded as he was by desire. It was difficult to be kind, he told me, when no one dared tell him that he caused unhappiness. Yet he believed that he had since won her affection, in part by giving her the freedom that no husband would have granted.

I returned my gaze to the board. Before I had beaten him, the sultan had resorted to ever more desperate stratagems to get a good game of chess. He had told opponents that he would put them to death if they lost; in their nervousness they played foolishly and lost all the same. The sultan was unwilling really to kill for such a failing; when that became known, the tactic lost any chance of success. He had then tried his hardest to lose, made one suicidal move after the other in an attempt to force his opponents to win; ever crafty, they always managed to outwit him and lose. This was a kind of success, since his opponents had to use all their skill to frustrate his designs, but he soon tired of such perverse competition. Abu Nuwas was the only one who tried to win, but he refused to play without wine, and he soon became drunk if he hadn't been already. The next day he claimed to have beaten the sultan and lived, such was his favor. His boasts should have encouraged others, but clever courtiers suspected the truth, and foolish ones believed his claim that only the sultan's special preference had spared him.

I thought too of a tradition about the Prophet.

Upon capturing the Holy City, the Prophet went to the tomb of his mother, who had died an idolater. He knelt down to pray but after an instant looked up, in tears. "I asked leave of God to visit my mother's tomb, and He granted it me," he explained; "but when I asked leave to pray for her, it was denied me." It is forbidden to pray for unbelievers. Yet, I thought, it is said many times in the Holy Book that no man may intercede before God. He alone is Judge, and the Prophet, to whom the Holy Book was spoken, must have known this better than any other. He knew that his prayers could make no difference; they were merely a form of mourning. When God forbade him to pray for his mother, He was really forbidding him to mourn for her.

"What are you thinking of, my friend?"

I reminded him of the chess stories and he nodded; I told him my thought about the Prophet and he was quiet. When he finally spoke, it was without lifting his gaze from his lap, dark in evening shadow.

"Abulhassan, ever since I had to kill Jafar for his disloyalty, you have been the only man, out of all my subjects, whom I have thought of as a friend. But we are told that we have no friend but God." He looked up, neither threatening nor melancholy, just serious. "Make your move. I have to meet my viziers soon."

"Camel to elephant four, sire. Check."

He was unperturbed—as if he had expected my move, or perhaps his thoughts were still elsewhere. "Sultan to queen two."

I paused a moment to scan the board one more time; no feint was evident. I took his horse.

VII

"Please rise, Abulhassan. I am happy at your presence."

"My lady, I am most grieved to hear of your continued illness. I have come upon the request of his majesty, who desired me to offer my humble science and aged ear to your service." I glanced at her servants as I spoke of my aged ear; Shemselnehar nodded at them.

"Leave us alone, please."

They left without blinking, but they had already seen far more scandalous. They all seemed to like Shemselnehar, but what were the chances that none of them would demand a private audience with the sultan? What were the chances that none of them already had? Yet Yazid would be ruthless in muffling the story, and if no one before me had dared beat the sultan in chess, it was likely that no one would dare tell news that would cause him such supreme unhappiness. Once before, I knew, one of Shemselnehar's servants had accused her of dishonesty. The sultan had simply summoned her and asked if the report was true. When she replied that it wasn't, without further questions he had the servant flogged and dismissed.

It was my first time in Shemselnehar's bedroom. Black satin sheets, pinned to the ceiling, flapped above my head in the evening breeze; giant windows opened onto the garden's orange trees and paths of colored pebbles. The sheets on the ceiling had a moonless night's constellations printed on them, and the room was so vast, and on that evening so dim, that one could have been outside, on a perfect, clear night, except that the wind made the sheets that showed the sky fold and billow, as if God were shifting about on His throne. The only lamp was a gold lantern at the side of Shemselnehar's bed; I could not see the room's sides except where the moonlight shone on them. The walls were covered in tapestries of yellow, red, and midnight blue that blended into the black sheets on the ceiling, as if the sun were setting in the desert at night.

Shemselnehar looked a different woman than the day before. Her skin was whiter, her eyes darker and larger; under her coal-black hair, in the flickering lamplight, her delicate features trembled. Pride and pretension had gone from her. In the warm night, a light sheet and gown were all that covered her, and as she sat and looked up at me, I found her eyes disturbing: she was appealing and afraid, yes, but also watchful.

"Are you really ill, Shemselnehar?"

She blinked. I had spoken kindly.

"Can I trust you, Abulhassan?"

"You can confide in me." I paused. Her expression had softened, but it remained watchful. "I don't know if I can help you," I said suddenly, "but I will not betray you."

She reached out her hand and took mine. "Dear Abulhassan, you can't imagine how much I need a friend like you right now. I'll never be able to thank you for your kindness."

I removed my hand from hers and looked into the darkness. Something trembled: the wall hangings, too distant for me to see distinctly, had shivered in the breeze. Her expression had been as sweet as her words, but her eyes continued to size me up. She was calculating every word and expression, I realized. She was so young, I thought, younger than my granddaughters. I had power over her; she had no choice but to calculate. She had not been so calculating a year and a half before, when the sultan had found her.

"May I sit down?"

"Yes, of course, forgive me, Abulhassan, I am inconsiderate as always."

I pulled a cushion to the side of the bed and sat on it.

"Nestor told me all about your escape last night," she said. "I'm so sorry. I should never have kept you so long. I can't forgive myself for the danger I put you in."

I waved my hand in dismissal. I didn't wish to talk about it.

"And . . ." She paused, watching my expression. "Have you heard from the prince?"

"No. But I was asleep most of the day . . ."

"Of course," she interrupted.

". . . and then I went to see the sultan."

"Does he suspect anything?"

"I don't think so." I paused. "He's worried about you, Shemselnehar. He cares about you very much."

She looked at me a long moment. When she finally spoke, her words were distinct, perhaps even proud as she looked me in the eyes: "I hate him."

I bowed my head. Around us darkness hid the walls in shadow, starry sheets billowed above, and the palace was silent. We were alone, in a flickering pool of lamplight. Her bed was several feet off the ground, and as I sat by her side I had to look up, as if I were appealing to her. "And did . . ." I paused. "Did you always hate him, Shemselnehar?"

"Yes," she said. "Always."

I was quiet. "You know," I said finally, "you know that he thinks you love him."

"I know what he thinks, Abulhassan. I've made him think that."

"Why, Shemselnehar?"

"Because that's what he wants, and if he doesn't get what he wants, I go live with all the other women he's tired of."

She looked down at me with a cool gaze. "Do you know what it's like in there?"

"No."

"Imagine a house full of women who have been discarded, most when they were sixteen or seventeen. Some of them have been in there for years and years now, without hope of a husband, without hope of seeing the world outside. Imagine too that they have no children to occupy them. That last part you should be able to imagine."

I reddened. When the sultan took the throne, he had been forced to kill his brother who had also claimed it. Twenty years before, his father had also had to kill his brothers. The sultan already had two sons. He had made them travel to the Holy City to swear friendship, but he, and the rest of the empire, still feared violence and even civil war after his death. The sultan did not want any more sons. I was responsible for providing the appropriate potions, and more when the potions failed.

Shemselnehar continued. "Imagine now that a new girl arrives in their midst, a new favorite, younger, who crowds out all the others. And imagine that on the day of her arrival the sultan announces that he will give her a palace, an honor he has shown to no other woman. She is his true beloved, he says, his one and only." She bent her head and blinked several times. "I was only fourteen, I had spent one night away from my parents in my life, and that was the night before, when the sultan took me in his bed. I arrived in the women's quarters in the morning. As soon as the eunuch left me, I started to cry, and then, those women, what they did, and said . . ." She shook her head. "I'm older now, and eventually, I'm sure, I'd manage to hold my own there. I'd find allies and then intrigue for useless privileges like the rest of them, but I don't want to become one of those women. I won't."

I reached to put my hand on hers but stopped; my hand remained poised in the shadowy air as I spoke.

"He is not a cruel man, Shemselnehar, he really isn't. I am sure he had no notion what happened there, and still doesn't. If you told him . . ."

"Tell him!" Her voice rose. "How can anyone tell him anything? Every moment that I'm with him I have to pretend I'm in paradise, when really his hairy belly makes me want . . ."

"Shhh . . ." I put my finger to her lips. I did not want to hear any more.

She covered her mouth with her hands and blushed. "Forgive me," she whispered. "Forgive me, please."

"It's all right. It's all right, Shemselnehar. I'm sure no one heard."

"I know, I know, but still forgive me. You're his friend." She looked at me with fear. She was worried that she had angered me, that now I would not help her.

I looked down at my lap.

Over the past year, the sultan had done everything he could think of to make her happy. He had tried to win her love. He thought he had succeeded.

Those first years with my wife, that had been love, hadn't it? It was so long ago. When she called me by name, and we worked together. And afterwards, when we reconciled, and she sat by my side as I worked? But she still called me "husband," and now that I was an alchemist, we hardly ever saw each other. Was there still love between us? What was love, anyway? I sat in silence, trying to remember my youth, trying to understand the present. . . .

"Abulhassan," she said softly. "You're crying."

"No, no I'm not. Am I?" I wiped my eyes. "No, my eyes

are just watering a little. I'm fine, really. But the sultan, he says that he loves you."

"Of course he does. He made me. All of this, everything you see, my name, it's all his."

"Your name?"

"What kind of mother names her daughter Shemselnehar? He made it up, like everything else."

In the classical dialect, Shemselnehar means light of the midday sun. I had never heard of anyone else with that name, but it hadn't occurred to me to question it.

"He's taken everything from me. You know my family is poor, don't you? When I see them or one of my old friends now they don't know how to talk to me, they think I'm a queen. I used to have friends, Abulhassan, just like other girls. We used to walk to the river to wash clothes and then we talked all day. I always complained about having to do the wash, I said my sister should do it instead, but I really liked it, because I could talk to Rehana, Marajil, Amine, all my friends. Now everyone in the world is afraid of me except Mona."

I closed my eyes. The sultan didn't even have Mona. He thought he had Shemselnehar, but all he really had was me.

"Shemselnehar," I asked, "why did you invite the prince into your palace?"

I opened my eyes. She was looking down at her lap. "I don't know," she said. "I really don't. I just did." She shook her head. "I liked him, and I was angry at the sultan, and I wanted to see how much I could get away with. And I thought that with you there . . ." She looked up at me. "Oh, Abulhassan, I don't know. I wasn't planning to kiss him, I just did it, but maybe I did always plan it, maybe I fell in love the moment I saw him. I don't know."

I bowed my head. "You know," I said, "Yazid is convinced that this is all a plot to disgrace the prince and so hurt his own cause. Nuraddin also has spies in your palace. If they haven't told the sultan yet, it's only because they don't think the moment is right. Either of them would poison all of us in an instant if he thought it useful."

"No." I looked up. Shemselnehar was shaking her head. "Not me, not you, and not the prince either. Both Nuraddin and Yazid have crossed me before, and suffered the consequences. They won't dare say a word."

I looked back down at my hands, gnarled from years in the laboratory; I had burnt each of them several times. They say that a man's hands show his life, in which case my life was one of fire and ashes, steaming stills and smoky furnaces.

"The sultan," I said. "He's a good man. He loves you. He wants nothing more than to make you happy."

"I know he's not a bad man, or at least he's not a bad sultan. I try, but I just can't get used to . . ." She paused. "To being with him."

I looked at her. "You're not really sick, I take it."

"No. I just couldn't bear to have him put his hands on me."

"Before you could."

"Yes, before I met the prince I could. But the not eating isn't fake. I don't want any food."

"You should try. Shemsel . . . or, what should I call you?"

She shrugged. "Shemselnehar. It's who I am now."

"What can I do for you, Shemselnehar?"

She looked at me carefully. "I don't know."

I waited, and her gaze dropped to her lap.

"Do you think . . ." She paused. "Do you think that the prince loves me?"

I closed my eyes again. I wanted to go home or, better

yet, to leave the City of Peace altogether. I would go back to Three Springs with my wife, where if princes or sultans or unhappy girls ever came, they would not ask an elderly pharmacist about love. Fatima and I would set up shop again, in the old square by the mosque, just the two of us, without any servants or apprentices.

I blinked. Shemselnehar no longer looked calculating; she was just afraid. I cleared my throat. "I don't know about love, Shemselnehar. I don't know yes and I don't know no. I just don't know—I don't know what love is. I do know that the prince is moved by you. He wants to help you, though I don't see any way that he can."

The call for the day's last prayer rang out, and we fell silent. In a moment the sultan, my wife, and millions of believers all over the earth would be bowing and praying to the same God. Shemselnehar and I sat in our flickering pool of light, waiting for the crier to finish.

"I think he does now," she said quietly. "I think he loves me. But will he if I'm no longer Shemselnehar? If I'm just a plain girl without a palace or pretty clothes, in a small town . . ." She looked at me a moment, then lowered her eyes: "In a small town in Spain or Africa, where no one knows us?"

So that was her idea—to run to the other end of the earth with the Prince of Persia. It was madness, but perhaps because it was just a dream, her desire moved me. I smiled as gently as I could. "So you think that the prince would take you to Spain?"

She looked at me.

"He said he will. But you don't think so? You don't think he means it? He swore upon the Holy Book."

"What?"

"He came today again. Didn't he tell you?"

"No. I told you I haven't seen him. How . . . ?"

"He came disguised as a doctor, this afternoon. He pretended he was blind, so that the eunuchs would think that his presence wouldn't harm my modesty. He had a big black silk sash tied around his eyes, and he came with his hand resting on Mesrour's shoulder—can you imagine?" Her eyes shone. "Can you imagine the risk he ran like that, for me?"

"Yes. Yes, I can."

"He said the sash was also good so that people wouldn't recognize him, but of course I did immediately, just from his chin and his lips. We talked for a few moments, whispering, he was supposedly asking me about my illness. He held my hand to test its warmth and then he ran his hands all along my arms. He felt my forehead and my neck too with his fingers, looking for lumps, he said, and then he had to take my pulse again while he squeezed my arm. And all the time the eunuchs stood at the side of the room, watching. To get more time he called for poultices, different medicines, he had to think and ask me more questions. He finally asked for the Holy Book, saying it would help cure me, and then he had everyone stand back so that he could whisper incantations, he said. And that's when he swore." She paused. "But do you think he meant it, Abulhassan? Do you think he loves me?"

"If he swore it," I said, "he meant it. He'll try to take you away."

She smiled at me.

It might seem strange, but though I had weightier matters to consider, ones of life and death for all of us, I thought about the other half of her question—the one about love. Can love be born in an afternoon? Can it vanish with a robe or a palace, change with a journey to Spain?

Arranged marriages were always better. If you marry for passion, your eyes are blind to your wife's faults; you think her perfection until passion fades. Then you must learn to live with a real woman, flesh and blood, who differs from the ideal that was half your invention. More often than not it ends badly. When your parents choose, and you don't even see your wife before the wedding day, your expectations are realistic. Wise parents choose a wife whose faults and virtues complement your own; you see them clearly and are prepared to live with them. When love comes, it is for a real woman, stubborn or superstitious or however else she might be.

"Abulhassan?"

"Forgive me," I said. "I was just thinking how traditional marriages make all this much simpler, but it's a little late for that."

Her face fell. "Yes. It is too late for that. You didn't have to tell me—I know I can never marry."

I stood up, took her hand, and before she could stop me kissed it. "Shemselnehar, you will never just be a plain girl, whether in Spain or in Africa, palace or rags."

She smiled.

"What can I do for you, my daughter? Curfew will fall soon, and my wife is surely worrying about me."

"Yes, yes, forgive me. I want to see the prince again, but somewhere outside of the palace too. I can leave quite freely, you know."

"Not when you have eunuchs and doctors watching you at all times. Not to mention Yazid and Nuraddin."

She paused. "Yes."

What she dreamed of could never happen, but I still wanted to help her. I needed time to think, and I needed for her and the prince not to get caught and not to see each other until I finished thinking.

"I want to help you, Shemselnehar. Meanwhile you should start eating again. You should try to make the sultan . . ." I paused. "You should try to make him worry less."

She closed her eyes a moment. "I have to," she said, "don't I?"

I bowed my head. "Forgive me, please. Forgive me, Shemselnehar."

"No," she said. "You're right."

My daughter Zaynab, my youngest, whom I could still see in a blanket hugging her red pillow, even she was more than twice the age of Shemselnehar.

"Perhaps it's not necessary," I said. "The sultan really does care for you. If he sees you are unhappy, perhaps, eventually . . ."

"Eventually what? I go back to the harem with the other women until I die."

"I could speak to him. He is not cruel. I'm sure he has no notion what it's like for you and the other women. How could he? No one tells him. He'll be horrified when he learns, I am certain of it. I know there is tradition, and the question of his honor, but . . ." My voice trailed off.

"But . . . ?"

I didn't answer. There was tradition, there was honor, and there was his heart. Shemselnehar's eyes were cold.

"Leave if you must, Abulhassan. Give my respectful greetings to your wife, whose virtue I have always admired—and envied."

"I'll talk to the prince, Shemselnehar. Send Mona to my shop whenever you want. In the meantime don't do anything rash. And for the moment, under no circumstances can you see the prince. Yazid will want to keep everything quiet, but Nuraddin, perhaps, is only waiting for evidence so strong that even your word could not convince the sultan. Don't let him have it. Don't see the prince, even if he wishes it. Tell him you have to wait until you hear from me."

She looked at me a long moment, and something in her gaze disturbed me, but then she nodded. I bowed.

At home my wife was waiting up for me. I just nodded at her and went to my laboratory, where I changed the ashes.

VIII

That night I fell asleep easily, but I dreamed. It was a kind of dream I had not had for years: of Three Springs sixty years before, when the civil war raged.

When the rebels first came and our governor closed the city walls, no one said the word "siege." We stood outside our shops and homes, looked at each other, and said little. Hooded herdsmen and farmers, trapped inside the city, wandered in small groups through the streets, silent amidst the low mud houses that baked in the sun. For months, as rumors of war had circulated, children had play-fought with sticks, shouted and kicked up dust in the alleys. Now they sat quietly, or cried, or petted the cows and goats and donkeys that could not go out to graze. The sun was fierce, but even at midday we took turns climbing the city wall. We stared at the rebels' tents and black flags, then climbed back down, silent.

Days passed. The animals ate what little grass was in the city and began to starve. Herdsmen had to sell, first singly, then by the herd. Butchers' knives rose and fell, rose and fell until nearby streets ran red. Little boys built dams for the streams of blood, carved out boats from small bits of wood and floated them in red lakes; they raced them down steaming rivers when the dams overflowed. The animals piled up faster than tanners could work the skins; older boys earned coppers chasing rats from the carcasses. The sky filled with smoke, and the air stank of leather and smoking meat. Everyone was coughing.

When the animals were all dead the smoke cleared, but the siege continued. Harvest time came. From the walls we watched our wheat ripen and then begin to rot. Despite the governor's assurances, desperation swept the city: that was our winter food out there, rotting before our eyes. Finally, late one night, two guardsmen who were also farmers opened the gates. The next morning black banners waved from the city walls. Between the banners were stakes, and on the stakes were heads: the old governor, judge, and chief of the guard were staring down at us; except for the two traitors, the guardsmen had also been executed. We carried the corpses to a dry gully outside of town, where I decided that since a man's body becomes heavier after death, his soul must weigh less than nothing.

The rebels were fighting, they said, because the old sultan had abandoned the path of true piety. In Three Springs, the rebel commander had a group of soldiers who had been away from their wives for months. He declared that since the old sultan was an apostate, the guardsmen who had obeyed him could not be numbered among the Faithful; the Holy Book's injunction against enslaving believers did not apply to their families. He gave the new widows and fatherless daughters to his men. The guardsmen had just been townsmen wealthy enough to own a sword; their wives and daughters were our sisters and cousins. Sons over twelve were murdered with their fathers; younger children were sold to a slave caravan that had been camped behind a hill, waiting for the siege to end so that it could commence its business.

We harvested our wheat and hunkered down for the winter. I was working for my father's older brother, the pharmacist. There was plenty of illness, but little money; we had few customers. When I foraged in the hills for herbs, I tried roots that my uncle had told me were worthless. I discovered one that made your stomach stop growling if you chewed it long enough.

The old sultan's troops arrived in the spring. Once again, siege was declared, and once again, farmers pined after their fields: we needed to plant. The rebel commander executed the first eight men he saw. He did not pretend that they had tried to betray him; he had decided that since we all wanted to, one man would make as good an example as any other. He planted the heads on stakes in a semi-circle, so that any man who approached the town gate had to pass among them.

At odd hours, in the midday sun or late at night, the rebel commander sent out his men to plunder and then retreat; nearly every night we heard the screams of fighting, dying men. Once a few of the old sultan's troops succeeded in entering the city, but the rebels closed the gate behind them. For the rest of the night we heard screams and then silence, screams and then silence, as the soldiers were found, one by one. The next morning we again had to bury corpses, but this time inside the city. Our wells tasted of blood; children and old people began to fall sick.

On the siege's thirtieth day, the besieging troops stormed the city with ladders. The final battle was fought on foot, with swords and knives, in the narrow streets where humble people like us lived. My mother, my uncle, and I huddled in my uncle's house, safe behind his bolted door. My uncle was a widower with no children, old and pious. Since my father had died when I was two, he had taken care that I remained on the right path. He was strict, but he only beat me when I did wrong. He talked little and when I tried to kiss his hand he pulled it from my grasp, but he taught me all he knew and he nodded his head when I did well. He never spoke of it, but I knew that he had been saving so that I could marry one day, and even during that last winter, when we were hungry, he had not touched the gold that he had buried under his floor—for me.

On the second day of battle, a man was wounded just outside our door. We heard him groaning, hour after hour, crying for water. By sunset, my uncle had had enough. As soon as we finished evening prayer, he silently gathered his dark blue cloak about him, pulled tight the hood that served him instead of a turban, and took a skin of water. He prostrated himself for one final prayer, the one that is supposed to protect against evil, then unbolted the door and stepped into the street, standing tall, not afraid of the archers. Two days later, when it was safe to bury him, my uncle smelled like the cattle carcasses. His skinny old body was so terribly heavy, so hard for me to carry, that I understood just how light his soul must have been.

The old sultan's troops won. The new commander said that the former guardsmen's widows and daughters had to be provided for, and gave them to his men. Since another rebel force was on its way, and the town would not survive another siege, he ordered us to come to the town square to learn to use the dead rebels' weapons. The next morning the sun came up on rows of thin, scared men, but not on me. My mother, my uncle's shop, and my honor would all have to fend for themselves. I had gone to the hills.

In the hills about Three Springs there is water but no food. I found the fleshy white roots I had learned about during the winter. They were too tough ever to swallow, but after I chewed for a few minutes they gave out a chalky juice. A little juice stilled my stomach; too much upset it, but nausea was better than hunger. I chased away birds to gather berries and nuts, but they were never enough and the berries gave me diarrhea. In town I could have cured my diarrhea in a moment; in those hills I hadn't the right plants. I swallowed raw coriander and always had a hand on my belt, but my pants and robe began to feel sticky and to smell. On my fourth day in the hills I stumbled on green shoots that looked familiar. I dug: they were carrots. I gulped down two and immediately threw them up; then I stilled my hunger, slowly. I praised God for His mercy and thought that I would survive after all, return to Three Springs one day to live in peace and plenty, marry and have children; but then the carrots were all eaten. I went back to the white roots.

The rebel troops came with their black banners; the old sultan's forces, my friends and neighbors, went out to meet them; and vultures began to circle before the first arrow flew. From the hills the people looked like ants, but I could see that many ants stopped and never moved again. No one won the battle, but more black banners were coming from the east. When I had fled Three Springs I had thought only that the war would kill me if I didn't run; I hadn't reflected that I, a deserter, could only return if the rebels won—if they succeeded in killing my neighbors and cousins.

As the men battled below, day after day, my stomach hammered down into my bowels and up through my ribs until even my head hurt, and I began to curse my body. I no longer knew what I believed, but I was sure that my soul would go nowhere pleasant if my body failed me. "Stop!" I yelled at my stomach. "Stop! I renounce you! I hate you! I am not you!" It kept hammering.

One morning I woke to find that the ache had spread to my eyes, and when I sat up my vision went blurry. It cleared after a moment, but it began to go blurry for hours at a time, and my head beat with each step I took. My feet had swollen during the night, and at the end of the day they were so big that I had to take off my sandals. My teeth ached as if they were hollow and had sand shaking about inside them; my gums had become so tender that the nuts made them bleed, so I stopped eating nuts and then forgot about the berries too. My diarrhea worsened, but I let the thin fluid seep into my pants. Now that I had stopped eating I seemed to have incredible energy. I had to keep moving and I clambered over boulders, stumbled through the brush and fell into trees, let rocks cut my feet and thorns scratch my shins. Even after the sun set I stumbled along, tripping and sliding and crawling until I rolled over onto my back and slept.

When I woke I saw that my feet and shins were covered with scratches and blood. I grinned and laughed, stood up, fell down, stood up again, ran through bunches of thorns and thistles until I saw the blood flow and I shrieked and screamed with joy. The mere sight of berries revolted me and I flung nuts at the birds, laughing and clapping: I had won over the war, over my body, over the whole universe. I stared down at the fighting troops and screamed: "Kill!" I yelled. "Kill them all! Ha Ha! Kill!" I smiled: I was telling them to kill and behold, they were killing. At noon I lay down by the spring where I found water and closed my eyes, happy. When I woke up I was drooling. A bowl of goat's milk lay at my side.

I reached for the milk, drank it, and went back to sleep. I woke again, ravenously hungry; I found another clay bowl of milk and again drank it greedily. I was still hungry, so I left the spring to go look for berries. Upon my return there was another bowl, a piece of cheese, and two carrots. After I ate this third meal, I sat still for a few moments. I suddenly realized that my clothes were ripped and stained with blood, urine, and excrement. The sun was setting, but I still stripped myself naked. I poured water on my clothes and beat them with rocks until the worst of the blood and excrement was gone. It was early summer, and the nights were warm. After I had laid my wet clothes on a boulder, I walked, naked, to gather sticks, dead bark, dry leaves, and calamint. I wouldn't have thought that my arms were strong enough, but I soon had a fire going. While my clothes dried by the flames, I filled the milk bowl with water, brought it to a boil, and added the calamint. After a little while I removed the calamint and cleaned my cuts with the water. As I washed my feet I found that I could encircle my ankle with thumb and forefinger, with room to spare.

Black and white banners fought for Three Springs; I received regular gifts of milk, cheese, and once even some smoked goat meat, covered in cold fat. I hid myself in the bushes by the spring one whole day, and another night I just lay there, pretending to sleep, hoping to see my savior, but he or she didn't come. Instead the stranger left a piece of cheese, wrapped in goat skin, on the boulder where I went to look down at Three Springs. I hunted for traces and found footsteps, so it was a person and not a djinn, but the steps always vanished into the brush. As I explored the farther reaches of the hills I discovered clusters of goat tracks; my savior was a goatherd who must have fled like me. Yet how could one hide a herd of goats? I had to be able to find them. But the hills were large, full of valleys and gullies and caves.

I was fifteen, the age at which men marry if they have the means; and the goatherd's footsteps were small enough to be a woman's. In Three Springs I had bought milk from goatherds; my uncle and I had sold them medicine. When they had no money, my uncle simply gave them his powders or syrups or poultices; he knew that they would come back another day, with cheese, or meat, or a pelt. So I knew goatherds well enough to know that they were a dirty bunch, with hard features and suspicious eyes. Even so I decided that my savior was soft and slender, with shining black eyes and a shy smile. I spoke my thanks into the woods, proclaimed my name and profession, announced that I had gold inside the city and would happily repay the help I had received. My only answer came from the leaves, which rustled.

One morning I woke and rolled over, looking for a bowl of milk that wasn't there. Surprised but not yet worried, I made my way through the brush. I came to the boulder that overlooked the city and where my friend sometimes left her gifts. There was no food, but when I looked down at Three Springs, the gate was open. Black banners flew along its walls; farmers, not soldiers, filled the fields.

It took me several hours to walk down to Three Springs. My clothes were ripped and filthy; I had lost my turban and my head was unshaven, covered with tangled hair. When I met my neighbors, I stared boldly, daring them to ask where I had been. They blinked until they recognized me, then said "peace be upon you" and went on with their work. If there was to be any hope of a harvest, the fields had to be planted and the irrigation ditches re-dug. When that was done, houses needed repair. After that, maybe, they would have time to mourn the dead, or ask questions. My mother too simply stared at me. She did not kiss me, and she did not say anything, ever, about how I had left her.

Work soon overwhelmed me. All the death had poisoned our wells; even strong young men were vomiting, falling feverish, and sometimes dying. Looters had taken my uncle's gold, plus all his silver and copper tools, but the dried herbs and powdered minerals were still there. As my uncle would have done, I mixed up batches of Dioscorides's theriac, pounded mitqal after mitqal of castor, myrrh, anthemis pyretheum, asafetida and coloquinth into powder. I told people to put the powder in their water before drinking it, but it didn't help. Hoping that heat would release the theriac's essence, I then told them to boil the powder-filled water. The plague subsided. My neighbors had no money, but a tailor made me pants, shirts and a robe from fine cotton; a coppersmith made utensils and a glassblower made jars to replace what had been looted. Yet when I put on my new clothes I thought of how my old ones had ripped; when I looked at my shiny tools and jars I thought of my uncle's death, and how his tools had been broken and stolen. I thought that my neighbors, now busy working to rebuild, had been killing a few weeks before.

In the evenings, I walked through the goatherds' quarter. The low, whitewashed mud houses turned orange, then brown, then blue as the sun faded and the moon rose; the pens, formerly full of snorting goats, were silent. I often wandered several minutes before I found a sign of life: a man sitting at the foot of his house, looking down at the dark road; a woman taking in washing for the night. I never saw any children.

"Greetings!" I said to a man one evening. "Peace be upon you."

The man did not stand to greet me. He just looked up, his eyes hard in the blue moonlight.

"I am Abulhassan the pharmacist, son of Taher the ropemaker, and nephew of Abulkasim the pharmacist, may their memories be blessed. You know me, do you not?"

After a moment, the man nodded.

"Well! I left the city during the war, as some know, and I had wondered if you knew of, well, of anyone else who had left the city, another goatherd, perhaps. I feel sure that I saw one, saw the hoofprints of goats in the hills."

The man looked at me in silence. I looked away from his gaze down the blue, empty street, up at the moon. When I looked back, the man snorted.

"If you've seen hoofprints, pharmacist, that's more than

any of us. None of us left. None except the dead, pharmacist, and those are too many to tell."

Since their goats were gone, the former herdsmen had to work in other men's fields for a few coppers a day. If one of their number was hiding in the hills, I realized, they certainly weren't telling.

My only hope was to tell what had happened, publicly invite my savior to come in secret to accept my gratitude. But what if it was some old man? Even an old man deserved whatever I could give him, but I hesitated. I had never said it, but everyone assumed that it was my remarkable knowledge of plants that had kept me alive. They flocked to my shop and looked at me, just turned sixteen, as if I were a wise man. I buried myself in work, earned as much gold as I could though I didn't know why I bothered; and I told myself that the goatherd was surely an old man. With a herd of goats and no one to sell to, he probably would have thrown away the milk that he gave me.

But when I dreamed that night in the City of Peace, the night after returning from Shemselnehar's Palace of Unending Pleasure, I dreamed of the goatherd. I was fifteen and stumbling through the hills, starving, bleeding, tripping over each bush as she walked calmly ahead. Her cloak was white like death; as she strode through brambles and dust it neither ripped nor dirtied. She was unveiled and at moments glanced back, but so slightly, so quickly that I had only a hint of her face. I thought I recognized my wife when she was young, then it seemed like Fatima as she is now, and then I realized that I didn't know, I had only glimpses, she might also be a woman I had never seen before. I couldn't be sure; it was impossible to see. I tripped and stumbled and fell through the brush; she kept turning slightly, too briefly. Suddenly stark naked, I tripped and stumbled and fell again, bled from my scraped shins, got up and kept after her. She looked back; I was getting closer. When I woke, my arms were reaching into the air. My hands were open, ready to grasp.

Just after morning prayer, Isaac, my youngest servant, came with my breakfast: bread, butter, dates, and salt—the same meal I used to eat in Three Springs. I smiled as Isaac spread a sheepskin on top of the rugs and placed the plate on top of it. He was not yet eight years old and had trouble standing still, but in my presence he always tried to keep a solemn expression, as he thought a grown man should. Now he was looking at me and biting his lip; he had so forgot himself that he hopped from one foot to the other. He had news that he was eager to tell.

"What is it, Isaac. It's all right, you can tell me while I'm eating."

"It's the Prince of Persia, Master. His servant Ozal is here to ask if you'll come see him at his villa in the city. Ozal came yesterday too when you were at his majesty's, and just now when he heard you were about to eat he said he'd wait till you were done for your answer."

I nodded, but my smile had faded. Lost in thoughts of Three Springs, I had woken without remembering my predicament. "Thank you, Isaac. Go tell Ozal that I have some urgent work in my laboratory, but then I shall be honored to visit my lord prince and the noble Lady Khadija."

"Yes, Master. Thank you."

Thank me for what? I wondered, but the boy had left, excited to carry his message. I broke off a piece of bread, dipped it in butter, then cut and added a piece of date. A pinch of salt, and I bit into my meal. I had to make a decision.

Two days before I had taken the prince into Shemselnehar's palace, where they had kissed in front of her servants. I
had seen the sultan the day after and lied to him, but if I went
to him now, I thought he would forgive me. The prince
would be banished or killed. Either way, I would be alone
again, with my furnaces, manuscripts, and memories—for after
the sultan killed or banished the prince, who was my son in
a sense stronger than blood, he and I would never again be
friends in the same way. I would no longer be capable of
beating him in chess. As for Shemselnehar, she would keep
her present unhappy life but without her present freedom. I
did not think the sultan would kill someone he loved so dearly,
though he had killed Jafar, whom he also loved.

And if I helped them? Could they possibly escape?
Strangely, it seemed to me that they might. The sultan had
ordered his spies not to follow Shemselnehar. Yazid would not
want them caught, and Nuraddin might be delighted to see
the Prince of Persia run away with the sultan's beloved. Yet
Yazid would do anything to stop a scandal; of the rumors that
surrounded the death of the prince's father, several involved
Yazid. As for Nuraddin, he might prefer to catch them in the
act, rather than permitting them to escape. And whether or
not the prince and Shemselnehar succeeded, if I helped them
I would betray my friend the sultan, and I would have to
bend my head under Mesrour's sword.

So I had to betray either the prince or the sultan, and only
by betraying the prince could I survive. Once before I had
abandoned all I cared about for a chance at life. Then I had
been young, and now I was old, but death still terrified me.
I agreed with the Holy Book that this life was but a trifle, but
I feared what might await me in the hereafter.

Would the prince and Shemselnehar be happy together,
somewhere beyond the empire? They might. Here in the cap-

ital the prince could never have any real responsibilities, not unless he intrigued with Yazid and the rest; even without Shemselnehar, he had thought to leave. He might be better off in Spain, far away in the north, where he could win honor fighting the unbelievers and serving the Sultan of Cordoba. And Shemselnehar? She had money, yes, but she was young and had never sought it; she wanted love, a husband and children, a life outside of the sultan's harem. I closed my eyes. I saw Shemselnehar as I had just seen her, intelligent, unhappy, pleading; I saw the prince with his boundless confidence and playful smile. Yes, they might be happy. And besides, was it happiness that was all important, or wasn't the dream of it also worthy?

I had finished my bread. I took the remaining piece of date and bit into it, letting the sweetness fill my mouth. I was alone in a small room, the same one where I had slept for the past thirty years, if not more. It was my library—outside the harem. How had that happened?

I had built the harem with a room for Fatima to work in, another for her to cook in, a dining room, two rooms for children, and a bedroom, all around a small garden with a pool, a fig tree, and lots of grass. Yet in those early years I worked late every night and rose before the sun. With young children to care for, Fatima spent many nights in the nursery, and then there were her unclean days, when she slept alone.

I had filled the bedroom with silk carpets and cushions, piled mattresses of softest cotton and covered them with even softer blankets. The lantern's copper frame glinted; its colored panes shone blue and pink light onto rich tapestries that covered the walls. Fatima looked at the silk rugs and fingered the tapestries. "Fine work," she seemed to be thinking, "but what's wrong with my wool ones, the ones I spend months making?" In Three Springs we had slept on a single straw mattress, placed on top of a single wool rug, on top of a hard mud floor. We both found the bedroom a pleasure, but too soft to sleep in; after a year we stopped trying. She slept in her work room, and if we fell asleep together it was also there, on a wool rug and straw mattress. So when, late at night, I left my laboratory, pushed open the harem's heavy door, walked over the grass, passed the silent pool and rustling fig tree and looked into that bedroom, it wasn't to sleep. If I found her there, she was waiting.

Some nights, when I found the bedroom empty, I went on to her room. Gently, I touched her shoulder. Some nights she did not wake; I waited a moment and then left without touching her again. Some nights I knew that she woke but chose to keep her breathing regular and her eyes closed; I again waited a moment and left without touching her a second time. Yet on other nights she blinked at my touch, once slowly, then three or four times rapidly; and then she smiled.

Years passed. I looked in the bedroom less often. I found her there less often. Night after night I slept in my library, on a straw mattress and a few wool carpets, all of which Fatima had made with her own hands.

My wife is a wonderful housekeeper. Every week, either she or a servant beats each of that bedroom's innumerable rugs and tapestries. The copper lantern shines with polish. Every spot on that room's floor and walls remains soft to the touch; everything is warm browns and reds, dark blue, pale silver, and dull gold. The objects all tell of wealth and pleasure, of luxury that glimmers under an ancient lamp's pink and blue panes. I know because I sometimes look through the doorway.

At first I was too poor to have servants, so I spent my days between my shop and my laboratory, the bazaars and the markets. Even on the Day of Assembly I worked, riding out to gather plants. Fatima was by my side, working with me in

the laboratory, but I never permitted her to serve my customers or trade in the markets, as she had done in Three Springs.
I wanted my customers to think me successful, and what kind
of successful merchant needs his wife to work?

The new sultan was young, rich from his victories over
the Greeks; gold spilled from the royal coffers out into the
royal city. At night wine, music, and men flowed through the
streets; barges with musicians and singing girls drifted down
torch-lit canals. Drunk, laughing men on shore flung coins at
the boats which sometimes missed, gold discs that disappeared
into the watery reflections of torches, men, and colored lights.
The men laughed harder: a few coins more or less, what did
it matter? Besides, the beggars would dive for them in the
morning, so it was really a tithe for the poor, God's will that
made a few coins go astray. We dyed our beards red and yellow, wore high heels and wove gold into our turbans. We
spilled wine on Chinese robes and laughed, claiming to have
another ten at home. Drink deep, hosts told their guests, drink
to his majesty and then break the glasses; they came all the
way from Constantinople, and the Greeks be damned. You
like those knives? They're from Khorasan, priceless, but take
them home, my friend, I'll buy more in the morning.

I would rather have stayed home with Fatima, but as a
merchant with wealthy clients, I felt obliged to go to these
banquets. I laughed, lifted up my glass, and did not drink;
when it came to wine, my wife was not so tolerant as the
new theologians. She surely would never know if I drank a
cup or two, but when I held a cup of wine in my hands and
then set it down untouched, I felt as if I were paying her
tribute.

For many weeks, the only time I saw my children was
the eve of the Day of Assembly, when I went to the harem
for dinner. Fatima had brought them up well. When I entered

they stood, bowed, kissed my hand, and remained standing until I told them to sit. My wife always prepared a plate for the boys, another for her and the girls, and a third, silver one for me; everyone waited for me to take the first bite. I asked the boys questions about their studies, told the girls to show me a rug they had woven, a robe they had sewn, or a cushion they had embroidered. No one spoke unless I asked a question. If they had requests, they told Fatima in advance, and if she decided that their wishes were reasonable, she asked me for them. After the meal they stayed seated until I stood, then quickly stood up themselves.

In fair weather, we ate in the harem garden, right next to the fig tree. When I was a boy, I spent hours climbing in a fig tree near my uncle's; if I wasn't at home or in my uncle's shop, everyone knew where to find me. A fig's low, tangled branches make a maze irresistible to any boy; I had planted a fig in the garden so that my sons would know at least one pleasure that their father had had in his village. Fatima told me that she had to chase them out of that tree, even the girls, but they never climbed it when I was there. On the Day of Assembly the boys wrestled, play-fought with sticks, and chased each other around the fountain; the girls made mazes out of string, sang as they danced, and chased and play-fought like the boys until my wife stopped them. I know what my children did because Fatima told me; they never played in front of me.

Fatima made all the decisions about our children. Having grown up without a father, I didn't have a model to compare myself to. It also would have been hard to protest; since I had shut her out of my shop, Fatima had decided that the harem was her domain. I could have given her an order, but to do what? Make them play in front of me? I had once before given her an order: to leave Three Springs. That command had somehow used up all my store of authority. Besides, my children were certainly polite and respectful, well brought up; and I always had work to do or a banquet to attend.

Sometimes, after sunset and before the day's last prayer, I went into the harem. Fatima always rushed to accompany me into the children's rooms. I let them kiss my hand, listened to them say a prayer, and blessed them. Then I left. I often would rather have stayed longer, but I somehow couldn't—especially not with Fatima standing there, watching me.

Some nights, working late in my laboratory, I thought of them asleep in the harem, and a wave of longing took hold of me. I left my scales and jars, my furnaces and stills, and walked out into the main garden. There I watched the stars and the goldfish; I looked at the wooden door that led to the harem. Sometimes that was enough, and I went back to my laboratory. More often, I pushed open the harem door. Quietly, I walked around the harem garden. I stared at the quiet pool, walked some more, then peeked into the bedroom, though on this night I wasn't looking for Fatima. I walked over to the fig tree and lightly shook its branches; I had grown too heavy to climb it. On warm nights I lay down in the grass and watched the stars. I thought not of my children as they really were, asleep a few feet away, but of Fatima on our marriage day; I thought of the caravan across the desert to the City of Peace with my then two children in my lap; I thought of the days when I took my sons to the mosque, where even if my own faith was weak, I was happy to kneel by the side of my sons.

Most often, my memories were enough. I stood up and left the harem, returned to my laboratory or went to my library to sleep. Yet some nights, no more than a few times in a year, I tiptoed into the children's rooms. I was careful not even to breathe too loudly since Fatima, who woke only sometimes when I touched her, was up like a hawk at a sound in the nursery. I watched my sons and daughters sleep. If one turned, or stretched an arm, or began to snore, I quickly stepped back. I had to remind myself that they were mine, and that I was allowed to be there. Before I left, I kissed their foreheads. It was the only time that I kissed them.

I presided proud as any father at my sons' circumcisions. I took each one after his fifth birthday to the mosque, to learn the alphabet and prayers; and as we walked through the City of Peace's streets, crowded with donkeys and water-carriers, merchants and beggars, lords on horseback and porters straining under baskets, I was perhaps even happier than most fathers. In those streets full of people and animals and noise, my son clutched my hand. When old women bent down to coo at him, he clutched my leg. Fatima was not there; my son was clinging to me.

As my sons grew older, I hired teachers for riding and swordsmanship; I handpicked tutors for mathematics, poetry, and philosophy. I taught my sons pharmacy and gave them tasks in my shop, but none of them cared for it. When I decided their professions, it somehow happened that for each there was an exceptional circumstance; and though I have three sons, I have had to hire strangers to work in my shop. My youngest son Isa, who travels and trades with caravans, sends letters when he crosses a caravan heading to the capital. "Most Beloved Mother," his letters always begin, "Most Honored Father."

Zaynab, our sixth child, was born eight years after the others; neither my wife nor I had expected to find the other in the bedroom that night. When I came into the harem, Zaynab smiled. As she grew older, she often sent Isa to find me. "With all due respect, my lord father," said Isa as he bowed, "your daughter begs the favor of your presence at

dinner. She has made a special pastry for you." My wife likes
to laugh at herself and at others, and she often grins, but she
rarely smiles as she did on those evenings, when I came to
dinner to eat what our daughter had prepared.

Like the others, Zaynab bowed to kiss my hand. If she
had something to show me, she respectfully requested permission from her lord father to do so. Afterwards she bowed
again, thanking me for the inevitable compliment, and requested permission to sit. I wanted to pick up my daughter
and kiss her, but what could I do with this bowing little person
who called me lord?

Zaynab insisted that she wanted to stay with her parents
all her life. Fatima and I said nonsense, but the truth was that
we were in no hurry to marry her, and at eighteen she was
still a girl. Since she loved music, one day I brought three
musicians into the harem for her. All were blind, of course,
but one was a certain pale young man who wore a black silk
band over his eyes. He smiled often, sweetly and somehow
puzzled, as if he knew he'd pleased you and was happy for it,
but didn't understand how he had done it. After he had finished playing, Zaynab asked him questions: about his com-
positions, his variants on the old songs, his innovative new
fingerings. His smile grew sweeter and even more happily
puzzled; but when my daughter asked him to show her a
fingering, my wife stood up and said that it was time for him
to go. Zaynab, the young man, and I all blushed—until my
wife had put an end to it, none of us had realized what was
happening.

Zaynab and Fadil were married three months later. I
bought my first book on alchemy. My wife, wrongly convinced that religion forbids alchemy, no longer came to sit by
my side in my laboratory. I missed her, but her stubbornness
also angered me; I was not about to abandon science's greatest

ambition because of her superstition. After a while, I even grew used to missing her: there is a kind of gentle sadness that becomes almost comfortable, or at least customary. Besides, I never failed to recognize her steps as they traveled through the courtyard, past my library or laboratory. It was enough to know that she was in the same house with me; it was enough, on days when I had troubles, to find a tangled knot of hair hanging above my furnace, or to taste a strange potion mixed into the rose water that she brought me.

Even though Zaynab and Fadil live nearby, I see them rarely. Some years I see them only on feast days, when I have Fadil's father to thank for their presence. Abu Yusuf had wanted his blind son to be a crier in the mosque; Fadil had had to run away to be a musician. The sultan had commanded Abu Yusuf to rescind his curse, but neither father nor son wanted to spend feast days together.

When they come, Zaynab kisses my hand and talks excitedly of Fadil and their children. She rarely asks a question, or even my opinion. When the meal is served, she goes with the other women and children back to the harem, while my sons and I sit out in the main garden. I ask Dawood, once a soldier, now a cloth merchant, whether he thinks the Mazdian rebellion in the peninsula will affect the cloth trade; Omar asks, respectfully, what his lord father knows about the rumor that the sultan is building a new palace; and we are all relieved when Fadil offers to play us a song, and we stop talking.

Aside from feast days, my routine was always the same. In the morning I wandered amidst furnaces and stills. My wife brought me lunch, and every week or two we exchanged a few words. ("Fatima," I said. "Husband," she said.) Then more furnaces and stills, coals, ashes, and elixir; I tried yet another formula that I did not expect to succeed. As the day waned I washed and went to my shop, where I solemnly bowed and gravely spoke just as I had for decades, dignified for the eyes of others. When my guests left, I went back to my laboratory for more coals, more ashes, a spoonful of cool mercury, a pinch of fiery sulfur.

The prince was a friend. Without him, the city would be empty.

The sultan too was a friend. As he had done for Jafar, he would wear white for ninety days if he ordered my death.

Once in my youth I had left for the hills above Three Springs, and once I had left for the City of Peace. In the fifty years since then my life had been respectable and dignified, one compromise after another not for the hearts, but just for the eyes of others. My own eyes were moist; I wiped them with my sleeve. I had to go to my laboratory. I had to shovel out cold ashes and shovel in fresh ones, obedient to a formula that asked only the barest of ingredients: mercury, sulfur, spiritual perfection, and ashes. In the laboratory I found that my hands were shaking; I was spilling ash all over the floor.

X

The gate to the prince's villa was like his mother: bleak and imposing. Slaves bowed at my sight, did not speak until spoken to, and spoke with a Persian accent despite evident Slavic or Frankish origin. I shivered as I was led down corridors of white walls, past tapestries of cold silver and dark blue, beneath verses from the Holy Book in heavy, dull gold frames. When I entered her room the Lady Khadija did not rise or speak; she stretched out her hand to be kissed.

"My son sent for you yesterday, Abulhassan." A heavy black veil covered her from head to toe; it shifted as she turned away to look at the verses on the wall. She apparently needed the Holy Book to suffer my presence.

"My lady, I beg your forgiveness. His majesty had required me."

She didn't respond. The Lady Khadija did not think much of the royal family, at least not in comparison with the king of kings whom she had married. After a moment, she spoke. "My son came back from your house pale, Abulhassan, and distraught. I don't know what happened, but Yazid came this morning." She turned to look at me. "The lord chamberlain."

"I have the honor of knowing him, my lady."

She looked at me a moment longer. Though I could not see her eyes through her veil, I could feel her contempt and suspicion. "He thought that I needed to watch my son, and he thought that I needed to watch you too, Abulhassan. Do you have any idea why?"

I swallowed. "No, my lady."

"And that Berber vizier, Nuraddin, he wished to see us too, though of course my servants told him that we weren't in. My steward, meanwhile, is convinced that several shady characters have taken to loitering in the street, watching our gates."

"Though I am honored by your ladyship's confiding her worries to me, I know nothing of these things. If my lady so desires, I shall speak to the royal guard when I leave."

She looked at me a moment longer. "My son is waiting for you," she finally said. "Here," she called to a slave. "Show this pharmacist to the prince."

I bowed.

A white corridor took me to the prince's bedroom, spare and clean. Wide doors opened onto the sunny garden; they let in blue sky, morning air, the scent of orange trees, and the song of birds. Amidst the summer brightness, for a moment I could not remember where I was or why I had come.

The prince stood on the far side of the room, on the threshold of the garden. Normally we exchanged warm greetings, smiled, sometimes even bowed with mock formality; that day we stood in silence. With Shemselnehar or without, the prince would have to leave the City of Peace. I would once again take my dinners alone, amidst my black furnaces and stills. I would wait for the angel of death and then the examining angels, with their dark skin and livid faces. They would question me on the life I had led.

"Aside from my servant," the prince said, "I also came to see you yesterday, but I asked your servant not to mention it."

I blinked. The prince's jaw was set; he too had decided something. "Yes," I said. "I was with the sultan."

He nodded. A hot summer breeze was blowing, and for a moment the orange trees' scent felt overwhelming, sickeningly sweet.

I closed my eyes and then opened them again. "I told him nothing."

He nodded again. "I know."

How did he know? I wondered briefly, but then focused on the matter at hand.

I addressed him by name. "Abulhassan," I said. "Tomorrow morning I will tell the sultan everything. By nightfall tonight, you must leave the City of Peace." I looked out at the orange trees and clear blue sky. "For God, Abulhassan, for honor, for children, a man may risk his life. But love is of no use to the dead." I turned back to him. He was looking at me intently, but I saw the hint of a smile on his lips. Increasingly uncertain, I still continued. "From here I'll go see Yazid, who will help you escape. After you're gone, I'll talk to the sultan. In a few months I'll talk to him again. I think I can say that when you return from your travels, you'll be able to resume your rightful place at court. I know you don't care much for that at the moment, but later on, you might."

He was smiling openly. I looked away. His smile was kind, but I still felt like a fool. He knew that I too cared nothing for positions at court.

"Abulhassan," he said. "My honored and justly beloved lord. Will you please come with me? There is something that I must show you. Please."

He was gesturing towards the garden, with its sunny sky and trees fluttering in the wind.

The garden's lawn and flagstones were littered with overripe oranges that had fallen and split open, overpowering the hot summer air with scent. The prince led me to a tiny house in the garden's center. On all six sides it had folding wooden screens that could be opened to make it a gazebo, but just then they were closed. He unlocked one and pulled it open. The floor had rich carpets and cushions, a pile of books, and a cold brazier. "Please sit, my lord," he said. "I shall return in a moment." I sat on a cushion and closed my eyes.

When the examining angels finish their interrogation, an initial judgment is made. Some learned men, who have spent their lives studying the Holy Book, tell us that the blessed dead all stay with Adam, in the lowest Heaven, until Israfil blows the trumpet for the Last Day. Others say that only saints and martyrs have such a privilege. The other blessed, the ranks of the faithful who led virtuous lives, simply stay near their graves, contentedly awaiting the end of time, when they shall stride across the bridge to Paradise.

"My lord?"

The prince had returned with Ozal, whose biceps pressed against the brass rings he wore about his arms.

"Ozal," the prince said, "you know this man, Abulhassan?"

Ozal nodded.

"Do not allow him to leave this garden. You and Hector shall take turns watching from my bedroom. If he tries to escape or to communicate with anyone, you will stop him with as little force as possible but as much as needed. Do you understand?"

Ozal bowed. The rings dangling from his ears jangled.

"Good. Wait in my room."

The prince smiled and sat down across from me. "You'll have food, books, everything you need here. I'll tell your wife that you're staying with me for a few days, to examine a manuscript. This way the sultan won't be able to punish you. Imprisoned here, you could do nothing to stop me, and he will surely forgive the kind heart that at first made you try to dissuade me, rather than going straight to him."

The carpets were thick and soft. Different shades of blue blended together, designs in silver and gold thread gave hints of light, and with five of the gazebo's six doors closed, I was surrounded by dark wood. I felt as if I were in the cabin of a ship, floating on a calm sea. I had to force myself to speak.

"You know that you'll never be able to live inside the empire again, or even enter it. If you leave with her, you leave forever."

The prince shrugged. "I'm not convinced that's true. For a while, of course, we'll have to stay away, but the sultan will not live forever. Whichever son takes the throne, with bloodshed or without, I think that he'll decide that the Prince of Persia's allegiance is worth more than his late father's jealousy over a concubine. Besides, she and I might like Spain. It's a new land, where I won't have to sit on my heels and waste my life—they still need men there to build cities and settle lands, to win honor and fight for the Faith." He took my hand, and I was so dizzy that I did not stop him from kissing it. "But I will miss you, my lord, you who have been like a father to me. It will be hard."

I looked out of the gazebo, at the orange trees and at the bushes of red roses; they gleamed and shone in the hot sun. I felt sweat seeping from my forehead into my turban. The prince was right. The sultan would not live forever.

"She will grow old," I said. "Her beauty will fade. You will be alone with her in a strange land."

"We all," he said softly, "grow old, my lord."

"You've only seen her three times."

"How often, my lord, did you see your wife before you married her?"

I took my breath in sharply, and for an instant my eyesight was fuzzy, but then I blinked and the orange trees, rose bushes, and hot blue sky came back into focus.

"That was different."

Of course, as tradition demanded, I had not seen my wife unveiled until our wedding day.

"Anyway," he said, "I saw her another time."

"I know, I know. You went disguised as a doctor."

"And then at night, I went back again. She invited me."

I stared. He was smiling like a boy who has gotten away with mischief. "At night?"

"Yes. We agreed not to tell you, because we knew you wouldn't approve. Mona came for me again in the boat, just before curfew. I left the same way the next morning."

I closed my eyes. It was too late, then. I felt a breeze on my face; it made the drops of sweat feel like ice.

"I assure you, my lord," he continued, "that we did not . . ." He paused. "We did nothing besides talk. We did nothing for which either of us could be punished."

It didn't matter. I believed him, and perhaps the sultan would too, but how could it be proven? Shemselnehar had invited him, he had said. Yes, of course, because now he could not turn back—the sultan could no longer just banish him. If the prince did not succeed in leaving, he would die. For a moment I was furious at Shemselnehar, but my anger passed as quickly as it had come. After all, the prince had accepted her invitation; she would not have needed to ask him twice. If he hadn't suggested it himself, it had only been from fear of offending her.

I opened my eyes. The prince was smiling into the sunlight. "I never thought that you could spend a night with a woman and do nothing but talk. She was unveiled and we were in that dressing room together, all alone, but I didn't even try to make love to her. I didn't think of it. I just looked at her and listened to her, and I felt as if I could look and listen like that for the rest of my life." He gestured with his hands as if he were trying to grasp something invisible that floated in the sunny air. "I don't know how to describe it, but when we talk, something inside of her is always firm. I feel like it's pressing against my own brain, my own soul. I can't tell you how exciting it is. It makes me feel like I'm awake, fully awake for the first time in my life, when with every other woman I've met I'm just sinking into soft mud." He shook his head. "I don't even know what we were talking about the whole time. The sultan, of course, and what we were going to do, but also being a child, playing with yarn, running a household, food, colors, stars, everything. Sometimes she made me feel like I was a little boy, other times she made me feel that if I stretched out my arms, I would fly."

I felt as if the world were swaying. I placed my hands upon the thick red cushions on either side of me and squeezed them for support; the silk was cool against my sweaty palms.

"Prince, why haven't you left yet? Rather than calling for me, you and she should already be on the road."

He frowned. "I know. It's what I told her." He stood up and clasped his hands together. "She said we have to wait, and she gave me all sorts of senseless reasons. There must be a good reason somewhere, but she won't tell it. At first she wanted us to wait a week, and just see each other here, in the capital, underneath the sultan's nose. The most I could get her down to was four days. A compromise." He released his hands from their clasp. "You were what made her give in, and agree even to four days. I spoke of the danger to you. I can't keep you imprisoned here forever."

I stood up and stepped to the gazebo's edge. I was looking out at the bright blue sky, but it was a memory that I saw: the last time the sultan had made me come to a royal banquet. The cushion that made obscene sounds had been only the start of Abu Nuwas's mischief. I had refused to drink, which others

had noticed and ascribed to piety, which is never welcome at
a banquet. At the end of the evening, swaying with wine,
Abu Nuwas had jumped on his table, which promptly crashed
to the floor beneath his feet. "I would like," he slurred amidst
equally matched cheers and hoots, "to recite a little something
in honor of Tabultassan son of Aher, that shining light among
men. I wrote it years ago, but always with him in mind, beloved!" He puckered his lips at me, grabbed a wine bottle and
whirled it about his head so that it splashed us all: "New
clothes for everyone! Harun's paying!" He grabbed another
bottle and poured it at his feet as he recited.

> Pour wine! Come, pour and pour again
> And tell me clearly: Here is wine!
> Don't make me drink in secret, when
> You can shout my name in front of all!
> I woke a barmaid from her nap.
> Who's knocking at my door? she cried.
> A brotherhood, we replied,
> Of empty glasses. Wine is what they need,
> And fornication without delay!
> My substitute, she said, will be a man
> With long languorous glances, shining like the dawn.

He shouted some parts ("Here is wine!" "Wine is what
they need!"), did others in falsetto ("Who's knocking at my
door?"), and slurringly sang the rest, save the last two lines:
those he whispered with his arms stretched out towards me,
thrusting his pelvis for an encore.

Cheers and hoots had faded; most of the table looked at
me with sympathy: Abu Nuwas, their eyes said, had gone too
far in abusing a pious old man; but dizzy heat had still risen
to my face. That same heat flushed my cheeks, my eyes even,

as I stood there in the prince's garden. The sky was bright blue and endless, without even a hint of cloud.

"So where," I said, "where will you meet her over the next four days? Will you continue to sneak into the palace?"

"I'll find a house somewhere."

Find a house somewhere? Eloping with the sultan's mistress was not the same as setting up with a courtesan. The prince was too reckless and too confident; he was going to get himself killed. My help would make the difference between escape and capture for both of them. It would save their lives.

"That will take time, prince, and then you'll have a landlord, who will guess that there is something suspicious and surely betray you. I have an empty house in the outer city. It's not far from a bazaar that Shemselnehar often goes to. You'll meet there."

"My lord?"

I turned to face him.

"I said you'll meet in my house. I want to help you. Aside from the house, remember that I can enter her palace openly, and that the sultan confides in me—I can warn you of approaching trouble and possibly deflect it. Accept my help, prince. It will save both of your lives."

He shook his head. "You would face Mesrour's sword."

The hot wind blew, carrying the scent of oranges against my beard and skin. "No," I lied. "Not me. I am his only friend. The Holy Book prescribes death only for adulterers. Even if he wished to be harsh, the law's punishment for me would only be lashes. But with me he will be merciful."

The prince stared, unsure whether to believe me. My words were improbable, but I had never before lied to him, and I knew the sultan better than any other man.

"Come, prince, do you not trust my word?"

"I trust it."

"And do you doubt my judgment, my knowledge of the sultan, or my affection for you?"

He hesitated, then shook his head. "I do not, my lord."

"Then you must let me do as I say. You must let me save your life."

In addition to beheading Jafar, the sultan had banished all his
male relations; but Jafar had been convicted of trying to seize
the throne. Not only was the crime tremendous, it would
necessarily involve his sons and nephews. In my case, so long
as my family knew nothing, there was no reason why my
treason should implicate them.

Yet the matter with Jafar remained mysterious. Most
thought that not even the sultan believed such an absurd
charge, and no details were ever given of the inconceivable
plot; but what else could explain the grand vizier's execution?
And if it wasn't true, why had Jafar confessed? With Abu
Nuwas the sultan drank, with me he talked; Jafar had shared
his childhood, his wars, and his adventures. One night each
month the two men had wandered the city streets, disguised
as merchants, dandies, beggars, and women. They had been
robbed, beaten up, and pitied; they had drunk cheap wine
with beggars, hawked eggs in the markets, and started a con-
spiracy against themselves. They had met djinn and fairies.

One night they knocked on the door of a party, claiming
to be merchants in need of shelter after curfew; they discovered three pretty women, three one-eyed dervishes, and a simple porter. The sultan's curiosity overstepped the bounds of
good manners; the women's servants put swords to their
necks. The sultan and Jafar stayed incognito, talking their way
out of danger as merchants, which was how they would have
died. One of the women who nearly beheaded the sultan is
now known to all: he made Zubaidah his queen.

Abu Nuwas was too reckless, I too cautious to share such adventures; they had ceased upon Jafar's death. Now when the sultan left the Palace of the Golden Gate, it was always in between two rows of nobles, eunuchs, and soldiers; Mesrour, whose sword had beheaded Jafar, rode by his right hand. The day of the execution was also the day that Zubaidah moved into her own palace, and the sultan began to acquire one mistress after another. "Not a day goes by," he once said to me, "that I do not think of Jafar."

I knew that Jafar's fate would be my own, but I was certain that ignorance would save my family. I told my wife nothing. At lunch that day the water's strange tang pleased me, but I swallowed the most un-fishlike bone tucked into the fish with melancholy. Years before I had bought a second house which I rented out; for several months it had been empty. I told my servants that I would not be in my shop that afternoon. They nodded: it had happened before.

That accomplished, I embarked on a day of madness—of drunkenness, if you will. I entered my children's old rooms and chose carpets and cushions, tables and lamps. I went out and bought two sofas, tapestries, more cushions and carpets, then goldfish, parakeets, turtledoves and exorbitant cockatoos. Why not? Considering what I had already committed myself to, nothing else seemed to matter, and I proceeded with a giddy happiness. It had been a long time since I had gone to the bazaars, and I wandered down the crowded, dark streets as if rediscovering a pleasure garden: the Street of Glass, where I bought mirrors; the Street of Clocks, where drops of water marked minutes and chimes rang on the quarter hour; the Street of Stars, where Sabian merchants sold astrolabes and almanacs; and the Street of Fate, where old women, thickly veiled in deathly white, sold talismans and other dark magic.

The bazaars were covered with dome after dome to protect from rain and sun. A hole in the center of each dome let in some light and air, but the bazaars still remained in eternal twilight. Their crowded streets seemed like underground canals that flowed not with water but people: silk turbans rubbed against cotton hoods; jewels and gold embroidery sparkled in the shadows; and straw baskets full of merchandise floated above it all, balanced on the heads of sweating porters. Every few feet the human stream passed through a column of blinding light that entered from the holes in the domes, and afterwards the darkness seemed even darker. In the dusky air, merchants bowed in front of their shops, gesturing for us to enter; others took lamps and shone light over their merchandise; and still others sent out boys who tugged at robes and sleeves, urging us to see furs from Siberia, glass from Aleppo, amber from India, porcelain from the Chinese Empire, swords from the Frankish kingdoms, spices and wood from Zanzibar, and strangely delicate cats from Siam. In every street, whether of jewelers or ropemakers, perfumers or tanners, men stood in front of braziers, their coals red in the dim light. They cooked up fish, aubergines, sweetened dough, or squash; smoke, frying food, and the spattering of hot oil mixed with the sounds and smells of men and women.

In Three Springs the bazaar was just a stretch of ground next to the mosque, where merchants set up tents in the morning and took them down at night. Perhaps the bazaars of the City of Peace, with their darkness and crowds, their foul smells and men thinking only of money, were more like Hell than like Heaven, but for me they were still a form of paradise.

No expenditures had ever given me such pleasure; I regretted that there weren't more hours in the day for me to buy things for my young friends. In front of that second house of mine, the neighbors gathered to watch: I, who was known throughout the city for my simple life, was buying porcelain vases and silver plates for a house I had never lived in. Children stared as porters carried in ebony tables and crystal cups, tiles from Tabristan and carpets from Armenia. "I've rented it to a rich foreigner," I told everyone. "He has no furniture with him, and he's paying me a premium to furnish it. After he leaves my grandson will use it, so I don't mind the expense." I didn't like to have slaves, but I was still prudent enough to want foreigners for servants, ignorant of my future guests' identity and too unsure of our language to gossip. I bought a cook and two housemen on the Street of Men, promising freedom within a month and pay as if they were servants, beginning with the silver dirhams I gave each immediately.

When I returned home, I stopped in my shop. A man was there, listening attentively to one of my servants. I blinked: it was Assad, one of the sultan's spies. My servant noticed me and stopped speaking; Assad turned, smiled smugly, and bowed. We had met before in the halls of the palace, he coming out of the sultan's presence as I entered or the reverse. I returned his bow.

"Good evening, my lord."

"Good evening," I replied. "I hope that you are not ill, Assad?"

"A sore throat, my lord, nothing serious. And your servant has been most helpful in his suggestions. He is truly a knowledgeable man." He lifted up a small flask. Assad was the least noticeable of men, average in all dimensions if a little chubby, with soft cheeks and eyes and a neatly trimmed beard, but his hands were short and plump like a baby's; they did not even reach all the way around the green flask.

"I am grateful that my shop has been of service to you."

"I am indeed in your debt, my lord." He bowed again

and left. My servant was busy dusting flasks, but they always tried to look busy when I entered. If the sultan had chosen to spy on me, why had he sent the one man he knew I would recognize? No, I told myself, Assad was a man like another; he had a sore throat. I went into my laboratory and changed the ashes.

The next afternoon I was in my second house's courtyard, waiting for Shemselnehar. She came through my gates just after the shops opened from their midday rest, since that was the hour when she usually went to the bazaar; Mona was her only companion. When she took off her veil, I saw that her small features were both determined and fearful. I clasped her hand in mine. "It's all right, my daughter. You are safe here." Both she and Mona were heavily veiled in silks of a pattern that any number of rich women use; they had taken care to pass through several crowded bazaars on their way. It was certainly possible that they had lost whichever spies had been assigned to them; it was possible too that whoever was watching my house would be unable to identify them with certainty.

"Oh," she said, "I don't doubt that. I know I'm safe here. But where . . . ?"

"He's inside, waiting."

"Has he been here long?"

"He arrived just after morning prayer, even though he knew that you wouldn't come till now. He said that he wanted to prepare the house, and to be here in case you came early." I smiled. "He left his house disguised as one of his servants. As he left his own mother didn't recognize him—she made him empty out the ashes from the kitchen."

She nodded, a little calmer.

"But right now he's in the parlor, over there, looking just like himself."

She nodded again but remained where she was, looking about her. "Abulhassan, is that a cockatoo?"

"Yes, it is. Or rather, she is. It's a girl."

She smiled at me, and in that happy smile, for just a moment, she looked like the young girl she was. "I love cockatoos. I love almost all birds. Even crows." She looked at the parrots and the turtledoves, then admired the poplars and all the different flowers. "Abulhassan, it's beautiful here."

"Thank you," I said. "I can't tell you how happy your smile makes me. For a long time now, I have had so little opportunity to give pleasure to others." She continued to look at the garden. I cleared my throat. "May I bring you to the prince?"

She turned and looked so serious that now I smiled; such earnestness was comic on so young a face.

"Yes," she said. "Please. But dear Abulhassan, my lord, it's strange. I've been pining to see him, and now I want to delay."

"Come," I said, still smiling. "No more postponements." I escorted her across the garden to the parlor. She turned, squeezed my hands, then walked through the doorway's purple beads. I returned to the garden with Mona.

Mona began to chatter about Spain, but I didn't listen; instead I watched the goldfish dart back and forth as the sun set and the pool's water darkened. Vague memories were coming, of early morning trips to collect herbs in the hills near Three Springs, then of my wife's sixtieth birthday, when I had taken her to one of the city's pleasure gardens. Our daughters had all come home from their husbands' houses to help dress her. I had thought she would protest, but the shrieks I heard from her room were all from the girls, arguing about how best to dress their mother. I had blindfolded her for the boat ride, removing the handkerchief only when we were in the garden. She had initially been frightened by all the people, but then she found the endless sequence of pools and flower beds, fountains and musicians, soft grass and thick carpets, to be like paradise. Not trusting me with such questions, she had turned to our daughters: Were they sure that this garden wasn't outlawed by religion?

"Abulhassan . . ."

The sun had almost set; it was cold. I wondered what was my wife doing just then. In the day and a half since I had decided to help the prince and Shemselnehar, I had not seen her once.

"Abulhassan . . ."

Mona's voice had a tone of urgency to it; when I looked at her, she was blushing. I cocked my ear and then understood. She and I must have walked around the garden while I was lost in memory. We were now standing next to the doorway to the parlor; strands of beads were all that separated the prince and Shemselnehar from us, and they had chosen to be bold like lovers who do not know when they will meet again.

Their pleasure was the final seal on my death warrant, but instead of fear, I felt a strange ecstasy. "Do you see the birds in the air?" says the Holy Book. "It is not their wings, but God's will alone that keeps them aloft." God is everywhere, they tell us; it is His conscious will at every instant that keeps every thing in existence. I have said that my faith is weak, and it was not God that I felt at that moment. It was me. I was in the parrots and in the turtledoves, flapping clipped wings; I swayed with the willow trees and each one of their leaves. I blew with the wind, I blushed with a virgin at the sounds of love, and the heat in my face was not shame but the drunkenness of release. It did not matter how distant I might have grown from my wife, how little my children knew me, and that my only friends would soon be lost to me: we were all one, I knew; they were in me and I was in them.

I took a breath and turned to Mona. "Come," I said. "Let's see how close we can get to the cockatoo. We're going to have to find you a husband in Spain, Mona: a warrior, bloodied from fighting the infidels. Men are men out there on the frontier, and when they see a woman they like . . . Well, you'd better start wearing thicker veils." She blushed deeper and, for the first time since I'd known her, had nothing to say.

A few moments later, Shemselnehar emerged. She was too heavily veiled for me to see her face. She grasped Mona's hand, Mona clutched back, and Shemselnehar pulled her friend after her. "Good-bye Abulhassan," she said without turning, and then they were gone. A moment later the prince came out. For an instant he looked embarrassed; then he shook his head. "Why did she run away like that? And she first made me swear upon the Holy Book that I would wait for her at the same time tomorrow."

The sultan had said that though I had known but one woman in my life, I still knew as much about them as did any man. I thought of my wife, of some of our nights and some of our fights, and I smiled at the prince. "It's because she loves you," I said.

I left him the key to the gate; they had no need of me now. Still, the next day I bought a hundred-year-old lute in case Shemselnehar knew how to play it. I came in the morning, when I thought that no one would be there, but Shemselnehar greeted me in the courtyard; she clasped my hands with tears in her eyes, then knelt and asked for my blessing. Only when she stood up did she realize that I had brought her a present. "No, my lord," she told me, "I do not know how to play. But I shall learn, I promise you, even if in Spain it will have to be with another lute." I had bought the lute on a whim; I hadn't meant to impose an obligation on her. I was not used to my gifts being accepted in such a way, rather than with a kiss on the hand and a "Thank you, my lord father." Yet she seemed happy to have the obligation.

That night, when I returned home, a messenger was waiting for me. He carried no papers; he just whispered into my ear that Yazid was awaiting my visit—and that he did not like to wait. "Tell him that he must wait a little longer," I said. "Tell him too that I believe that he will be pleased."

The morning after, I went to the prince's house; I told him of the messenger. "When are you leaving?" I asked. "What are you waiting for?"

"Another few days," he told me. "She insists. The sultan is going away next week, so there won't be a chance of his coming at night and not finding her. It will give us more time to escape before anyone notices." She had told the sultan that she thought that Yazid or Nuraddin was spying on her. "I shall speak to them both," the sultan had said. "Firmly. They should know better than to have anything to do with you." Shemselnehar believed that they were safe inside the city, and that her servants would never betray her; they knew that if it were a case of her word against theirs, the sultan would always believe her. I was the only one whom the sultan might trust more than her, and everyone had seen me with the prince in the palace. The real danger would come, Shemselnehar felt, when they were fleeing and the sultan could mobilize the army to find them; they had to choose just the right moment.

I did not argue; for me more delay meant more life. I saw the prince or Shemselnehar every day, when I brought them some new present for the house; they always asked me to stay, but I did not accept. It would appear strange to my neighbors if I spent hours in the house of my tenants, and the way they clasped my hands and looked into my eyes was enough to keep me happy. It was true too that those days were strangely peaceful. Not only did I not sense anyone spying, but the streets around my second house, where the prince and Shemselnehar met, were quieter than usual.

Sobriety came with my wife. When we met, she looked at me, knowing that something was happening; I looked away, knowing that I could not tell her what. I thought back on the moment of ecstasy that I had had in the garden of my second house; when I saw Fatima, or even when I thought of her, that vision felt empty. What good was a sense of oneness with the universe if I could no longer confide in my wife? This escapade was driving me farther from her, not closer, and I did not know how to change that without risking her life. I began to avoid her company, but when I found a strange knot woven inside my shirt, or a talisman against the evil eye hanging next to my window, I was often tempted to kiss it.

And my children? The Festival of the Sacrifice was approaching. If I were still alive, all my children and grandchildren would gather in my house; I might even have a great-grandchild by then. They would run to hug my wife, chattering and tugging while she kissed their cheeks or forehead and they kissed her, lovingly, just as the prince and Shemselnehar did with me. But when my own children came up to me, their kisses would show no more than respect. I would soon die. My wife, I thought, would understand, and perhaps she even did already, but my children and grandchildren would never forgive me. I thought of visiting them, but I never visited my children without an occasion. My presence would be strange; we wouldn't know what to say to each other. Besides, for their safety, shouldn't I avoid them during these days of treachery? Nor, for safety's sake, should I break my normal habits. Instead of visiting my children, I once again received indifferent young nobles in my shop, where I dispensed prudent maxims and my knowledge of philosophy.

On the Day of Assembly, the messenger from Yazid returned. "My master is still awaiting your visit," he whispered. "If you do not come, he will draw appropriate conclusions—and take appropriate action."

"Tell your master," I said, "that any action he takes against myself or the prince shall be an action against his majesty, and that if he continues his threats—for you are threatening me—the consequences for him shall be terrible." I gazed at him with what I hoped was contempt. "If I have not gone to his majesty to speak of your visits, it is only because I suspect that Yazid is too wise and too loyal to send such a message, and you are simply some troublemaker speaking in the lord chamberlain's name without his permission. Leave my house, or I shall call the royal guard on you."

That night I told the prince of this second visit. "You must leave," I said. "Now. Yazid will not wait much longer, if at all. He's much better at this sort of thing than I—he'll see through my bluff. Leave," I said. "The next time you see her put her on back of your horse and go."

"She refuses," the prince said. "She absolutely refuses. The sultan has postponed his journey, she says, so we have to wait too. She says that until we flee, we are safe."

I stared at him. "Do you believe that?"

The prince's customary confidence fell from him; he looked frightened. "I don't know," he said. "I don't know if I believe it. But what choice do I have? She won't go."

XII

The next day, just after morning prayer was called, after I had eaten my bread and dates, and after I had changed the ashes around my egg of sulfur and mercury, I walked down the street to the baths. I always went at the same time—the morning after the Day of Assembly, when the baths are emptiest— and I only stayed long enough to wash myself. Many religious men are suspicious of the baths, so the brevity and timing of my visits were approvingly noted, considered part of my rigid morality. To miss my bath, I thought, would be to draw attention; it also might be the last bath that I took.

The baths on my street were perhaps the most opulent in the city; I paid my five silver dirhams and walked down the stone steps into the earth. The baths were made of white marble except for the ceiling, where strips of translucent marble intertwined with colored glass; the sunlight entered pink and blue. In the changing room I left my clothes with an attendant and covered myself with a cloth. I then passed through room after room of steam, colored pink and blue by the light. In some rooms the steam was thin and tepid, and I could see scattered men sitting on the benches along the walls; in other rooms the steam was so thick and so hot that I felt as if I were blinded and burning, alone with nothingness on all sides, and if I lost my balance I would not slip but fall into the deepest of pits.

After the last room of steam I came upon the rooms of water: each room had a pool, beginning with cold, moving through warm, and finally reaching hot. I passed into the last room, with its scalding water. It was too hot for most men; that morning only one other was in the pool. I bowed to him and then gingerly stepped in, letting the heat burn and then tingle; old muscles woke after days of sleep. Servants offered soap and bundles of branches to stimulate the skin; a barber entered and began to shave my head, skillfully keeping the hairs on his razor so that they did not fall into the water; and only then did I notice who my companion was. Were it not for the slave's brass ring in his ear, I likely never would have recognized him.

"Lord Nuraddin!" In my surprise I sat up; only the barber's skill prevented his razor from entering my scalp.

In the steam that rose from the hot water, the sultan's grand vizier bowed his head. "A pleasure, Abulhassan, my lord. Peace be upon you." He looked at me mildly, with the slight, crooked smile that never left him. When he had come out of his mother's womb, I sometimes thought, he had not cried but smirked.

"Peace be upon you too, Lord Nuraddin. Forgive me that I did not recognize you."

Still smiling slightly, Nuraddin shook his head in dismissal. In the clouds of blue and pink steam, his brass ring glinted.

Nuraddin had been born in the empire's western reaches. Captured in war and brought to the capital as a slave, he had entered the sultan's service and risen rapidly. The sultan had freed him, so he no longer needed to wear the ring in his ear, but he had chosen to keep it. "It is to remind myself," he once told me, "that we are all slaves of the Almighty God, the Most Just—and we are all slaves of his majesty too. It was against my will, you know, that he freed me."

Nuraddin was as ugly as his predecessor Jafar had been beautiful. Jafar had looked at you with a smile in his eyes, as if he knew your secret qualities as a man; you wanted to tell him your hopes and dreams, your worries and triumphs. Nuraddin made you feel nervous, as if he knew all your secret defects; you wanted to flee, but you were scared to turn your back.

Nuraddin had pale skin, a long, sharp nose, and eyes that somehow seemed even longer and sharper. As much as Yazid enjoyed wealth, Nuraddin did not care for it. Unmarried, he lived in a modest villa, and he made a point of visiting markets and baths in person, accompanied only by a few guards in disguise—and no one, looking at this thin, pale man with a crooked smile, would ever guess that after the sultan he was the most powerful man in the realm.

The barber resumed shaving my head. Steam rose up in the dim pink and blue light. Nuraddin watched me with his eternal smile.

"It has been a long time since I have seen you, Abulhassan."

"You have been well, my lord, I hope."

"The times are difficult. If the taxes are too high, the peasants abandon their land from misery. If they are too low, the army cannot be paid." He shrugged. "The problem, you see, is delicate. I sometimes fear that it is insoluble."

Among his other duties, Nuraddin was in charge of collecting taxes; he was the most hated man in the empire. Yet he was remarkably competent, and knew so much about so many people. There would be no way to remove him except by killing him.

"Your duties must be trying, my lord."

Nuraddin's smile widened. "Oh, but you see, I enjoy them."

I could think of nothing more to say. Nuraddin continued to look at me with his knowing, contemptuous gaze. The barber finished shaving my head and began to trim my beard;

he spread a fine net in front of my chest to catch the hairs that fell. A boy passed through with a censer of incense, and so burning sandalwood mixed its sweet, brown smoke with the steam.

Nuraddin tapped the steaming water with the palms of his hands, as if he had to tame it.

"You know, Abulhassan, that one of my worries has been the City of the Dead."

"I have heard something of that, my lord." In part of the City of the Dead, graves had been dug up and the deceased had been hurled into the river; the land had then been sold a second time.

"It makes one think about death. So many deaths in this city, Abulhassan. It's remarkable. I sometimes think that at this rate, there won't be anyone left alive." He glanced down at the water, which he patted again. "But the Holy Book tells us that our true home is not here, but in the hereafter. All we need worry about, then, is an honorable path to the next world. The quicker the better." Still smiling slightly, he looked up at me. "What do you think, Abulhassan?"

"My lord, I am in ignorance about such matters."

"A shame, Abulhassan. A shame indeed. Does not the Holy Book order us to think about the Last Day? Death should be on the mind of every man."

The barber's hands were soft about my chin and cheeks, but I could feel a slight tremble in them. "I think about it, my lord Nuraddin, and what the Holy Book tells me, I know. Unfortunately, much of the Holy Book is beyond the understanding of a foolish man such as myself. I can only trust in the Most Merciful."

"So you think yourself foolish? I tend to think of you as quite wise. The sultan does too, I'm sure of it. He greatly admires you."

"I am flattered by the sultan's belief, but we are all fools in comparison with the wisdom of the Most High."

With his smirking smile, Nuraddin nodded approvingly, as if I were a child who had passed a test. "Very good, Abulhassan."

He closed his eyes for a moment and again patted the water with the palms of his hands. The barber removed his hands and then his net; his job was done, my white beard smooth and square. I wondered if I should excuse myself, but something about Nuraddin's hands, patting the water, kept me from moving. He opened his eyes and then stopped his hands; they now rested on top of the steaming water.

"It's a strange thing, Abulhassan, or at least it's strange for a man of action such as myself, but sometimes the best way I can serve the sultan is by not doing anything. Take this incident in the City of the Dead, for example. What can I do? Of course, I had the perpetrators caught, drawn, and quartered before I also beheaded them and put their heads up on stakes. That much my duty commanded. But what about the sacrilege that they had already committed? I cannot find the dead whom they threw into the river—I cannot undo what has already been done, and yet that, in addition to punishing the criminals, is what true justice would require." He paused, smiling crookedly as always. "And so I must leave some dead in their stolen graves, and I must leave other dead in the river—there are dead people all over, my dear Abulhassan, and most of them are in the wrong places. It is difficult to accept, for I believe in justice, but . . ." His smile widened a fraction. "But as you said so wisely, we are all fools in comparison with the Most High, so sometimes I must do nothing except believe in Providence." He smiled at me a moment longer, then bowed his head. "It has been a pleasure to see you, Abulhassan. I fear that it may be a long, long time before

I see you again, but who knows? God is great."

Though the bath was public, mine as much as his, and I had not washed properly, I understood that his words were a dismissal. I stood up, wrapping my cloth more tightly around me, and bowed. "It has been a honor for me, Lord Nuraddin."

Without lifting his head, he smiled into the steaming water. I left, passing through the rooms of cooler water and then the rooms of steam, all colored in pink and blue light.

That afternoon I again greeted noble young men in my shop, where I found myself directing the conversation, again and again, to the virtues of marriage and the mysteries of death.

In my lab, I began a new formula of al-Siddaq's. Besides mercury and plain sulfur, it relied on cohobation (redistilling the same liquid again and again), iron sulfide, and egg yolks. I lit a fire under my largest still, watched the flames lick the clay flask until the liquid turned to steam, then watched the steam gather in the still's glass head before it trickled down another tube into a receiver. When the receiver was full, I returned the liquid to the still's base and began the process again. It would take three days to complete the ninety-nine distillations required—one for each of the names of God. I would then combine iron and sulfur in one furnace while I mixed egg yolks with my purified mercury and sulfur in another. The main difficulty in this process, I knew, was creating a perfect form of iron sulfide: "The hardness of the earth," says the recipe, "must entirely swallow the warmth of the spirit, else the red elixir shall never be potent, and the old man will remain."

Assad paid my pharmacy several more visits, always complaining of his throat, but there was nothing for him to learn in my shop; he must really be sick, I told myself. From the sultan I heard nothing; our weekly chess date passed without a message for me to come. That had not happened for many years, but if he knew, I told myself, why would he be silent? My main concern was Yazid, whose messenger had not returned. He knew that the prince and Shemselnehar were having an affair, which would inevitably harm his cause. My hope was that he had accepted my bluff, that he believed that the sultan was using Shemselnehar to disgrace the prince for his own purposes. But who was I to believe that I could bluff the lord chamberlain, veteran of decades of palace intrigue? And even if he did swallow my lies, who knew what he might not do to stop this affair from becoming public?

Mona finally came to my shop. The sultan had gone on the journey of which Shemselnehar had spoken. She and the prince were still not leaving, but they would any day now, before he returned. For the moment, they were taking advantage of his absence to spend a night together. They wanted me to come for dinner.

After evening prayer, I hired a gondola. My second house was downstream from the first, so the gondolier soon left the canals to join the river, crowded with high barges and ferries between which we glided. Bargemen and ferry pilots yelled jokes and directions over my head; sometimes they greeted the gondolier. Standing, he was high enough that they could see him; I was invisible, both because I sat in such a low boat and because in the world of river men I was a transient, cargo like the bales of cotton they brought to the sea.

My second house is outside the city walls, but the neighborhood is identical to those in the city proper; we passed villa after villa along the river bank until we reached a gap: the street on which my inland house lay. I absentmindedly gave the gondolier a gold dinar, let him help me out of the boat and kiss my hand without reacting. Only as I walked down the street did I reflect that I had raised myself out of anonymity for the gondolier, and might live on as the story of the extravagantly generous passenger.

The house gates were locked. I rapped, and Kristof, one of the Frankish housemen I had bought, opened and bowed briefly. He was a tall, heavy man with dull eyes. He shaved off his beard so that he looked like a boy, but he wore no turban and did not shave his head; his hair grew long, red and shaggy like a dog's. I had already seen him several times, and the fear that had been with me for days did not make me easily amused, but I still had to smile at his appearance.

"They wait in house, lordship." He turned and led the way through the garden without any further words or gestures. I smiled wider at his accent and also at his brusqueness; the prince and Shemselnehar's household seemed far less formal than that of his mother or her master.

Announcing my name, Kristof left me in front of the bead curtain leading into the room I had set up as their parlor. "Enter!" cried a duo of voices, but first I handed Kristof a handful of dirhams. Whether the prince and Shemselnehar escaped or were caught, he would soon be a free man; he would need money to return to his own people.

Strings of purple beads still lay on my shoulders as the prince took my hand and kissed it before I could stop him. "Welcome, dearest Abulhassan, my lord to whom my life shall always belong. Welcome to our unworthy home."

"You have fine manners, Abulhassan Ali, calling his house unworthy." Shemselnehar smiled at the stammering prince and then at me. "We are the ones unworthy, is what he meant to say, and rightfully so. No, please," she said as I withdrew my hand from hers, "please, my lord, allow me to kiss your hand, as your servant ought, for if you do not let me be your servant you will force me to live my life with the sin of ingratitude around my neck."

Smiling, I was about to relent but then drew my hand back. "No," I said, still smiling, "I have enough servants, enough people who kiss my hand, but I accept your gratitude with pleasure."

"My lord," the prince said, "I only meant . . ."

"I know what you meant, and it is your home, and it is as it should be."

On the walls I saw the warm, rich silk tapestries I had bought the week before, the green, white, and yellow wool one I had seen in Shemselnehar's dressing room, and my youngest son Isa's childhood favorite, dark blue like the evening sky. On the floor were the Chinese and Persian rugs I had bought, Shemselnehar's worn red pillow, and the old purple cushions that Dawood, my second son, had loved until he had decreed them unmanly; he had tried to give them to Laila, my second daughter, who had spurned them as ugly. How many years had they been gathering dust? The prince bowed me to a cushion next to a plain sheepskin. As he sprinkled water over my hands from a gold vase, I saw Shemselnehar bring over a clay pot with a conical top, like those that poor women cook in. Not until she had put it front of me and lifted the top did I realize that she had actually cooked in it. I leaned over: carrots, onions, chickpeas, camel meat: the fare of poor folk.

Suddenly I was a child back in Three Springs. I reached down and greedily scooped up a piece of meat with the bread Shemselnehar gave me; it was not every day that my mother could afford even camel meat. Shemselnehar looked on, proud at my appetite. My mother had been younger than Shemselnehar when she had me, perhaps her very age when my father died.

I had given them a house with eight rooms, but Shemselnehar had chosen to do everything in this one: she had cooked in the ornate fireplace and spread out a dinner sheep-skin over the costly rugs; they had moved the sofas to the side and made a bed in the corner out of cushions and carpets. Memories I did not know I had came with the smell of on-ions: sleeping at the feet of my parents, rebuffed when I wanted to climb up to warmth; a man who smelled of sweat towering, then taking me into his arms; coils of rope and raw hemp on the cool floor, such pleasure to play in: our one room home was also my father's workplace.

"Shemselnehar, your father was a grain merchant, was he not?"

She blushed. "He still is, my lord."

I blinked. The reference to her humble origins must have embarrassed her, I thought.

"Forgive me, I was thinking of my own father." But apol-ogizing was worse; it implied that I considered it shameful. Yet she was looking at me only with attentive sympathy, a dutiful hostess with a dear but distracted grandfather. She had qualities of girl and of matron that she hadn't had before; she appeared both demure and efficient. Yes, as I looked at her and the prince, I saw a young married couple, rich in silk and jewels. He was proud but doting, ready to obey her slightest wish, but also attentive to her sadness: though she was glow-ing, her eyes and the corners of her mouth were old. The night before her bed had been the sultan's.

I reached my bread into the pot, scooped out an onion, then a carrot and some meat. "You don't know what pleasure this meal is giving me," I told them. They smiled; the prince put his arm around her.

After the meal I asked for a moment alone in the garden, to collect my thoughts; then we would have a cup of wine and talk about Spain. Spain . . . Perhaps they would make it there and even be happy; they certainly had no less of a chance than any other couple.

I paced around the dark garden and sat down by the pool. It was almost a new moon; in the starlight I only caught an occasional glitter of the goldfish in the dark water.

The banging on the gates was so unexpected that it took a moment for me to turn my head. Then I lay on my back. I heard the gates crash open, padded footsteps, a brief squeal that must have been Shemselnehar, then silence. I stayed on my back. Darkness and the pool's rim hid me from the house; I could only watch the sky and shooting stars. The ancients thought them gods paying each other a visit; my wife believes them heavenly arrows, shot by angels at those devils who in their desire stray too near to Paradise, from which they are eternally exiled. I heard bumps: the guardsmen were still in my house. Why not stand up, I asked myself, face the inevitable with dignity when cowardice will only grant you a few hours of life? I didn't move. Heavy objects were dragged along the ground, then the gates closed; all was silent. When I entered the parlor I found a room bare except for a few worn red and purple cushions, a clay cooking pot, and a green, white, and yellow wool tapestry that showed a field of daisies. It took me a moment to understand. No guardsman had entered my house.

XIII

I untied my servants and crept out into the street; there was no sign that anyone had noticed. The thieves would set free their hostages once they realized who they were, I thought; the only dangers I saw were that this misfortune would delay their departure further, and that news of it might reach the ears of the sultan. Strangely, it did not occur to me that the thieves might be more than just thieves.

From what the prince and Shemselnehar told me later, I pieced together most of what happened.

The thieves put swords to their necks. Both understood what was happening; neither struggled while men tied their hands and feet; and the men were surprisingly gentle. "Leave her," the prince whispered to them. "My family will ransom me for a fortune, but her, if you dare . . ." He could not finish the sentence because the thieves slipped a gag over his mouth; they left the pair bound and gagged while they stripped my house.

The lovers and my possessions were split up among several boats, slender like gondolas but with a seated paddler on each end. Shemselnehar was calm as she lay in the boat's bottom. The men smelled of sweat and onions; carpets, plates, and vases pressed against her on all sides, and the thin boat tilted crazily in the river current; but the thieves had not bothered to cover her, and she could see the stars. God would not forget her, she thought, and she came up with a story that would even spare me involvement. She was quite collected until the man in the rear leaned forward. His lower face was hooded, but she could see the folds shift as his wide jaw broke into a smile.

"My, my," he said, "you're a nice little one, aren't you?" Laying down his paddle, he drew his sword.

"What are you doing?" hissed his partner.

"You can steer. I want to do a little interrogation."

"Wait till we're back. Don't be a fool."

"Shut up and steer. And don't call me a fool." The man placed his sword to Shemselnehar's neck. "I am going to take off your gag," he said, "but just for a tiny moment. If you make any noise, I'll cut your head off. Like that." He swept his free hand through the air. "Understand? Nod if you understand. Good. I'd hate to cut such a pretty neck."

"Yahya, I don't like this. I don't like this at all. And what's this about cutting off her head? The chief said to be extra careful with her."

Yahya pulled Shemselnehar's gag down to her chin. "What sweet lips you have. Who are you?"

Shemselnehar gasped for breath a moment. "Have mercy on me, my lord, I am a simple dancer and an orphan. All my fortune is in the jewels I am wearing, presents from admirers, but please, take them all, just let me live."

The black folds around Yahya's jaw shifted again; he brushed the sword against her neck. "Is that so? All right, dancer, what's your name?"

"Safie, my noble lord."

"If your name is Safie, I'm a Companion of the Prophet. You're as much of a dancer as I am. No dancer is dressed like that." Shemselnehar was dressed elegantly and modestly, like a young, married noblewoman.

"My kind lord, it was a whim of the man who hired me.

Ask in the city, everyone knows Safie the dancer." She paused. "One of my admirers will surely pay a ransom if you contact him discreetly."

"Come on, Yahya, put the gag back on her and start paddling. You can make her dance back at the camp, after the chief says so."

"I thought I told you to shut up. And I want to make her do more than dance. If we wait till we get back to camp the chief'll never let me do anything. Anyway, if she really is a dancer, she's used to it. That's right, Safie, isn't it? I'll bet she even likes it. Unless, of course, she's not really a dancer."

"Yahya, the chief said to be very gentle with her. I don't think she's a dancer."

"That's what we're about to find out. Because if she is a dancer, she's not going to be the complaining sort."

Shemselnehar took a moment to reply. "I am a dancer," she said. "But I have maintained . . ."

"Your virtue?"

She nodded.

Yahya snorted. "Well, that at least we know how to test." He leaned so close that she felt his breath, smelly and moist; she turned her head to the side.

"Please, my lord, have mercy, in the name of God I beg you . . ."

"Bah." He pulled the gag up over her mouth. "Grunt if you feel like telling me who you really are. If not, I'm just going to assume you're telling the truth, and that's going to make me happy. Real happy, even though you got kind of thin hips for a dancer."

A moment later Shemselnehar grunted, but her answer had to wait: they beached the boat. They lifted out Shemselnehar and brought her several yards into the dark woods, low and sparse from the sandy soil. They left her at the foot of a tree; she saw them carry the other loot past her and then the boat, which they hid in a clump of bushes. She grunted. Yahya looked around at the quiet river and the shadowy trees, then drew his sword and pulled down her gag. "Well?"

"Yahya, the chief'll cut your throat!"

"Who are you, Safie?"

"My real name is Laila, my lord, and my father is Ali, the cotton merchant, and his father is Abulhassan, the pharmacist and the sultan's confidant. Have mercy on me, my lords!" She turned her head to Yahya's partner. "My father will kill me if he knew where I was that night, but my grandfather will pay a queen's ransom, but only if he knows I am unharmed! If I am no longer a girl he will disown me, and not pay a copper. I beg you, my lord, have mercy on me and contact my grandfather. It was his house that we were in, and you saw how wealthy he is."

Yahya pulled up her gag and snorted. "Nah. Safie, I think you really are a dancer, and you were looking so respectable because you were trying to trick that nobleman into marrying you. I know your type. Your grandfather a rich pharmacist . . . you can do better than that. Why not make him a general? Or the sultan himself?" As Shemselnehar tried to speak through the gag, he knelt down.

"Yahya!"

"I'm busy."

"I've heard of that Abulhassan, he's the sultan's best friend. If she's telling the truth, we're all dead. The chief told us to be careful with her!"

"She's not telling the truth. She's a dancer and I'll take her as my share. The chief never lets us go into town and I'm sick of it. And even if she is telling the truth, she'll keep real quiet about what's about to happen, because I bet she wants to get married some day. Right, Safie?"

"I don't like it, Yahya. I really, really don't like it."

At this moment, the thieves' chief arrived on the beach; Yahya and his partner explained that one of her ties had come loose and she had tried to escape; and Yahya's partner carried her to the camp.

Tied to a tree at the edge of the camp, the prince saw Shemselnehar brought in: Yahya's partner carried her in his arms, gently, rather than over his shoulder. Yahya, his hood off, looked sullen.

The thieves' camp was in the forest bordering the river. Despite their proximity to the capital, the woods had remained intact by royal decree. Yahya's partner deposited Shemselnehar next to another tree, only a few feet from the prince, who saw her captor sit her up and tie her to the trunk. She looked around rapidly. Her eyes met the prince's for a moment, but then she looked away.

The thieves were tying my possessions into neat bundles, labeled "House of Ali" as if they had been merchandise newly arrived by caravan. The haul was tremendous, the mood jubilant. Shemselnehar and the prince saw a mass of movement in the dark woods, a glint of sword or silver here and there as the men rushed back and forth, slapped each other on the back, and whispered, "Ho, here's a beauty!" "A hundred dinars for this one! No, more!" or just "Whoo-ooo!" They clashed their swords in play and lopped branches off the trees. "Wine!" one called out fairly loudly, "Let's wake some tavern owner and get some wine!"

"Enough!" hissed a voice. Shemselnehar felt wind and then a shudder as a man was pressed up against the side of her tree; the chief had his sword at the man's neck. "I decide if and when we get wine, and in the meantime, quiet! If you asses bray enough to attract some guardsman we'll have to kill him, and I'd rather kill one of you. As soon as we're done we'll go somewhere far away, someplace where you can drink and whore your guts out. But now I want quiet! Understood?" He let go of the man, who stumbled and then ran. Amidst utter silence, the chief stepped back and looked down at Shemselnehar.

"Sorry about the rough treatment, my lady. Nothing personal, you understand." He grinned. "You see, it's just hard to kidnap someone any other way." The chief had a wide, pockmarked face and a broad nose. He wore no turban and had wild gray hair, long like a woman's; his eyes were sarcastic and his teeth were perfect, white and shiny—disconcerting in a man whose hair had already turned gray. He now walked over to the prince and looked down at him; the prince thought that his gaze was sad, apologetic even. "We'll rig up some more comfortable accommodations in a moment," he finally said, "though perhaps not quite what your lordships are used to."

Silent and shadowy, the thieves finished bundling the loot as leaves rustled in the cold wind; both the prince and Shemselnehar shivered with the chill.

Poles clacked and tents began to sprout; the chief and two men untied the prince and took him away. A moment later the chief came back for Shemselnehar and carried her into a small, round tent, where he rearranged her ties—"Just want to make sure your bracelets fit, darling"—and then left her next to the pole in the tent's center. The tent's floor was a simple wool rug, but it was warm and soft; a hooded lantern covered her in light but left everything above in darkness. Shemselnehar curled into a ball, closed her eyes, and felt the canvas brush her forehead with the breeze. Several minutes later the chief returned. He sat down next to her; the lamp lit up his knees and lap but left his upper body in semi-darkness. Even so, she could make out his white teeth and bright eyes in the shadows.

"You know," he said after a moment, "I could sell you at the market in Kufa. Even if you can't sing or dance—and I'll bet you can—I could get a thousand dinars for you, easy." He looked at her a moment longer. Gagged and bound, Shemselnehar looked back. "I might do it," he said finally. "I also might not. It depends on what you say, so think carefully. And if I think you're lying, it's to the slave market with you—for me that's the safest choice. Are we understood?"

She nodded.

"All right." He leaned forward. "I'm going to take your gag off now. I can see that you're smart enough to know how to behave." He took off the gag and she was quiet. The chief nodded, satisfied. "What's your name?"

"Laila."

"All right, Laila, you can relax. No matter what, I'm not going to hurt you. You're worth too much. I look at you, and I see a thousand dinars of pure, red gold. You understand?"

"Yes."

He leaned forward so that his pockmarked face and shiny teeth entered the light. "What's that on your cheek? Did one of my men hurt you? If he did, I'll cut off his head and hand it to you. None of them are worth your fingernail, you can tell me."

She paused. "No," she said. "No one hurt me."

He looked at her a moment longer, then shrugged and leaned back into the shadows. "So. Do you have a ransomer, or is it the market in Kufa for you?"

"My grandfather, Abulhassan son of Taher, the pharmacist. He'll pay whatever you ask without hesitating. He loves me dearly and he's very, very rich. It was his house I was in last night."

"Abulhassan the pharmacist, eh? And your name really is Laila?"

"Yes. But my grandfather always calls me Sunshine, so tell him that."

"What about your father? Or a husband?"

"I am not married. And my father . . ." Shemselnehar hesitated. "Far from ransoming me, he would disown me if he knew where I was last night."

"Really? So your father doesn't approve of that young man you were with last night? He's not your betrothed?"

Shemselnehar managed to blush.

"Hmm," said the chief. "So we've a romance on our hands here, have we? You like a young man and your father doesn't approve. What's a girl to do? Run away? Or perhaps lose her honor, then come to father with the only possible means of reparation? Were you planning something like that?"

Shemselnehar blushed more deeply. "Something like that."

The chief leaned forward. The lamp lit up his face from below, so that his features were all distorted and shadowed around his smiling white teeth; his long gray hair swayed at his sides. "So you're really a conniving little whore, aren't you? Trying to trap a man and disobey your father. What would this world come to if every girl were as lustful as you, a regular bitch in heat? There'd be no families, no husbands, and no fathers. Between the two of us, you're the real criminal here—the only thing I steal is money, and what's money compared to honor? I ought to cut off your head right now out of pity for your father and that nice-looking young man. Right? Shouldn't I?"

Shemselnehar stared. He leaned back, sweeping his long hair behind him, then removed his sword from its sheath and lay it on the carpet between them, right underneath the lantern's cloaked beams. The blade shone. "I'm beginning to think," he said, "that I'm going to have a chance to restore some honor to a family. It's not every day I get a chance like that. But first, tell me—who's the young man?"

"He's also named Abulhassan, like my grandfather. He's a merchant."

"Of?"

"Grain."

"Is he a particularly important merchant? Rich or anything?"

Shemselnehar shook her head. "No. He's just starting."

"And that's the problem, eh? Your father wants a rich man for a pretty girl like you."

She nodded.

"Do you love him?"

She hesitated, then nodded again; the chief leaned forward once more and rested his fingers upon the blade of his sword. "Well, if you love him, you'd better come up with a better story, because as things stand he's going to lose his head." He smiled, his features again distorted by the lamp light coming from below; his white teeth were dazzling. "You see, Laila, I was paid a thousand dinars to break into that house and capture him—what we stole was just extra. And I'm to get another two thousand if I show up at a certain spot tomorrow with your beloved's head, severed from his body. Nothing you've said has convinced me that I shouldn't fulfill my part of the bargain. The only reason I'm hesitating is that I'm a cautious man—I don't like to cut off young men's heads unless I'm sure that I won't get in trouble—and that I can't get a better offer. As a matter of fact, I wasn't even supposed to take you, I was supposed to leave you in the house, but as I said, I'm a cautious man."

Shemselnehar was quiet for a moment. "My grandfather," she said, "Abulhassan the pharmacist, will ransom us both for far more than two thousand dinars." Her voice gathered authority. "And if you dare kill that young man, you cannot imagine the trouble that you will fall into. Yes, I have been lying, but it is because if I told you the truth, you would not believe it."

The chief leaned back against the wall of the tent. There his upper body was in complete darkness; Shemselnehar could only see his knees, covered in a black cloak, and the shining blade of his sword. His voice came out of the darkness. "What is the truth?"

Shemselnehar shook her head. "I won't tell you. Send for Abulhassan. He'll ransom us. You won't regret it. But if you dare to hurt me, or him . . ." She let her words trail off. Although she was a sixteen-year-old girl, bound hand and foot, freshly kidnapped, and he was a mature man with tens of deaths under his belt and a sword within reach, she now was threatening him—and she did it with perfect confidence.

The chief sat in the dark for a moment. "Well," he finally said. "I suppose that I will send for him. Or do you have anything else to tell me?"

Shemselnehar shook her head. The chief stood up. "That's that, then. Oh, if you want me to wrap that rug around you so you'll stop shivering I can do it."

"Yes. Please."

"Done. I'm also going to have to leave you bound, but I'll leave off the gag. But remember, I'll be back in a short while, and I'm a light sleeper. It's possible to put a person in great pain without leaving any marks. It's rather fun, even."

He stood up and left the tent. She curled up in the blanket. Her legs weren't so bad, they were just tied together at the ankles and she could move them, but her shoulders were going numb from her hands being tied behind her back. Several minutes later the chief came back in. Without glancing at her, he rolled up in the rug next to hers and began to snore.

The next day, before morning prayer had sounded, I woke to a hand on my shoulder. It belonged to the angel of death. On my back in the barren parlor, wrapped up in a wool rug I had borrowed from my servants, I stared wide-eyed at Azrael's flowing robes, whiter than any earthly mourning. Their folds revealed only his eyes, calm and compassionless: I had died full of sin and doubt.

"Softly, my lord." He paused a moment. "I have come for Abulhassan." He paused again. "Son of Taher." Though deep, his voice was gentle like a woman's and curiously melodious, as if a lute string vibrated just beneath his words. It was strange for Death. Azrael also would not call me lord; nor would his hand feel warm on my shoulder. I blinked. Of course: desert dwellers, whom I had seen daily in Three Springs, dressed in such loose white robes. On occasion, with caravans or camel herds, they also visited the capital.

My visitor waited, his hand calm on my shoulder.

"I am he," I said finally.

"I am Saleh. I have a trade to propose to you. It could bring sunshine back to your eyes." He stressed the word "sunshine."

Still lying on my back, I nodded at this apparition of white. I was alive. I knew who he was and I had expected him, yet my voice still trembled from my initial vision. "I am always eager, my lord, to engage in trade that may bring profit to all concerned."

He stood up and glided back a step. "Put on good shoes,

my lord. The journey is long." I nodded, examining him more closely as my grip on reality strengthened. He was small and moved lightly. Despite his desert garb, I could better imagine him on a mountain, scampering soundlessly over boulders like a goat.

I had spent the night alone in the parlor waiting for just such a visit. I must have fallen asleep towards morning, but all I had seen in my dreams was immense, pulsing blackness.

Saleh led me through the wakening city. The call to morning prayer rang out, gates opened on shops, and the smell of bread filled the air. A hooded figure turned his head to us from a mound of oranges: it was Assad, the sultan's spy! He turned back to the oranges and tested two for firmness, his stumpy white fingers barely reaching halfway around the orange globes. He let them drop and said something to the peasant woman; she shook her head indignantly. I thought of calling out his name but was afraid; and when I glanced at the man's raw, mud-caked ankles and callused bare feet, I told myself that it was just some laborer, and I was imagining Assad just as I had imagined Azrael.

Saleh and I headed further and further out as the sun rose, stopping only to buy bread and milk for breakfast. We soon entered winding streets that smelled of excrement, so narrow that they would be dark till noon; we had to flatten ourselves against the wall as water carriers pushed past, sweating and cursing under their yokes. The alleys twisted and turned, full of slippery mud patches and pungent rubbish heaps barely visible in the gloom, but the water carriers never spilled a drop.

A wide, dusty street hosted the kind of bazaar I had not seen since Three Springs: used copper utensils, unpainted clay pots, figs, bread, and hordes of beggars. They surrounded us. "My noble lord . . . for the love of the Most Merciful God . . . a few coppers, anything . . . I'm starving, my lord. . . ." Horrified at the wilted limbs that tugged my robe, the drooling lips, the leprous cheeks, I reached into my purse for silver—rich as I was, I did not even carry coppers—and gave a dirham apiece to the ten nearest beggars. They kissed my hands with tears in their eyes, wished blessings upon my grandsons' grandsons. The others swarmed: they pulled on my robe and held on, pawed my cheek, and tugged my beard until I called out to the first ten to protect me. At once unwithered arms punched, crutches swung, good legs kicked while their owners hopped on lame ones. The lucky beggars called their comrades scum, unworthy even to kiss the hand of the noble lord; then they broke ranks as I reached the street's end, ran or limped after me with their cursing friends in pursuit, and cried for another dirham until Saleh drew his sword.

We entered another warren of dark, smelly alleys. They curved, and Saleh turned at every corner; unable to see the sun, I did not even know if we were going north or south. One cat hissed and the next scampered up to rub my ankles. Inside dark houses, behind windows that were just holes in the walls, bareheaded, unveiled women stirred cauldrons that stank of onion; they looked up as we passed, following us with their eyes. A group of children had caught a rat and made a circle around it, keeping it from escaping with their surprisingly fast feet as they laughed and called out to each other. The circle filled the street; we had to wait for the rat to escape in order to pass. In another alley naked children played with fish bones and pebbles; at our approach they stopped to stare. Several smiled and waved, and one asked for a copper, but it occurred to none to move to the side. We had to step over them to get past, and then a moment later we were in a square.

A line of men, lean like vultures, stood against the walls,

hands at their sides. Many turned narrow eyes to us; they looked hungry. These were the "flesh-eaters," I realized, the men who had been pushed off their farms, or who had come to the capital in search of fortune and failed to find it. They wore dark blue cloaks, red shoes if any, and no turbans: their heads were unshaven like slaves'. The sun had just risen an hour before, but out of dark houses came the smells of wine and vomit. Cocks fought in one corner; men cursed and cheered as blood ran along the ground. We crossed the dusty square and in the far end saw a boxing match. Both men were bloody. Was it to the death? "Go! Go! Harder! Hit him! Kill him! Yes! Again! Yes! No!" "Ten coppers more on Othman!" "Two to one on Said! Takers, takers! Any takers! Two to one! Takers, takers! Half dirham, you're on!" The Holy Book strictly forbids such gambling; the brazen contempt for the law shocked me as much as the misery did.

We traveled through more dark streets and another dusty square. I could not believe how big the City of Peace really was. A million inhabitants, the sultan had once said, and growing fast: there were thousands more squares like the ones I had just seen. My eyes teared. "Saleh," I said, "I beg of you, I am an old man, let us stop and rest a moment."

He looked at me closely. "Patience, my lord. We are almost there."

We now went in a straight line and reached a canal almost instantly. Saleh called for a rowboat, the sort used to take small cargo upriver; I sank into its plain wooden bottom as if it had been a gondola swollen with cushions. Saleh whispered his instructions, but he needn't have bothered; I was thinking only of rest.

A moment later he touched my cheek. "You owe the boatman five coppers, my lord." The boatman was shriveled, perhaps older than I and still rowing a boat. I gave him a dirham and told him to keep the change. I refused to let him kiss my hand although, dizzy, I accepted his arm to help me onto shore. We were still in the outer city, on a street of modest homes, three or four stories tall—the kind of homes that various families share, each with just a part of a story. Saleh brought me to another boat in which a man waited, also hooded like a camelherd. They helped me in and we set off; Saleh leaned forward when we reached the middle of the river. "My lord, I must ask you to lie down. I will cover your eyes." I believe I slept until we landed, though if I dreamed it was only of lying in a dark space, close like the boat's bottom.

They carried the boat inland, hid it, and led me into the forest. We reached a clearing. The other man, huge like a bear and silent, produced a thin rug from his pouch and spread it out on the ground. "Sit, my lord," Saleh said. "Are you thirsty?"

"Yes," I croaked.

The bear reached inside his robes and brought out a water skin; I eagerly gulped tepid water.

"It will be some time still," Saleh said. "You may lie down, if you wish."

The carpet was thin, but the sandy ground soft; a cool breeze made its way through the trees. I moved the rug to the edge of the clearing, into the shade. It had been years since I had slept like that, on a rug in the forest with only trees for a roof. I closed my eyes: Azrael, I thought vaguely, would watch over me.

I woke to a warm hand on my cheek. It took me a moment to understand: without his hood, Saleh was a small youth with only the fuzzy beginnings of a beard; his narrow face and thin nose seemed cunning, but his light brown eyes were innocent. "Come, my lord, we are almost there." Squatting, he stretched out his hands and pulled on my arms until I sprang up.

"Thank you, my son."

The bear had gone ahead. Wordless, Saleh rolled up the carpet and led me once more through the forest, to another clearing. Three small tents stood at different edges, and eight or nine men sat in a circle, talking quietly; in their midst, four clay pots with conical tops lay on hot braziers. Sunlight fell through the trees in patches; it changed pattern as the branches moved in the breeze. One man saw us and coughed; the rest turned scarred faces, ragged beards, and unshaved heads to eye my silk robe and my long, groomed beard. Saleh had unrolled the thin rug; he bade me sit with him by one of the pots. The men began to whisper to each other, to nod and shrug in my direction, but then they froze: the chief had emerged from a tent.

I stared at the man's pockmarked face, his gray hair long like a woman's and dirty like a goat's, and his perfect, clean white teeth. He curled his lip between a smile and a sneer. "Welcome." A boy, even younger than Saleh, had accompanied him out of the tent. Dressed in black satin, he was pretty and delicate like a girl; deep black hair hung down to his chin. We remained rigid in the chief's presence, but the boy hummed and tossed his hair as he lifted the high cone tops off the pots and distributed fresh bread from a sack. The chief sat and began to eat. "In the name of the Most High," muttered the others, and we too ate. I had no appetite, but I ate a few carrots when the chief glanced at me; they sat in my stomach like rocks.

When all the men had belched, the boy brought round a water skin and several cups. The chief looked at me. I met his gaze. He was an intelligent man, I thought. We would be all right.

"You are Abulhassan son of Taher, the pharmacist?"

"I am."

"Owner of the house in which I took a young man and woman hostage last night?"

I nodded. "Yes."

"Are you prepared to pay a ransom to have these two freed unharmed?"

I tried to make my smile appear condescending. "If necessary, yes, but for your sake, I rather think that you'll waive that requirement."

The chief sneered at me, his white teeth shining. "Now why would I do a thing like that?"

"Because the young man," I said, "is the Prince Abulhassan Ali of Persia, son of Abu Bakr." I paused. The chief's eyes had flinched; the men murmured. "The young lady," I continued, "is the famous Shemselnehar, the beloved mistress of his majesty." The men gasped. Several stood up.

The chief was pale. "You lie."

I shrugged.

"What was the sultan's woman doing in your house with the Prince of Persia?"

I shrugged again. "I don't see why that concerns you. Frankly, I think you've already learned and done far, far more than is good for you."

One of the thieves spoke up, timidly. "Chief, I was in the hospital once and everyone knew Abulhassan son of Taher, the pharmacist. They said he was the sultan's best friend, he saw him weekly and was even allowed into the harem . . ."

"Shut up! How do we know this is that Abulhassan?"

"I asked," Saleh said quietly, "for the house of Abulhassan

son of Taher, the pharmacist. Everyone knew him."

"You shut up too! Tarik, bring out the boy!"

One of the thieves ran to a tent. The rest fidgeted. They had all incurred death sentences long ago, but kidnapping a prince and the sultan's favorite mistress . . . The army would search the province tree by tree. When captured, their execution would not be a merciful swing of the axe but days, months even, of tortures learned from the Persians and the Chinese, who have ancient traditions.

Tarik and a man who had been in the tent came out, carrying the prince. Gently, they laid him at the chief's feet.

"Remove his gag!"

Tarik removed it. Still bound hand and foot, lying in the dirt, the prince licked his lips and was silent.

The chief stepped forward. "Hassan!" he barked to one of his men. "Say something to him in Persian!"

Some of the best pharmaceutical books are in Persian. I scarcely ever spoke it, but my reading knowledge was enough to let me understand the gist of Hassan's trembling speech: "My noble lord," he said (in about twenty words; the Persians are even worse than the Greeks when it comes to titles) "are you really Prince Ali, called Abulhassan?"

"Yes," the prince said calmly. "I am."

Hassan stepped back. "I think," he said, "that he really is . . ."

"Enough! Ozair, get out the girl. And untie her feet, let her walk!"

The chief stared at me, then at the prince, then back at me; I ignored him. When Shemselnehar arrived I smiled at her, as calmly and fatherly as I could manage. "I have told them your identity, my daughter. They will let us go." She nodded and looked down at the prince, who was still bound hand and foot.

"Who are you, really?" the chief barked.

"I am called Shemselnehar," she said quietly.

The chief stared at her. Perhaps he looked at her delicate features, at her dark eyes that shone with intelligence, and at her long, thick black hair; perhaps he noticed her tiny wrists and hands, her skin that glowed even after a day in the dirt. Perhaps he remembered her haughty refusal to tell him her identity the night before, and her supreme confidence that if he knew it, he would not dare hurt her. Although likely a man of other pleasures, perhaps he also admired a figure that required no props for its perfection; and likely he thought something like this: "Yes, if I were absolute ruler of the largest empire in the history of man and of each individual in it, and if I were to choose a woman, she might be it."

"Untie her hands," he said. "And the prince, untie him too."

The prince stood up slowly, without any sign of his usual ebullience. Shemselnehar watched him, and her eyes too looked passive, somehow defeated. His hands nervously flicked leaves and dirt off his robe as he met her gaze; when the leaves were gone his hands continued, brushing a clean robe.

I turned to the chief, who shuffled his feet, perhaps considering a bow. His men stood in a clump behind him. Except for the young boy, I was the only one still seated. The boy squatted on his heels by the lunch pots and stared with happy eyes at Shemselnehar, at the prince, and even at me. We were wondrous creatures in beautiful clothes. Why was everyone, even his master, afraid?

The chief cleared his throat. "We didn't know, my lords."

"Of course you didn't," I said. "Saleh, will you give an old man a hand up?" Saleh strode forward, light and calm.

"Thank you, my son."

"I wish," the chief said, "that I could return all your possessions to you, but, you see, many of them are no longer in our hands. . . ."

I frowned, but then shrugged. My children would already inherit plenty—if the law would even permit them to inherit from me after my execution.

"Wait, though. Hassan, get my silverware!"

A moment later Hassan returned with a small chest that the chief knelt to open. "Here, come over, my lord, this is yours, and this too, wait, no, not this, but here, the knife . . . Please, take it." He had a good memory. My ladles and knives were mixed in with hundreds of others. I even saw some of those miniature farm implements that the Greeks and Franks use for eating; they need them, apparently, because they don't wash their hands. "Here you go, my lord, this is all of it, I think." He plopped the mass of silver into my hands. Had I really bought so much? It seemed enough for twenty.

"Thank you."

"No, wait, Saleh! Tie it up for his lordship into a package. And here, wait! Here, have some more, my lord. Everyone can use some extra knives. This one's from China, my lord, and those are pearls in the handle." He admired the knife a moment, then gave it to Saleh with what looked like real regret. I was about to tell him not to bother, but he had already picked out a matching set. "These ones, my lord, came from a caravan from Khorasan, you can see the carvings. They were meant for a prince's table, my lord, a prince's table!" He stopped a moment and reddened slightly before hurriedly reburying his hands in the chest. "And this one, I *bought* it, my lord. In the bazaar. It's from India. Have you ever seen ivory carved this way before?"

"Very kind of you," I said, as he picked out another

twenty or so knives. At least ten entirely different styles were represented.

"Saleh! Tie a handle on the package for his lordship, so it's easier to carry."

Saleh did as asked.

"Now, my lords, I wish, well, if they had only said who they were! And no one mistreated them, right, my lord and lady?"

Shemselnehar and the prince both nodded.

"Because," he continued, "you understand, well, but who could have sent us? Who would want to kill the Prince of Persia?"

We all turned to look at him. "What?" I said.

"I didn't tell you? No, of course I didn't. I was paid to break into your house. I was supposed to kill the prince and set her ladyship free. The man who hired me was dressed in desert garb, my lord, I couldn't tell a thing about him. But I was supposed to meet him out by the Street of Tanners to-night, in front of the shop of Sarkis, the Armenian. Perhaps you should send the Royal Guard there, my lord."

"Yes," I said. "Without a doubt."

"And may I ask you, please, to swear that you will not send the army after us? You understand, we hadn't dreamed that our, our guests were of such quality. And of course we didn't harm them—I turned down two thousand dinars just for that reason, that I worried that the prince might be some-one important."

I nodded absentmindedly; my mind was full only of this attempted murder.

"Yes, yes," I said. "We shall not send the army after you."

We agreed that they would break camp and leave us horses. We swore upon the Holy Book to wait until sunset before leaving ourselves.

The thieves began to pack. Tents collapsed with a whoosh, poles clacked together, carpets were rolled up, and saddlebags were carried to horses tethered out of sight, somewhere in the soft forest. As they moved about, the thieves looked at me or the prince with open curiosity, but Shemselnehar they gave only furtive glances; many covered their faces with their hands if they walked past her line of vision. The prince's gaze passed from the fearful thieves to Shemselnehar and back again. She finally sat down in the dirt and leaves, bending her head as if about to take a nap, and the prince turned his gaze to me. Despite the danger he had just escaped, his gaze showed no fear; it showed horror and astonishment.

He stepped forward. "Abulhassan." He came even closer, and leaned over to whisper in my ear so that Shemselnehar could not hear. "Abulhassan. What you said in my garden, about the sultan sparing you when I leave with Shemselnehar. That wasn't true, was it?"

I looked down at the sandy ground, dappled with the sunlight that broke through the foliage. "No."

He stepped back. "Why?"

I paused. "It's what I wanted. It's what I chose."

Without answering, he turned and walked across the clearing to Shemselnehar. He knelt, took her hands, and spoke into her ear. His words were too soft for me to hear, but his manner was urgent. She paused, looked down, and then shook her head rapidly. He grasped her hands tighter and kept on speaking until finally she looked up and nodded slightly. He spoke again, and all of a sudden, she smiled. Though her eyes were dry, she still gave the impression of smiling through tears.

Behind them treetops gleamed bright green in the afternoon sun; shafts of light shone between the branches. As the wind picked up, tickling my cheek and sweaty brow, several leaves glinted in the afternoon light and fluttered to the ground.

The thieves had finished packing. They approached and bowed as a group. "Remember," said the chief, "you have sworn upon the Holy Book to wait till sunset."

"We remember," I said. They left into the cool green forest.

As soon as they were gone, the prince strode back to me. "We are going to leave tomorrow morning, my lord. We would leave tonight, from here, but we cannot abandon Mona."

I nodded. The prince went back to Shemselnehar, who was still sitting on the ground with her head bent. After a moment, I sat down too, and closed my eyes.

Where I sat I was half in sun and half in shadow; it was pleasant to feel warm light on my right arm while my left remained cool. Suddenly I shivered: something was by my side, I was sure of it then and I still am today: it was a djinn or even an angel. I opened my eyes and looked about. I saw nothing, but it was still a moment before the shiver passed.

I reached for the waterskin the thieves had left us; I gulped down cool water, then sprinkled drops on my cheeks and wiped my brow. "You must tell me what happened to you," I said to them.

Shemselnehar told how the thief Yahya had threatened her in the boat, brought her to shore, pulled his sword, leaned over her with lust . . . and then the thieves' chief had come and nothing had happened. She told the story calmly, even indifferently, as if it had happened to another woman. "It was very lucky," she concluded, "that the chief came then. Very lucky." Yet something in her tone, so resigned, indicated that it wouldn't have mattered much if the chief hadn't come. She had to spend almost every night with the sultan.

We were all quiet for a moment. When the prince spoke, it was scarcely more than a whisper. "We are going to leave tomorrow. We are going to reach Spain, and there we will be married. I failed you yesterday, and because God is the only one who can protect us, fate may force me to fail you again in the future. But if you can forgive me, if you can accept that I am imperfect, I will devote my life to you."

"You really will marry me," she said, "even though . . ."

"Yes. If you'll have me. They can write whatever they want in the contract, I don't care."

She was quiet for a moment; then she looked up. "How will we live in Spain?" Something in her tone indicated that, for the first time, she was thinking that they really were going to leave; only now could she permit herself to imagine the details.

"Modestly, at first," he said. "Of course we'll bring what gold we can. . . ."

"Diamonds," she interrupted. "Diamonds will be better. I'll sew them into my clothes tonight."

"Certainly," he said. "But we'll need some gold for the journey. Silver too. Always paying in diamonds or even gold would attract suspicion."

She nodded. "And in Spain?"

"I'll offer my services to the Sultan of Cordoba. He might grant me some land, but it's so far away that my title might not mean anything to him. If that's so, then we'll buy a house in the city, or some land just outside it. With the gold and diamonds we can bring, we could live like that for the rest of our days if we needed to, but they are fighting a war there. I'm sure I'll find a way to win some honor and some wealth, if that's what we decide we want."

"I don't want that," she said. "I don't want honor and wealth. You could die in a war."

He smiled at her. "I could die in many ways. Risking death is not the same as dying. Some men, wiser than I, have even suggested that it's the same as living. But I won't do anything that would make you unhappy."

She shook her head. "We'll have a small house and lots of friends, and then we'll have children too."

He smiled wider. "It shall all be as you wish."

"What does it look like in Spain? Is it cold up there? Do they dress like us?"

Still smiling, he closed his eyes for a moment. "We could be in Damascus in a week or two, then catch a boat in Tyre. Depending on wind, of course. . . ." He opened his eyes. "In two months, I think, we'll buy our little house. Then you'll find out everything."

Shemselnehar did not return his smile, but stayed serious, trying to imagine her future. It seemed to me that she was succeeding.

XV

The call for evening prayer rang out from the other side of the woods; the words, calling the faithful to come and submit to God, were faint but clear. Shemselnehar shook her head, as if she had forgotten where we were; the prince stopped smiling. Our respite was over. We had to go back into the sultan's city before curfew; Shemselnehar had to spend one more night in his palace; and then we would all, in our different ways, leave the City of Peace.

The thieves had left us three horses, in their haste forgetting that one of us was a woman. Shemselnehar should ride behind me rather than the prince, I thought, in case we were identified; but while I stared at the horses, trying to decide which would be the tamest, Shemselnehar untied the largest one and hopped onto it. The half-wild animal had a bridle but no saddle; it reared to throw her, but she dug her heels into its sides and pulled on the reins. It was soon prancing beneath her amidst the trees, snorting.

I was flabbergasted. Did young women ride about on horseback these days? No, she was an exception; the sultan had indulged her whim. So Shemselnehar could ride, but a woman on horseback would still attract attention. We decided that she should veil herself tightly and tie her horse to mine, like father and daughter. We rode slowly through the darkening forest.

We soon hit a wide road, the one that begins down at the sea; it carries goods and people from all over the world to its center, the City of Peace. To our right was the forest and then the river, to the left wheat fields and serfs' huts, the estate of some great lord. Ahead was a caravan of thirty or so donkeys and half as many men. They greeted us cheerfully, not even blinking at our sudden appearance from the woods with a woman on horseback. Everyone knew that the capital's rich had strange customs; they had surely seen stranger in their travels.

Amidst this peace and prosperity, where was the misery I had seen that morning? Had I dreamed it? Or did the sultan keep it away from the roads as well as from the inner city? Inside the city walls, beggars were clean and polite; they never strayed from the steps of mosques.

We rode on into the darkening evening, slowed by my poor horsemanship. When we were finally away from the caravan, Shemselnehar turned to the prince. In the dim light, her gray veil had become vague as a shadow, barely discernible as it hid her face. "Tomorrow," she said, "I'll dress like a man so that I can ride behind you. And you'll call me Aisha."

The prince, like me, was staring at her shadowy veil. We rode side by side on the empty evening road. "But," he said, "Aisha is a woman's name."

"Of course! In public you'll call me something else."

We rode on in silence for a moment. In the dim light, with the dust kicked up by the horses, the still air seemed brown.

"But you told me," the prince finally said, "that your real name is . . ."

"Yes, yes," she interrupted. "I know you know. But from now on, or once we've left the city, I'll be Aisha."

We passed a brown old man with a short, milk-white beard and a dark blue turban, leading a donkey laden with firewood; he bowed his head to us in respect. I realized that the sultan too must know her name. Was it Marida, the name written in a child's hand in her dressing room? I tried, but for me she could be neither Marida nor Aisha; she was Shemselnehar, the one loved by my friend, the sultan. He loved her imperfectly, and perhaps he loved her for the wrong reasons, but his love was still real.

"When we're in Spain," she asked, "will you miss your mother?"

The prince frowned. "Perhaps," he said finally. "Certainly not at first, but perhaps after a while I will. But it doesn't matter."

She did not answer. As she rode, her dark veil bobbed up and down with the movement of her horse.

Stars were beginning to fill the sky; there was a sliver of moon, rising above the City of Peace. Huts were getting closer together; boys began to run out and tug at the hems of my and the prince's robes, extolling the virtues of caravansaries and inns. Women veiled in white from head to toe emerged from a cemetery on our left. It was the day of the week to pray for the dead, I realized. Who of the many should I pray for? My father, my mother, and my uncle were buried with the rest of my ancestors back in Three Springs; I would be the first in this part of the world. The world looked dim, and I dimly thought that we should hurry to arrive before curfew; most travelers were turning off into the roadside inns. But Shemselnehar had started to speak.

"It was on a road like this, I was walking back from the cemetery with Amine. We saw an emir riding towards us, dressed in gold and burgundy, on a beautiful black horse. He was going past us, of course, but then I let my veil drop. I was fourteen. We had all giggled about doing it, but none of us had dared before. I wasn't expecting anything, it was just because it was so exciting. The emir pulled his horse to a stop. I was terrified, of course, and I covered myself as quickly as I could, blushing, for real. Was he going to take me up on his horse and steal me away from my parents forever? Maybe he wasn't an emir, but a bandit. We hurried away.

" 'My lady,' he called out, 'please do me the honor of telling me your name. I mean no harm, only the greatest of honors.' I walked even faster. Even if he wanted to propose marriage and make me a great lady, I only wanted to go home. He laughed and turned his horse around to follow us. 'Very well,' he said. 'I respect your decision, my lady, and will not insist. But may I ask the name of your honored father?' We hurried on, and he continued to follow us a moment, at a respectful distance. Then I heard his horse stop, neighing as he pulled the reins to turn it around. Without stopping or turning, I called out my father's name. Amine turned to me and clutched my arm, but then she let go again, suddenly, as if she were scared. I heard the emir turn round his horse and ride off. The horse kicked up a lot of dust when he turned; I felt it against my veil. Amine and I didn't speak the rest of the way back. In fact, we never spoke again.

"The very next morning I was in the kitchen, helping my mother, when my father came in, slowly, looking very pale and pulling at his beard. He just looked at us a moment. 'Veil yourselves, both of you,' he said finally, 'and come out.' His voice was shaky. I knew it had something to do with the emir who'd seen me the day before. I was very scared, and I was glad to veil myself so that my mother couldn't see me blushing. In my father's room were a dozen eunuchs, dressed in black, the royal livery, with gold. The room wasn't very big. They filled it up, and they made everything, my father's wooden table, the wool carpet, my father himself, they made it all look poor. They bowed to me and then one, Mesrour, stepped forward and asked me to unveil myself. I looked to my father. He nodded, but it wasn't reassuring, and Mesrour's eyes were mean. It was the worst moment of my life, but I did it. The eunuch glared at me as if he hated me. I didn't know then that it wasn't me, that Mesrour hates all women except very old ones.

"He nodded and turned to my father. My father is a very small man, thin too, and Mesrour was as big as three of him. 'His Royal Majesty, Commander of the Faithful, would like to see your daughter. She will be returned to you as she came to him. Only then will he decide what honor he wishes to give her and you, and you may decide whether to accept the honor or to refuse his majesty.' My father bowed, very, very pale.

" 'I am,' he said weakly, 'speechless.' He paused. 'I am speechless in the face of this honor from his majesty, may the Most Merciful God preserve him and shower His bounties upon him.'

"Mesrour nodded. 'Get the girl dressed.'

"Of course, the sultan was horrified when I later told him how Mesrour had been, but it was still his fault, he knew Mesrour and should have known the kind of things he would say.

"My father went back with my mother and me into the harem. My mother was taking out my finest robe and veil. 'Salama,' my father said, 'try not to make her too pretty.' My mother turned and stared at him. 'Are you mad? Do you know what the sultan's favor could mean for us? And do you think we can get away with dressing her in rags for the sultan?' My father sat down against the wall, on the mattress which at night I slept on and in the day I rolled up to make a kind of sofa. He just watched. He didn't understand what was happening, and he certainly had heard that if the sultan liked me he would make me and my whole family very rich. But he also knew that I would become far away from him, that I would never marry the son of one of his friends. I had never wanted those boys, I thought I was too good for them, but I was still very scared. My father stayed on that mattress. It was my mother who brought me out to Mesrour.

"When we went outside there was a big crowd in the muddy square. Most of us had never seen a eunuch before, and here were twelve, in the sultan's livery! I saw Amine, Marajil, some other girls, and there were mothers too, some boys, one whom my mother had said was saving up so he could marry me. There was a palanquin waiting for me, all gold and ivory. There amidst the mud houses it looked like it had fallen from Heaven. I acted very proud as I walked to it, though it was lucky no one could see my face. And when we got to the palace, well, there I really thought I was in Heaven. We'd all heard how beautiful it was, but it was even better than the stories about it. Birds I hadn't even seen in the bazaar, where I used to spend hours walking amidst the different cages! My father had some gold that he kept buried under the house, but there even the vases were gold. And the space—I got dizzy when I was in the main hall. My father's house was only five rooms, and when you went out the front door there was another house right there, and then another. And everyone in the palace bowed to me!

"Then we went into a smaller room and everyone knelt and bowed, so I did the same without even looking. A voice told everyone but me to rise and leave, and then it told me to rise. Since my face was still covered, I dared look at him. He was much different from what I had expected. He looked old and tired, but kind, not like Mesrour at all, and not like my father either. He was very big. 'Please take off your veil, my dear.' His voice was kind too, and though I knew he really wasn't, he made it sound like he was just asking me, and not giving a command. I did it, looking at the ground. 'Look up at me.' He was smiling now, but the smile didn't make me happy; something in it scared me. I was so young I didn't know what that something was, but I knew that his smile was for himself, not for me. 'Take off all your veil, not just the part that covers your face.' I let it drop to the floor. 'Turn around. No, slowly, yes, that's good.' Even when I had turned all the way around, I still looked at the floor, but I felt that he was smiling even wider. His voice now had something harsh in it.

"He clapped his hands. I heard someone rush into the room and fall to the ground.

" 'Rise, Yacub. Find her a string of diamonds and get Habiba to choose a new robe for her. Then have Mesrour take her back to her father and tell him I want her. Bring him ten thousand gold dinars and if he says he doesn't want the money, that the honor alone is enough for him, tell him I insist that he take it for his family, that it's part of my dowry. Go.' Ten thousand dinars! If he was lucky, my father might earn a hundred in a year. I almost started crying.

" 'Come here, my dear.' I stepped forward. Everything was blurry and shiny, all the gold and pearls everywhere were blinding me. He took my hand.

" 'Are you scared of me?'

"I shook my head. He laughed, but kindly, the way my father did when I did something silly. I could feel that my fear was making him smile even wider. 'Well,' he went on, 'I think that you are scared, but I will try my best to be kind to you. You can never tell, but I believe that you are going to make me happy. I'm asking your father to send you here this evening. In my experience, it's best for it to happen quickly, but you will see your family as often as you wish.'

"Habiba came. She was an old lady who looked at me neither kindly nor coldly; she'd seen so many she no longer paid attention. She didn't say a word to me, not ever, but I remember that her fingers were warm when she took my hand. He sent me off with her to change my clothes, then called me in again to see me in them. He told Habiba to choose another robe and saw me a final time before approving and calling for Mesrour. He hadn't even asked my name.

"Mesrour's eyes were still mean, but now he bowed to me, called me 'my lady' and begged permission to lead me out of palace. He took me through antechambers, the grand hall, and the gardens. Everyone bowed again, but to the ground now. My father had said that he would buy me a few bolts of silk for my trousseau when I got engaged, but I had never worn silk before—and those were diamonds, tens of them, hanging on my chest. I had never even seen diamonds, and once I was in the palanquin again I just stared at them, one after the other. Instead of thinking about my family I watched how they changed with every shadow.

"This time there was a really big crowd waiting outside my father's house. Everyone stared at me as I stepped out of the palanquin, and then they murmured. I heard a little boy ask his mother what those beautiful lights were hanging from my neck and his mother told him, frightened, to hush, hush, hush! 'Why? Why do I have to be quiet, Mommy?' And his mother, really scared, put her hand on his mouth and carried him away. I pretended not to notice. I walked in, accompanied by the eunuchs, the way I thought a great lady would walk, very straight, my head high, but I wasn't sure what to do with my hands. I finally put them together behind my back.

"My little brothers stepped a few feet back, my mother whispered a prayer, though it was probably of gratitude, and my father couldn't stop pulling at his beard. He took a step forward, by instinct, to hug me as he usually did, but then he stopped short. His hand stopped moving and just held his

XVI

"Halt! In the name of his majesty!"

During Shemselnehar's story night had fallen, the call for the day's last prayer had sounded, and we had reached the walls of the city. We had planned to enter separately, but we had to gallop together when we saw the guards beginning to pull the gates shut for the night; they stopped us just inside. We turned to face the guardhouse at the foot of the wall. The sultan had once shown me a plan of the city: the walls were ninety-eight feet high and thirty-nine feet wide. Now they seemed higher, dark giants that dwarfed us, hiding even the stars. On top of the walls, distant like faint suns, lanterns glowed yellow inside huts and turrets; others moved slowly, as soldiers paced from one side to the other. At the base, torches sent shadows flickering partway up the dull brown mud before they too faded into darkness. The torches belonged to guardsmen who were approaching, making a semicircle in front of us; in the shadows behind us, other guardsmen held crossbows.

The lieutenant was a short, squat man; he had shaved the center of his beard and let the sides grow down in black tufts, like fangs. His face looked red, but in the torchlight my own face and long white beard probably seemed red too. "Dismount, my lords, if you please. The lady may remain seated." His words were polite—perhaps we really were lords—but his narrow eyes and harsh voice showed his suspicion. "I apologize for the inconvenience, my lords and lady. If needed, my men will be happy to escort you to your homes. But first tell me who you are, and why you are galloping into the city at this hour." His eyes had taken in our fine but soiled clothes, the unsaddled horses, the clanging bundle of silverware, and the presence of a young woman, on horseback, amidst two men at an improper hour. Even though she was heavily veiled, Shemselnehar remained several feet behind, in the shadows.

"My lord," I said, "I am Abulhassan son of Taher, the pharmacist." I paused. His flame-lit face showed only impatience; he had not heard of me. "I live on Kufa Street, but I have a second residence, outside the city walls, near the Mansur mosque. For years I have rented it to strangers, but recently I decided to give it to my granddaughter, Laila," I gestured back at Shemselnehar, "on the occasion of her marriage to the silk merchant Ali. Her brother, my grandson Abulhassan," I nodded at the prince, "had come to help us last night when thieves broke in. They robbed my house and took the three of us hostage. Having other affairs, they waited till this afternoon to interrogate us. Upon learning my identity, their chief, who had heard of the great favor which I have the honor to enjoy from his majesty, set us free." That last sentence, I thought, must have sounded absurd. The lieutenant was eyeing the bundle. "They had already sold most of my goods, but out of good will, they gave me my silverware back."

The lieutenant's mouth had curled into the beginning of a smile. "Permit me to see it, my lord."

I took the bundle down and unwrapped it for him. Despite my best efforts, heat rose to my face, though perhaps in the torchlight it passed unnoticed. Inside the bundle was every sort of knife imaginable, the choicest items from tens of different robberies. "To make up for what they had taken of mine, they gave me some extra knives, my lord."

The lieutenant's contemptuous smile had broadened. "My lords, my lady, you will pardon me, but it is my duty to confirm what you have told me. My men will go to your home to find someone to identify you. For the moment, you must come with me. Perhaps my captain will know you and your silverware." I think I showed fear at those words; his captain would probably know all of us.

"Come here. You." Shemselnehar had ridden into the semicircle of torches and was speaking to the lieutenant. He blinked, but came. "Closer," she said. "I don't like to speak loudly." He came closer. "I am Shemselnehar," she said. "Robbers kidnapped me last night, on my way back to the palace from a friend's house. They had already taken that noble lord, Abulhassan, whom you have before you. He is indeed the intimate friend of his majesty. They freed me when they understood who I was, and they freed those two because I told them to. I know Abulhassan well. He is an old man, pious and old-fashioned. He told you that story because he has never understood the nature of his majesty's love for me, and he worries for my reputation and for that of his majesty. Take him and his grandson back to their home, and take me to the palace. I have suffered a great deal over the last day; I have no intention of suffering you."

The lieutenant stepped back. "My noble and gracious lady, how can I know . . . ?"

"That I am I? Take me to the palace and find out. If I am lying, you will have embarrassed yourself. Your men will laugh at you, perhaps, for several days. If I am telling the truth, and you do not do as I say, you will have been disrespectful to me and thereby to his majesty. Since even the thought of blood makes me ill, it is possible that, if I ask it, his majesty will spare your life. I am not prepared to unveil myself to you."

"Of course, powerful and merciful lady, I would not even dream . . ." He turned around. "You! Take these men

wherever they want. And you! Come with me! We will accompany her ladyship to the palace of his majesty."

It was well indeed, I thought, that the prince and Shemselnehar were leaving the next day. The thieves had not shown
up with the prince's head on a platter; whoever had ordered
the prince's death already knew that his plans had been foiled.
And how could the sultan not hear that Shemselnehar and I
had shown up at the gates with a young man and a story of
having been kidnapped?

Shemselnehar untied her horse from mine. "Good night,
my lord Abulhassan." She paused. "May you enjoy the rest of
the just and the justly well-beloved."

I bowed. "Give his majesty, may God preserve him, the
humble greeting that he knows to expect from his unworthy
servant. And to you, my gracious lady, good night. May God
preserve you in all your endeavors, wherever they may lead
you."

One of the guardsmen had reached to take the reins of
Shemselnehar's horse; she pulled them out of his hands. "I can
ride very well, thank you. You may simply ride on either side
of me, and a little behind. I know the way." She set off without looking at the prince or at me, as was only prudent. In a
moment she had disappeared into the darkness, but I could
see that she took the road that circles the city just under the
looming wall; the lieutenant and four other guardsmen scram-
bled onto horses and followed. I watched them disappear into
the darkness. That had been our good-bye. I turned to the
guardsmen. "My home is straight ahead," I said. "And we
need not gallop. I am not the horseman that her ladyship is."

My gates were locked, of course, and we had to bang for
a moment before a pair of figures came scurrying through the
courtyard: Isaac and . . . Assad, who bowed briefly. "Good

evening, my lords, and forgive my hasty departure. Even his majesty's servants should not be out after curfew." He continued out the gates that Isaac had opened. I blinked and turned to my servant. "His throat, master, he came . . ."

"Never mind, Isaac. Where is my wife?"

She was asleep. We had only come back a few minutes after curfew. The other nights she had waited up for me, worrying.

"Isaac. Is she ill?"

"No, master."

"Did she give orders to wake her if I arrived?"

"No, master. She just went to sleep. She didn't say anything. Should I wake her?"

"No," I said. "Let her sleep."

The guardsmen left, and it was time for the prince to go too. It was already after curfew, and the longer he waited, the riskier his ride home would become. He also had preparations to make for the next day, and yet, as we stood in my courtyard, with the stars shining down on the still pool of water, full of golden fish, he hesitated. The look on his face was unbearable.

"Go," I told him. "There is nothing to say. You have my blessing. I know you will remember me and honor me, but now you must ensure that you live to do so, else my death will be in vain. Go."

He stayed where he was, silent. I shivered. The same foreign presence that had come in the forest was again beside me, and I knew that the prince also felt it. It must be the recording angels, I thought, hovering about my head, getting closer in order to catch this moment in all its detail. Which angel would write this deed? Would it go in the book of life or in the book of death?

"I shall never forget you," he said. "I shall never cease to mourn your absence, though I shall always try to imagine that you are still beside me."

I bowed my head. When I lifted it, he had gone. I stood in my garden for a few moments, though if I looked either up at the stars or down at my goldfish, I don't remember it. Then I went into my laboratory.

It was cold and dark. The last time I had left it so long unattended was five years before, when I had camped out in the countryside to look for herbs. I had formerly taken such trips regularly, and I had even enjoyed my nights alone in the hills; I used a tent much like the thieves'. After that last trip I had begun the experiment that required me to change ashes morning and night; between that moment and now, I had been in my laboratory each morning and each night.

I chose not to light a lamp. I let my eyes adjust as best they could to the dark, then made my way through the shadows. I weaved past furnace after furnace, many taller than I; I stepped over stills and bellows, cauldrons and vases, mortars and pestles; I walked past walls whose alcoves contained more stills, then bars of lead and iron, jars of glass and clay, and neat piles of books. My manuscripts were safely rolled inside leather sheaths, but the leather became covered with dust and ash after only a few hours: despite my open windows and door and my four chimneys, my laboratory's air was always foul. That night the furnaces, stills, and stoves were all quiet; the fire that was their soul had gone from them. Yet I knew my laboratory as some holy men know the Holy Book: if you read them a verse, they can tell you its chapter and number, then chant the subsequent verses until you ask them to stop. I had no need of a lamp.

For the first time in five years, the nest for my golden egg had gone cold along with the other stoves. Nimbly, I inserted my hands into the cold ashes and dug until I felt hard glass. I closed my hand around the container's neck; it was just wide enough for my encircling fingers to reach my thumb. I lifted it up through the ashes, slowly. Through the window's wooden grid, stars and a sliver of moon gave a little light, but no gold glimmered. Sulfur and mercury were still sulfur and mercury: they were sun and moon, male and female, as far from unity and perfection as at the beginning. Gold is harmony, male and female molten and transcended; it is perfection, indestructible, the reconciliation of all opposites and the end of change, says Jabir.

I lifted the pot of ashes off the stove and emptied it. According to the recipe, the ashes must be changed gradually, a handful of old ones shoveled out, a handful of new ones shoveled in: a gradual metamorphosis that ends in complete newness. But I never should have let the ashes go cold; there seemed no point in exactitude now. I put the glass container back inside the pot, then put kindling into the stove's mouth. A little oil, and I struck a spark. All was red. I kept my eyes upon the fire until I could make out individual flames, and then I fed in wood.

When most was ash, I took the small shovel and filled up the pot. I added some charcoal and closed the stove; in the sudden dark I was blind again. Without waiting for my eyes to adjust, I lifted up the pot and placed it on the warm stove top. Without exterior heat, ashes turn cold in just a few moments.

The next morning the prince and Shemselnehar would run away. Soon after, soldiers would come for me. If I really did have two guardian angels to record my deeds, they were about to flutter away; when Azrael comes, the books close. Other angels come, to accuse.

Yet if there really were an angel of death, what name would he whisper?

Abulhassan, of course, is not my real name. When I was born, the custom was to give each child one name for the home, and another for the street. It was to protect against sorcery: a witch needed your real name to curse you, so you should hide it from strangers. For boys, Abu is the usual beginning for such street names: Abu Nuwas . . . Abu Becr . . . Abulhassan. Today, in the City of Peace, most parents do not give their children a street name except as a formality: the prince's parents gave him Abulhassan, but they never hid his real name, Ali.

For the people of Three Springs, sorcerers lurked in every shadow, djinn in every sand storm; secrecy was the rule. It was common for mothers to do as mine did: she did not tell me my real name at first, for fear I might blurt it out. My father died when I was two. When I was eight or nine, she decided that I was ready to know my name; I informed her that I did not want to hear it. In part I was just throwing a fit, but I had already begun to rebel against tradition and against her. She wanted me pious and cautious, a ropemaker like my father. I had apprenticed myself to my uncle, a pharmacist. For my mother, pharmacy was little better than sorcery. My uncle was my father's brother; by law she had to accept his decision, but she knew that I had been the one who asked for it. Now I told her that I was Abulhassan and no other. She could keep that other name for herself, or give it to the witches if she felt like it. When I married, I wrote Abulhassan on the contract. My mother died six months after my wedding. When Fatima and I left Three Springs, we left behind any relative who might have known that name.

Names float through my dreams. One of them, perhaps, was pronounced at my circumcision. The three most common are Omar, Dawood, and Isa, the names I gave to my sons, but there are tens of others. Harun comes up frequently.

A few months after our marriage, when Fatima had overcome her girlish timidity and begun to ask questions, she confronted me. What was my name? It was absurd to be married to a man whose name she did not know. "Abulhassan," I snapped. Fatima looked at me and smiled. I had been rude, and she was still smiling at me. Her bright eyes looked up into mine and smiled too; they said that I was silly, but she liked me just the same. I told her the truth. "But you can go ask my mother," I added. "She thinks of you as her daughter. She'll be happy to tell it to you. But keep it a secret, even from me. I'm Abulhassan now." She nodded, still smiling: I was the funniest creature alive. "Yes, Abulhassan." My mother was very sick then. She really did adore my wife, but back then Fatima was afraid of most people, and my mother could be intimidating. I always assumed that she did not go ask her, but who knows? Perhaps she did.

XVII

Something about the Commander of the Faithful . . . praying at home . . . I opened my eyes, bewildered: I had fallen asleep cross-legged, in front of the furnace. The call to morning prayer was sounding, but with a difference: the sultan, Commander of the Faithful, ordered all the faithful and all those of other faiths to pray in their homes. Curfew was extended until further notice; those who entered the street without written permission would be flogged forty times, the punishment for disturbing the peace.

I tried to stand up and winced; my legs had been crossed for hours. Footsteps thumped as people bustled through my house, speaking to each other in questioning, alarmed tones; I could only listen as I stretched out one leg and then another, slowly and painfully. I finally got to my feet and entered the garden; all my servants were clustered at the gate. Soldiers were walking down the street, but they showed no intention of entering my home.

"My lords, what's happened?" Farabi, one of my servants, called out to the soldiers.

"Nothing! There were troublemakers about last night, and we're looking for them. Stay in your homes."

My servants turned to me, expecting another, more authoritative appeal to the soldiers, but I turned away. I was ravenously hungry.

The Magians, they say, are divided into seventy sects, all quarreling amongst themselves; the Jews have seventy-one, and the Christians seventy-two. The Prophet continued the tradition, predicted that we would have seventy-three. At all times one of these seventy-three, and only one, will entitle its followers to salvation. Most commentators consider this tradition apocryphal, but our religion does have a bewildering number of interpretations. We are not so bad as the Christians, who cannot even decide if their prophet is God or not. Our controversy centers on the Holy Book.

All agree that the Holy Book is the word of God, revealed to the Prophet by the angel Jibril. The first verses were given on the Night of Power; others followed as God's wisdom decreed. The Traditionalists and the Separatists also agree that the Holy Book's words are perfect truth, its commandments to be followed absolutely. Their difference is ontological. The Holy Book, say the Traditionalists, has always existed. It is eternal, uncreated since it has always been part of God, long before the Prophet, the angels, or even this world came to be. Impossible, say the Separatists: the Holy Book was created as was this earth and its creatures. God composed it when He gave it to Jibril. How else could the Holy Book refer to contemporary events? One day the Prophet's wife is accused of adultery; that night a portion of the Holy Book is revealed that declares her innocence. How could such a verse have existed before the Prophet, his wife, or even this earth?

All is written, respond the Traditionalists; all is predetermined. God, in His wisdom, always knew that there would be the Prophet, just as He knew that I would be writing these words at this very moment. He knew before He even created light that the Prophet's wife would be unjustly accused of adultery. No, say the Separatists, man has free will; and each side quotes passages from the Holy Book.

Is not, ask the Separatists, one of God's names the Eternal? By making the Holy Book coexistent with God, like God, are you not falling into the sin of idolatry? The Holy Book is part of God, answer the Traditionalists, one of His attributes; hence its miraculous, inhuman beauty.

The Holy Book is beautiful, certainly, say the Separatists, more beautiful than any other writing known to man or djinn; but it is still blasphemy to say that its style is miraculous. Men could not know its prophetic stories or match the wisdom of its laws, but they could write verses of equivalent beauty. Blasphemy, respond the Traditionalists: the Holy Book clearly states that its beauty can be matched by no man or djinn.

For the Mystics, these questions do not exist; nothing exists, except God. Everyone and everything always has been and always will be; free will is irrelevant when all are One. True religion is to break through the veil to see Him in every creature and thing. In this quest the Holy Book is but a tool, though a most valuable one. It is written: to God belongs the East and the West; therefore, whichever way you turn to pray, there is the face of God. His throne, says that most beautiful of all verses, extends over all Heaven and all earth; He supports it at all moments without tiring. In the heart of man, said the Prophet, lies the throne of God. Turn inward, say the Mystics, find Him and thus the whole universe in your heart. Some say they have succeeded. "I am the Truth!" proclaimed one; "I am I!" cried another; "Praise be unto me!" demanded a third. All threw themselves at a melancholy ruler's executioner: the axe fell.

In private, the sultan reads the Mystics. He permits others to do the same, and does not object if individuals proclaim the merits of meditation and self-mortification. But when they claim direct access to God, such access granting permission to disregard the Law, the Commander of the Faithful must step in. Once a mystic proclaimed that fifty prayers a day, rather than the five prescribed by the Holy Book, had allowed him

to reach God; he urged others to imitate him. He was a char-
ismatic man; soon thousands were saying those fifty prayers,
following their leader and refusing to obey any commands
from the sultan or his governor; the army's bloody interven-
tion was required. The sultan learned his lesson. His tolerance
has its limits.

He has tried to walk a fine line between Traditionalist and
Separatist. Say your prayers, declares the Commander of the
Faithful, obey the laws: this is sufficient. Yet the question of
free will has practical implications. Without calling it by name,
the sultan has accepted the Separatists' looser interpretations
on concubinage and wine; he is widely suspected of being a
secret Separatist, which he is—as is Yazid. Nuraddin, the Berber from Africa, the ascetic grand vizier, is a Traditionalist.
The debates can turn violent. Separatists have demanded the
expulsion of Traditionalists from public office; bands of Traditionalists have broken into taverns and banquets, where they
dump wine into the gutter, beat the dancing girls, and flog
any man who has consorted with them.

The evening that the prince and Shemselnehar were kidnapped, while the sultan was traveling up the river to Raqqa,
such a raid took place. Yet these raids happen often; generally
they are spontaneous, and neither Nuraddin nor any other of
the Traditionalists' leaders has ordered them. Usually the sultan's guard tracks down the perpetrators and there is an end
of it; there are no revenge attacks, and few people ever hear
that anything happened. Though Nuraddin and Yazid cannot
control the fanatics who make up their bases, they have great
influence with each group's leaders. Only on rare occasions
does anyone want civil unrest, especially since the sultan is
well aware of his henchmen's alliances; if Yazid or Nuraddin
cannot convince him that the unrest really was out of their

control, the guilty party will suffer the consequences—unless, of course, the sultan has his own reasons for letting his subjects indulge in a day or two of violence.

The afternoon after this raid on the tavern, while Shemselnehar, the prince, and I were sitting in the forest, two of the Traditionalists' leaders were found lying in the street, beaten to a pulp. Such a response is uncommon enough to make one suspect orders from someone higher up, but it might have occurred before anyone important had heard of the initial provocation. But at night, a few hours after the three of us had returned to the city and encountered the guard at the gate, a mob broke into a leading Separatist's house, dragged him into the street, and would have avenged their own but for a passing patrol. The patrol called on them to desist. They did, but only to turn their violence on the guardsmen, crying that the sultan was a Separatist who allowed their leaders to be beaten. Reinforcements were sent. Many men were arrested; others escaped, perhaps to rouse their comrades. Word of the Traditionalists' attack quickly spread among the Separatists, whose leaders called for restraint, but not very loudly; men began to gather in squares and in courtyards of friendly mosques. Nuraddin called up the army to scatter these gatherings. He also dispatched messenger pigeons to the sultan, although, strangely, he did not order the curfew; it was the sultan himself, hurrying back to the capital, who ordered it via pigeon.

There could be no question of the prince and Shemselnehar's leaving under such a curfew. Every moment they stayed in the city was a moment of danger for them, but my death was postponed. I had offered my life so that they might escape, and now that escape was in danger. In return I had only a few extra days, perhaps mere hours, until curfew was lifted.

What does a man do with a temporary stay of execution? I changed the ashes, ate a meal devoid of any special tang or bone, and did what I had not done in years: I walked over to Fatima's room. On my way through the garden, I stopped to look at the goldfish. It had always been my regret that I could not have both ducks and goldfish, and what self-respecting alchemist could do without goldfish? In my own way, I am just as traditional as my wife. Yet I had often spent evening hours sitting by one of the quieter canals, throwing bread to the ducks. I even quacked at them, softly, when no one else was around. "Quack! Quack!" went the wise old pharmacist, the mysterious alchemist, the white-bearded confidant of the sultan: "Quack!"

Shemselnehar used to wander through the bazaar of birds, admiring and desiring the pretty feathers and strange beaks. I too had spent many an hour strolling up and down the Street of Birds. What I loved was the blur of feathers, the cacophony of chirps, squawks, and shrill parrot speech, the bustle and chaos that differed from that of people in that it could not harm me. The merchants resented me for buying so rarely, but I liked that blur only outside my home.

Leaving the goldfish, I crossed the rest of the garden.

"Fatima. It is your husband. May I come in?"

"Yes."

I stepped through the blue beads as if falling through water.

The house was full of silk rugs and cushions, but my wife sat cross-legged on a red and black wool carpet. It looked new; she had surely woven it sometime over the past year, while I was poking through ashes. The walls too could have been in Three Springs: they had only a few wool tapestries and parchments, with the names of God and of the Prophet written upon them. The room's only costly item was a copy of the

Holy Book; it lay, on a silk cushion, on top of the only table. At the side, next to a pair of chests, a thin mattress was rolled up neatly, just like the one in my library.

Fatima looked at me as I stood in front of the strings of blue beads, which were still swaying and rattling from my entrance. After a moment, she put down her work; she was embroidering a red cushion, the kind that little children use. She looked back up at me.

"May I sit down, Fatima?"

She nodded. I glanced at the space next to her on the rug, but chose instead to sit on the mattress. She turned to face me. She squinted a little, but I could still see her bright eyes: they were narrow and watchful, but never cold; a lifetime with me had killed her open trust, but not her heart. "It is said that when God gave the Prophet a glimpse of the afterlife, he saw that Heaven was mostly the poor, and Hell, mostly women." I paused. "Even amidst my worldly success, you have retained the soul of a poor woman."

"Are you becoming religious now?"

I shook my head.

"If you were trying to pay a compliment, you could do better."

I blushed.

"Fatima. I'm very sorry for how I've been these past few weeks. You must have been worried—and hurt."

She shrugged. "Yes." She picked up the red pillow and looked down at it; she was using gold thread for her embroidery. "It was little Abulhassan's birthday yesterday."

"Oh, Most Merciful Lord." Despite my protests, Zaynab had insisted on naming her son after me; I had forgotten his birthday. My wife normally would have reminded me, but in my guilt and my concern for her safety I had been avoiding her. Of course Zaynab would have said that his grandfather was busy, and of course the little boy wouldn't have cared, but Zaynab cared, and I cared, and my children and grand-children all would have been there. My whole adventure with the prince and Shemselnehar suddenly seemed hopeless, fool-ish vanity, in which I was tossing away everything that really mattered. "Oh, Fatima, will she ever forgive me? Or, no . . ."

The tone of my voice was so desperate that my wife dropped the pillow to look at me. "Of course she'll forgive you."

I blinked and regained control of my voice. "Yes. Yes, of course she'll forgive me."

When our first child was born, Fatima and I had our first big fight. Tradition states that a woman is unclean for forty days after giving birth; the newborn baby is taken from her arms and given to a wet nurse. I thought the tradition barbaric. Wet nurses are never as careful as mothers; the Magians, who don't have such a tradition, have far fewer babies who die in their first months of life. Often sisters or cousins nurse each other's children, but no one in the family was available, so we had to find a servant, a woman without even an aunt's solic-itude. I insisted that Fatima nurse Omar herself. She refused. She cried as he was given to another woman—but it was how things were done. Even if she wouldn't really contaminate Omar by nursing him, the rest of the village would think she had; he might become a pariah. I called her silly, superstitious, and an unworthy mother; she did as custom required. All our children survived, in part because Fatima took remarkable care in choosing and then supervising the nurses.

Instead of calling her names, what if I had called her beau-tiful? What if I had insisted that she was pure and even desir-able, and to prove it taken her in my arms and said that if she were unclean, then we would both be unclean? I had been the unclean one. Certainly I had cared for the life and health of my son, but it was vanity that had made me yell: my wife was being foolish and stubborn, resisting my words of wisdom. What if I had accepted the inevitable, and instead of berating her, comforted her for a mother's sorrow at separation from her child?

"What are you thinking of, husband?"

"Omar's birth."

Her eyes blinked and widened. When I was a child, my mother had told me that bright eyes meant a restless heart.

"I'm very sorry," I said quickly, "for the way I've been. If you knew, you'd forgive me. Well, perhaps you wouldn't, but you would understand why I couldn't talk, and why I still can't. It's too dangerous, Fatima."

"You can't tell me," she said softly, "about how you are helping the Prince of Persia and the sultan's concubine have an affair?"

I said nothing.

"Servants talk," she added.

"Mmm." I looked at my hands for a long moment. It was surprising how little I had to say.

"Fatima," I finally said, "I know I don't deserve it, but I have . . . I have a request." I looked up at her but could not read her eyes. "It's been so long, Fatima." I paused. "Will you call me by my name?"

She looked straight at me. "What shall I say to you?"

"Say to me, Abulhassan, you weren't very . . . or, Abulhassan, you forgot your grandson's birthday."

She smiled. "Abulhassan son of Taher, you forgot our grandson's birthday."

I smiled too, giddy. "And tell me," I added, "tell me: did you ever, so long ago, my goodness, fifty years, did you ever go ask my mother what my real name was?"

Her smile widened. She hadn't many teeth left, but her

smile was still as beautiful as when we were young, and her eyes were playful and open as I had not seen them in so very long. "Yes," she said. "Husband, I did."

"And do you remember what she said?"

"I do, husband."

"What . . . what was it?"

"Abulhassan."

I knew that she was lying.

XVIII

For the rest of the day, each call to prayer called to pray at home. The criers read out those verses of the Holy Book that condemn sowers of schism, command unity among the believers, and decry as perverse those who fight over parabolic passages when God, in His mercy, has given us so many verses of inarguable clarity. In the afternoon water-carriers made their rounds, distributing water at the sultan's expense. Guardsmen rounded up suspected troublemakers; religious men from both parties went from house to house, urging restraint. The streets, usually full of dust and commotion, were as still and empty as at midday in Three Springs, when the sun drove all creatures to cover. Kicking up dust that hung in the air behind him, a water-carrier passed by, straining under his leather sacks of water, his gasps loud in the still air; a religious man hurried past, wrapped up in his cloak; and then the tramp of soldiers was heard from down the street. Dressed in black, carrying sabers and the sultan's black banner, they marched up and down and then back up again.

In my laboratory, I had changed the ashes in the morning; now it was time to start a new experiment. If I didn't want practical work, there was a Greek manuscript, recently acquired, with fragments of Zosima's conversation with Alexander; I could pore over those foreign characters and find some allegory to guide me. I had no desire for any of it. The curfew would end soon, and then Shemselnehar and the prince would leave, if we weren't all captured before then. True, there were many recipes that required only a few hours;

I had neglected them in recent years. Yet I no longer felt like blackening myself with bellows and forge, fiddling with iron and sulfur. What else was there to fiddle with? This world, says the Holy Book, is strewn with flowers for the unbelievers. I went to the storeroom and took out equal quantities of dried violet, water lily, camomile, blue lily, and clove. In my laboratory I mixed them in a mortar that I used to pulverize gold, then placed them in a pot full of water. I lit the stove, staring as the water boiled down. It was a pity that I didn't have fresh flowers; they would have looked so pretty in the boiling water, bubbling blue and white and violet. When the liquid was thick enough, I removed the pot and let it cool as I unwrapped my turban, unclasped my robe, and pulled my shirt over my bare head. The instructions are for a patient's spouse or friend to help, but by myself I rubbed the pleasant-smelling lotion onto my head and then my chest. The flower lotion is al-Shirazi's recipe, against melancholy. It is one of my most reliable medicines, and customers report that its effect is immediate, but that day it gave me no relief: I felt as heavy as before. I dressed. As I finished tying my turban, a thought occurred to me: perhaps the cure's potency lay not in the lotion, but in having one's wife or friend apply it. Well, done is done, and I left the remaining lotion by the furnace; but I went back to my wife's room, to see how the cushion was coming along.

The next morning, the callers announced that curfew was over, but except for the heavily patrolled mosques and bazaars, assemblies greater than five were forbidden. Shortly after, as I was changing the ashes, Isaac came to tell me that a servant of his majesty had come. It was not a normal messenger, he told me, but a great lord. It was evident what he had come for, and I wished to meet this moment with dignity, but I also wanted to finish changing the ashes. I hated to lie at a moment such as this, but the truth would be disrespectful. "Beg his lordship to wait a moment, while I dress." Since the recipe requires one to shovel out one load of old ashes, then shovel in some new, then shovel out some old again, the process is imperfect. Ashes mix: after the first load, each shovel of old ashes inevitably takes some new out with it. It is even likely that some old ashes remain, no matter how careful one is.

The messenger was Musa, the sultan's secretary: a small, thin man as old as I. His eyes had seen so much blood that they wore a constant air of pity, weary but genuine. He was a friend. He spoke little, but his face expressed much; that day I saw nothing besides his universal pity and his pleasure at seeing me. Perhaps I was not yet discovered, or perhaps the sultan had chosen not to tell the man he sent for me. Musa was the one man in the palace who did not listen for gossip or scandal.

We embraced.

"How are you, my friend?"

I shrugged, strangely calm. Perhaps, for all my certainty about my death, on some level I did not believe in it, or did not believe that it mattered. "As well as can be expected," I said. "And yourself?"

He shook his head. More blood, I thought: the rabble-rousers had been drawn and quartered. Gentle Musa, the sultan's official witness, bearer of his seal, had been sent to record the executions.

"On other occasions," he said, "I would insist on a glass of your wife's delicious sorbet and demand happy news of your sons and grandsons, but his majesty is anxious to see you as soon as possible."

I nodded. He took my hand and thus, hand in hand, we set off for the Palace of the Golden Gate.

The sultan was in the small garden, just like the last time I had seen him. There was no sign of Yazid; Musa announced my name, then left me on the threshold. Was it another good-bye? I made my way through sunny willows, past goldfish that sparkled in the sun's rays. The sultan did not rise to greet me. He sat by the chess table, looking out on the bright river and the swaying forest on the far bank. The summer sky was bright and clean, as if it too had been under curfew for a day and now reveled in its freedom. That sky promised life to all hopes, but nature is ironic. I hesitated a moment, then bowed. "It is Abulhassan, sire."

Still looking out at the gleaming river, the sultan nodded. "Sit down, Abulhassan."

I glanced at the board: the sultan had not moved yet. The Holy Book lay on a marble table to his right, but he was looking at another book, which lay open on his lap.

" 'A group of students,' " he read, " 'once drank such a heavy dose of anacardia kernels that one of them lost his wits entirely and came naked to class. When amidst the laughter he was asked for an explanation, he gravely replied that he and his companions had tried the anacardia infusion, which had made them all mad with the exception of himself, who had happily kept his senses.' " He closed the book and looked back out at the river—not at me.

He nodded at the Holy Book. "Are your hands clean?"

"Perhaps I should wash them, sire, before I touch it."

"Never mind, I have the verse memorized." His voice softened as he looked up at the sky. " 'We proposed the Faith unto the Heavens,' " he recited, " 'and the earth, and the mountains; and they refused to undertake the same, and were afraid thereof; but man undertook it.' " He looked down at the sunny water. Why did he refuse to look at me? I was trembling. "Faith is a mysterious and most difficult thing, Abulhassan. All kinds of faith. Are you familiar with the notion of original sin?"

" 'Every person that comes into this world is touched at birth by the devil, and therefore cries out.' "

The sultan smiled slightly. "No, that's the Prophet. I mean the Christians' idea."

"I know of it, sire."

"The Christians, as usual, are almost right. The true origin of our burden is what I just recited: man dared to undertake faith."

I was silent. For over a decade I had listened to his confidences. When he was young, I had heard, he had been the most cheerful of men. His generosity, still legendary, had been reckless before he ascended the throne. He once spent a month's rent from his estates to give a feast in a poor neighborhood; each of the first one thousand guests found a pearl in his cup. The next month he simply returned the rent to the serfs, dividing it among them. His father the sultan had been pleased at the generous thought; he nonetheless forbid him to repeat such a gesture and issued a royal proclamation, explaining that his son's extravagant generosity had been to celebrate the birth of a new prince. The sultan had not hesitated to marry a common woman who had nearly chopped off his head: Zubaidah, the orphaned daughter of a merchant, had at first raised silk worms in her garden to support herself. She had then gone to sea with a load of cargo, trading as men do. When the sultan met her, she had just returned from such a journey.

Traces of the sultan's former self lived on in his warmth and in his pleasure in giving, but his face was worn. He now looked at the chessboard between us without seeing. "My gamekeepers tell me that I own a griffin and two unicorns, but they cannot show them to me. I do have a bear who knows how to fight a sword with his paw. I have fought him myself, many times, always to a draw. He beats nobody, but not even the empire's best swordsmen can beat him; he never falls for a feint and parries every blow as if he were swatting a fly. If only he'd learn to attack, he'd be invincible. Was he trained? Was he enchanted? My daughter Amine refuses to appear before him unveiled: he is really a man, she says, turned into a bear by a witch, and she must not appear before a strange man unveiled. She prays daily for him to return to his real state. He was a great prince, she says, fit for her to marry. And Shemselnehar is unhappy. Very unhappy."

He finally looked at me, and I could read nothing in his eyes except loneliness and an appeal for me to end it. "Abulhassan. Do you have any idea why?"

I shook my head. He looked down at the chessboard.

"Nuraddin came to me," he said, "a little over a week ago. He told me that he had heard strange rumors about Shemselnehar. I stopped him before he could go any further. 'Your ears,' I told him, 'ought to be listening for thieves in the markets and traitors amidst my servants, not to rumors about women.' "

He lifted his gaze to me as if I might have something to say, but I had no response for the sadness in his eyes.

"Nuraddin begged my pardon," he continued, "but then yesterday Yazid wanted to speak about her too. I also ordered him to keep quiet and leave her alone, and I reminded him that you too are off limits for his spies and plots. I was quite stern—I think I frightened him. I was especially angry because I had just told him a few days before to leave her alone. She had told me that she thought she was being followed, and I'm sure that she was." He grimaced. "Since I met her, she probably always has been." He thought for a moment; his hand tapped the chessboard. "Abulhassan. Go talk to her, will you? I think that she'll confide in you."

"Yes, sire. I'll talk to her." Did he not care that, after my last conversation with her, I had told him nothing?

"Perhaps the real problem is just the confinement. I've ordered her not to go about without eunuchs for the moment. Half my people want to riot because they think the laws too lax; I can't have her walking about the streets unaccompanied. It's just for the moment." He looked at me and smiled faintly. "But you are quiet today, my friend. What are you thinking about?"

"Death, sire."

He leaned forward, concern on his face. "Are you ill?"

I shook my head. "I don't think so, sire. But I've been having dreams, intimations." I felt the warm sunlight on the back of my neck. Beads of sweat were forming.

His face relaxed. "And I thought you were opposed to all superstition."

I shrugged.

He nodded, then looked down at the chessboard again. Its white squares shone in the sun. Was I the only one who found the day sweltering? "Death has been on my mind, too," he said. "Yesterday was bloody. It could have been worse. I only had to execute two people, but that's still too many. Most were just poor bastards, hungry and idle; I let them go with a flogging. These two really seemed to believe that God had sent them to restore His law to my empire. I didn't have a choice." He stared at the chessboard. "There are three pillars to my life, Abulhassan: my belief in God, my duty to my subjects, and those few people whom I trust. Events like those of the past few days bring them all into doubt." He paused. "Could I have prevented this bloodshed by making the laws stricter? Was this all some machination by Nuraddin or Yazid,

that a firmer hand on my part could have stopped? I have put
men to death, hundreds over the years, for crimes that are not
explicitly called capital by the Holy Book. I think I'm doing
right, but what if I'm not? Will God forgive me? Or will He
call my laws too lax? Am I living in self-indulgent illusion?"
We were quiet. The chessboard gleamed.

"You didn't make a move, sire." I reddened at my inanity.
I wiped the sweat off my forehead with the back of my hand.

"No. Suddenly the game has stopped interesting me. I
hope that will change, and soon." He looked up and all of a
sudden his face turned into another: cunning, with narrow
eyes. "Why," he said, so softly, so gently that at first I thought
I was dreaming it, "why so many 'sires' today, Abulhassan?"
He knows everything, I thought; he's playing with me.
"Why," so softly, "why, Abulhassan?"

"My death," I stuttered. "I feel it all around me. I am not
myself. I have been talking to Azrael in my dreams. He is
patient, but he is not sympathetic."

There was a tense pause, and then his eyes lurched back
into sadness. He looked down at his hands. "When you die,
Abulhassan, if it is before me, it will be a great, great sorrow
to me. I can only hope that we will meet again in the next
world."

"If there is a next world, it is not for such as me."

"I tremble at the thought of my own Judgment, but,
though I know you think so, I do not think you really are an
unbeliever." I blinked. He smiled. "You have told me that
faith is needed for alchemy."

"Some say so." I shook my head and looked at the chessboard. I saw only burning white and deep black, then shaky
blotches, as when you close your eyes very tight. "Yes. Some
look merely at the chemistry, but others insist on spiritual perfection and total faith: faith in God, sometimes, in all cases in

the formula. 'Those who question the marriage of sun and moon shall never witness the contract.' " I looked up at him. "Of course, I've been a failure. Perhaps because I lack faith. I only go through the motions."

The sultan's smile remained, but it expressed a limited happiness: his cheeks sagged and his forehead was wrinkled.

"Do you know about the imaginary feast that Jafar gave a beggar?"

This was the second time in two meetings that the sultan had mentioned Jafar. How had that other friend betrayed him?

"I've heard rumors, but not the whole story."

He smiled a little wider. As he spoke, that smile took over his entire face. He was remembering Jafar.

"The beggar came to the doors of Jafar's palace. His clothes were simple but spotless; his beard was well trimmed and his shoes shone. He had come, as beggars do, to ask the servant by the gate for leftovers from the kitchen. As I learned when wandering in disguise with Jafar, beggars can be a pretty familiar lot, especially with servants. This one bowed to the ground before the servant as if he were a lord. 'My gracious and honorable lord, forgive a humble man's importunity, but hunger knows no manners. A poor beggar asks the boon of you, my lord, of asking the cook for any scraps that might otherwise be thrown away. Even a crust of bread, my noble lord, is a bounty to a starving man.' The servant happened to be Jafar's chief steward; he knew how much Jafar liked surprises, and this well-spoken beggar intrigued him. Despite his neatness, he was evidently half-starved. His noble speech probably repulsed more men than it attracted; men find it difficult to pity those who seem their superiors. 'My master,' the steward said, 'is a most wise and generous man. I will bring you to him. If you are indeed the honorable man you appear, he may well give you more than a crust.'

"The beggar bowed. 'I am indebted to you for your kindness, my lord.' "

"The steward brought him to the main hall and announced simply: 'My lord, a visitor for you.' He then left the two alone, though I suspect he watched from behind some pillar. The beggar prostrated himself in the doorway.

" 'Rise, rise, my friend, and approach.' The man approached, then prostrated himself again in front of Jafar, who was sitting cross-legged on a carpet.

" 'May God keep you, my noble lord,' the beggar said, 'God who is merciful to those who show mercy to their fellow men. I was reduced to indigence by His will, and now must beg for my bread. Though I shrank at such an importunity, your kind servant thought it best to bring me before you, an honor which I took the boldness of accepting, so if you are angered at such an interruption, the responsibility must all be mine. I have not eaten since yesterday, my lord. If you could spare a loaf of bread, or a few coppers, your reward will surely be great in the next life, as the Holy Book says: "No harm shall befall those men who believe in God, and the Last Day, and give alms out of that which God hath bestowed on them. God knoweth all." ' "

"Jafar was as surprised at the man's speech as at the modesty of his request. He also noticed his clean dress, his half-starved frame, and the pitiful look in his eyes: this beggar had seen little mercy. 'What,' said Jafar, 'in the greatest city in the world, a man such as you is hungry? As his majesty's grand vizier, I am ashamed. You have done well to address yourself to me, and if you do me the honor of sitting down, you shall be my guest for lunch.' The man offered him a thousand blessings, and blessings upon his blessings, while Jafar called out, 'Boy, bring us the water and basin. Thank you!' But there was no boy and no basin. Jafar stretched out his hands, rubbed them together, shook them, and grasped the air as if it were a towel. 'Come, my friend, don't be shy. A man as neat as yourself must want to wash his hands.' 'Thank you, thank you, my lord, and forgive my timidity.' Without changing expression, the man stuck out his hands and went through the same pantomime.

" 'Boy! Bring on the first course! Ah, thank you. Here, break off a piece of bread, my friend, and dig in! The slave who made that bread cost me five hundred dinars.' Jafar stretched out an empty hand to the beggar, who obediently clutched at air and smiled. 'Mmm. It smells magnificent, my lord. Mmm!' He ground his teeth together, swallowed saliva, and smiled. 'Your slave was worth every copper.' 'Excellent! Now dig into this dish,' said Jafar, placing emptiness in front of the man. 'That's right! Don't be shy, my friend. You won't ever taste such tender lamb again!' The man diligently scooped up imaginary lamb with imaginary bread, swallowed his saliva, and praised Jafar's cook. 'I am pleased that you like it, but for a man who hasn't eaten all day, you eat like a bird. I beg you, don't hold back.'

"Jafar next called for goose cooked with vinegar, honey, raisins, chickpeas, and figs. 'Limit yourself to a leg, my friend, there are so many more dishes coming, it won't do to fill up all at once.' 'It is difficult, my lord,' said the man, who was turning pale from hunger, 'with such a delicious bird.' Three or four imaginary dishes followed, then the main course, a lamb cooked with pistachios. 'I insist, my friend, you will eat this dish from my own hand.' And Jafar lovingly fed the poor beggar handful after handful of air. 'Magnificent, magnificent, my lord!' Jafar then called for a stew. 'Marvelous,' commented the man. 'In my luckier days, I too had a good cook, but nothing to compare with this: in each bite I can taste amber, clove, nutmeg, ginger, and other herbs I cannot even recognize. Yet the spices are so well mixed that each one seems to increase rather than drown out the others' flavor. A masterpiece, my lord!' The poor man's stomach growled, but he patted it contentedly as if he had belched.

" 'Well, my friend, if you are satisfied, I will call for dessert. Boy! But are you sure you've eaten enough? I believe that you have been holding back from modesty and are still hungry.' 'My lord, your hospitality is magnificent, and I wish that I could eat more of such delicacies, but I cannot.' 'I insist, my friend, at least try this cake.' 'You are most kind, my lord, but forgive me if I prefer these almonds. I have never seen such large ones.' And the man went through the motions of cracking almond shells.

" 'After a good meal, there's nothing better than a good glass of wine. Boy! Bring out the red!' 'My lord,' said the man, 'I beg you to forgive me if I refuse: religion forbids it.' 'It is impolite to be more scrupulous than one's host,' said Jafar. 'My lord, you are right, and forgive my well-intentioned lie: it is not religion, but my own weakness that urges prudence on me. I have no tolerance for wine, and am afraid lest I commit some indiscretion.' 'Nonsense, I insist that you drink with me.' 'Very well, my lord.' Jafar uncorked an imaginary bottle and poured wine into imaginary glasses. The man examined the air in front of him. 'What a fine, deep color, my lord.' He leaned over to smell it. 'Mmm! Aged in oak, was it not? And I smell cherry and cinnamon too.' He bowed his head to Jafar. 'I beg you, my lord, to permit me the honor of drinking to your health.' He took a sip, smiled, and then rapidly finished off the imaginary glass. Jafar filled it up, the man finished the second glass and smiled widely. 'That was delicious wine, really great stuff, old boy!' Jafar blinked, surprised at such language. 'What? You don't think so? Come on, old boy, smooth as silk, drink up!' He slapped Jafar on the shoulder. 'Come on, all men are equal before God, right? Drink with me, you fool! Drink!' And he actually slapped Jafar's face.

"Jafar stood up. 'Are you mad? Shall I call the guards on you?' The man's face fell; all his boisterousness turned to shame. 'Forgive me, my lord, I beg of you. I had warned you that I have no tolerance for wine, and you see the shameful result. I had foreseen such consequences, and I beg you to forgive me my weakness.' At this Jafar pulled the man to his feet and embraced him. 'My friend, men of your talents are rare; I hope I shall be able to convince you to work for me. But first, let us have a meal, a real one this time.' He clapped his hands; real servants brought a meal as magnificent as the one he had described. The man had formerly been a merchant, and Jafar ended up making him head of his household staff."

The sultan and I were both smiling. My friendship with the sultan was so old, my habit of happily listening to his stories so strong, that I had forgotten how I had betrayed him. The lull lasted but a moment. Suddenly his face fell: he remembered why he had told the story. My guilt and fear returned, and I hunted for something to say. "Did the man stay long with Jafar?"

"Until his death. Since Jafar's goods were confiscated, the man was left with nothing. He decided to go on pilgrimage to the Holy City, but in the desert nomads raided the caravan and took him hostage. He had kept his fine clothes from Jafar's service, and his captors refused to believe that he hadn't anyone to ransom him. They thought he was holding out. He was too frail and old to be enslaved; they finally cut open his lips with a knife and left him to die amidst the dunes. By miracle, a caravan came upon him. His lips are still horribly deformed today; it is painful for him to talk or eat. He was working as a petty scribe when his brother, a remarkably talkative barber, brought him to my attention. But that is another story."

Suddenly his hand darted forward. I blinked. "Soldier to sultan five, Abulhassan."

I stared. Merciful God, it changed the game completely. I would have to move my elephant, then when he moved his horse I would have to move my queen; my right flank would be entirely open. I trembled. I had fallen into a trap. How could I help seeing it as a metaphor?

"Perhaps I am regaining a taste for the game after all. You may think of your next move at home, Abulhassan, for next week. I must hear the latest reports from my spies now. I hope that your work goes well, and that you do not neglect the spiritual goodness on which your experiment with ashes depends. I feel confident that Azrael will remain patient. But be sure to see Shemselnehar."

I bowed.

XIX

The eunuchs did not know me. They put their hands on their swords and smiled when I told them I was to see Shemselnehar, but out of respect for my rich clothes and white beard, one of them left to get Wasif. Mesrour's assistant was a small man, thin for a eunuch, with high, sharp cheeks; always harried, his forehead twitched and his sharp eyes darted without pause. Today he had the grim air of a man weathering a storm, and I thought that those quick eyes examined me. Mesrour always looked at you as if you were a bug, but Wasif's typical air was gruff fellowship. Certainly he was annoyed at having been disturbed. "Forgive them, my lord. They are new," he said curtly. He turned to his men. "This man, Abulhassan the pharmacist, is the one exception. On the sultan's orders, he may come and go as he pleases." They bowed. "Good Day, Abulhassan. Peace be upon you."

"Peace be upon you too, Wasif."

I walked through the orange groves, along the patterned, empty paths of gold, white, and red pebbles. In front, the palace's great windows were curtained; about me the birds kept silent in the heat. The trees gave only superficial protection against the burning midday sun; an overripe orange fell and split open in front of me, oozing hot, sweet smelling flesh onto the pebbles.

I pushed through silk netting into the main hall and almost fell: it was pitch black like my laboratory at night, but this space I barely knew. I did know that the dome was a hundred feet high at its peak, the base perhaps twice that in diameter;

but in the dark I felt as if I were out in the wilderness, that the shadows were not sofas and tables but thorny, poisonous bushes, or nocturnal animals that watched me in the dark. "Hello!" I called out. All remained silent, but had a shadow shifted? "Hello! It is Abulhassan the pharmacist, humbly come to see her respectable ladyship with a message from his majesty."

"Abulhassan! Wait." The sound of flint scratching echoed like a growl; then a lantern glowed on the far side of the dome. The bubble of soft light hurried towards me: it was Mona. As she passed with her lamp, silk couches and jade tables glowed briefly, eerie gold and ghostly blue; the carpet's gold threads shone in a circle around her feet. When she came up to me I saw that her eyes were swollen from crying.

"Mona," I whispered, "has anything happened?" My whisper filled up the dark hall meant for concerts; I felt as if she and I were all alone, in our small circle of light.

"I'm not going to Spain, Abulhassan, I can't. This is my home, and I'm too scared. It's not fair. And I'm scared now."

"Shhh . . ."

"Oh, it doesn't matter, everyone knows. The axe is going to fall. And even if they get out, what's going to happen to me?"

"Hush, Mona, don't talk like that. I'm staying too. The sultan is not cruel, nothing will happen to you. And of course you want to stay, it's natural, and Shemselnehar must have understood."

"She's just so scared herself. I feel like I've betrayed her, but I can't give up my life just to watch her and the prince!"

"No, of course not, you're right, just don't talk so loud. You'll be fine, and if you need it I'll ask my wife to find a place for you. She's not going anywhere either. But why is it so dark in here?"

"She ordered it. She said it's out of respect for the troubles outside, that we shouldn't be showy, but it's really just because she feels like it. The new eunuchs are also all posted outside, and she doesn't want them to see in. She doesn't know them like the old ones."

"Well, take me to her, Mona, please. And you'll be fine, and you're doing the right thing to stay here. I'd miss you terribly if you left. You've always been my favorite among Shemselnehar's servants."

She smiled weakly. "But please do say something to your wife."

"I will."

She turned and led me through the shadows, beneath an invisible ceiling, surrounded by gold.

Lanterns burned in the corridors. After the hall's cool darkness, the burgundy and midnight blue carpets and tapestries felt close and hellishly bright. Mona hurried me through.

"Mistress, Abulhassan." Without waiting for an answer, she turned and hurried back down the corridor.

"Come in, Abulhassan." I pulled open the teak doors to enter; I pulled them shut behind me.

The stars had fled the ceiling, and the desert had left the walls: Shemselnehar had replaced the old hangings with billowy white sheets that shuddered in the breeze, and I suddenly remembered that it was bright day outside. Yet her shutters were half closed; lamps burned low in the corners and on the ceiling. She stood at the far end, by the windows, wearing a simple, loose black cloak that made her eyes look black too. Light and wind fell on her from the shutters in stripes and bursts; the light striped her black cloak white, then the fabric billowed in the wind and the zebra pattern curved and rippled before settling again. There were a full twenty feet between us, but her fearful, haughty gaze made me stay by the door.

"Do you come from the prince?"

I shook my head. "From the sultan."

She looked surprised.

"He didn't say anything enlightening," I continued. "Whatever he may suspect, or know, I don't think that he's about to act."

"Then you have no news of the prince?"

"No. I assume he's waiting at my other house. When I leave you I'll send a messenger to tell him why you haven't come. He must be frantic with worry. How long did the sultan say he'd keep eunuchs around you?"

"A day or two. But you assume, you don't know that he's waiting there."

"No, I suppose I don't, but . . ." I froze. Someone had sent thieves to kill the prince; why wouldn't that someone send some other assassin now?

"What?" Shemselnehar said. "What's wrong?"

"Nothing," I said. "I'm sure he's there. I was just remembering something about my wife—but the prince is there, I know it."

She bowed her head. I took the liberty of approaching her, walking forward amidst the rippling white sheets until my legs too were striped with white light. She looked up.

"I'm going mad, Abulhassan." I waited. She looked back down. "Every servant in the palace knows about the prince and me, perhaps even that we're running away to Spain. So far everyone's been too afraid to talk—they think that the sultan won't believe them and I'll take vengeance. But these new eunuchs . . . These ones don't report to Yazid, but directly to Mesrour, who wouldn't hesitate the blink of an eye to inform the sultan—and Mesrour the sultan really might trust more than me. All I can do is pray that they only stay a day or two, and that that's not too long. And I'm scared about Ali—the prince, I mean."

She now looked me in the eyes, with an appeal like that which the sultan had just shown me, except that hers was only pleading, without any threat.

"Abulhassan, I've been at least as scared of him as of the sultan. I know that by now he has to flee the city, whether or not he wants to, but he could always go without me. The sultan might let him go like that, his family is so powerful, and in any case he could go faster, more secretly without me. What's to stop him?"

She looked down. "And once we're in Spain—if we ever arrive there, which I know we might not—what's to stop him from leaving me then? I won't have anyone, not my father, not even Mona. It would make sense for him to try to marry some rich woman there, and then I'd be even worse off than here, because I wouldn't have anything. In Spain I'll be helpless, and I hate being helpless—I hate it with the sultan, and I'd hate it even more with the prince, because already . . ." She paused. "Already I go mad when I don't see him, even for a day. Already I'm mad with fear that something has happened to him, that those thieves or someone else is going to try to kill him again, and it'll all be my fault. He was perfectly happy before he met me, wasn't he? I don't even know what I'm more scared of—that he'll abandon me or that he'll be hurt."

"Shemselnehar," I said, "why did you insist on waiting, instead of leaving with him immediately?"

She shook her head. "I've been scared we'd get caught, and then, though I know it's madness, I've also been scared to leave here. I'm certainly not happy here, and I know it will only get worse when the sultan tires of me and locks me in the harem for the rest of my life, but at least I know it—I know what awaits me here. And then, as I just said, I've been scared of the prince. Here I have power over him. I could always go to the sultan, pretend that almost nothing happened and that it was all the prince's initiative. He'd believe me." I stared at her.

"But of course I'd never do that," she said. "Never. I would die first. I've bought poison."

"You won't need that," I said. "I have complete faith in the prince. He will wait for you and he will marry you in Spain. I think you have far more power over him than you realize, Shemselnehar, and it's the sort of power that you are unlikely ever to lose, even after your hair is gray and your teeth have fallen out." I hadn't meant to say that last part, but she was smiling, tentatively. I smiled back. "I'll send a servant to confirm that he's at my house, though I'm sure of it. In any event, I need to tell him what's happened. He really must be sick with worry."

She kissed my hand. "Thank you, my lord."

I looked at her a moment, then bowed, but she put her hand on my shoulder to stop me from going. "Wait, Abul-hassan. You lost a fortune when your house was robbed, and I have all this gold that I can't take with me."

I smiled, but shook my head. "It is kind of you, but no, thank you."

"But why? I should give it all to you. Don't think that I'm trying to repay you, I know I can never do that, but it's not even of any use to me."

"I have been a merchant, Shemselnehar, and I do not refuse gold easily. But for where I am going, it will not be of any use to me either."

She blinked, as if waking from a trance. As I watched, the expression on her face changed from confusion to understanding, then to horror. For her I had always been the sultan's friend, one who had power; she had never had any reason to worry for me. "Most Merciful God," she said. "How . . . ?"

"When the eunuchs leave," I told her, "and you hear from me that the prince is ready, as you will, you must leave without any hesitation. You are not the only ones for whom it is too late to turn back."

Her eyes still wide, she nodded slowly.

I bowed.

I dispatched Isaac to my other house with a sealed letter for the prince, then I went to my laboratory. I stopped on the threshold. Someone had been in it. Still in the doorway, I looked around. No change was apparent. But I knew my laboratory so well; I was as sensitive to it as to my own skin. Something had been moved and then put back into place, almost right, but not exactly. I sought out each of my servants, even the apprentices: no one had gone in; no one had seen anyone go in. I went back, and this time I entered. I tiptoed from furnace to stove, still to cauldron; I brushed the edges of pots and flasks to compare levels of dust. Was the mercury flask dustier than the flask of sal ammoniac? Yes, it certainly was, but perhaps I had used the sal ammoniac more recently? But that pestle, it had been lying on the left of the mortar, but it hadn't been tilted that far towards the descensory furnace, had it? Everywhere I found so much food for improbable suspicions that I began to dismiss my intuition as paranoia. The pot of ashes? Weren't the ashes different? Hadn't the pile been smoother, more even at the top? My body went light. I jumped forward and greedily dug my hands into the pot so that ashes flew about me; I grasped the flask's neck and jerked it out. The sulfur was still sulfur, the mercury mercury.

Isaac returned. The prince was waiting at my other house and would stay there; as a precaution, he had gone there using a different disguise than he ever had before. I sent Isaac on to the palace with a message for Mona: "Tell your mistress that her medicine is all prepared. It will keep until she arrives. She can come fetch it whenever she is at liberty."

I continued to poke around my laboratory. First I wiped off the dust that I had just examined on flasks and pots; then I wiped off stovetops, stills and furnaces. I placed mercury, then arsenic, and then salt on the scales of two and then on the scales of five, though I knew their weights by heart. Suddenly impatient, I pushed the minerals to the side and opened up my dissolving furnace. A dissolving furnace has for its center a cube of water. For certain experiments flasks or sealed pots are suspended inside the cube, which is then sealed, and the water heated past boiling. In mine, the water was brown. I ladled it into a bucket, scrubbed the inside, filled it with fresh water, and closed it again. I was preparing to scrub out the inside of another furnace when I heard Isaac cry out "Master! Master!" The beads in the doorway clattered. Mona ran in, breathless.

"The sultan knows everything, Abulhassan! Just an hour ago six of the girls who were there the night when she and the prince kissed left as a group, then five minutes ago Mesrour came and told my mistress to come with him, immediately, and he wasn't at all respectful, he just said, 'Come, you!' " Mona stopped short and took a breath. She awaited my wisdom. Isaac, who stood right next to her, stared at her and then at me and then back at her.

"Go home," I said. "Nothing will happen to you. If you ever need anything, address yourself to my wife." She nodded. I hurried through my shop into the street, then down to the canal. "Ho!" I yelled at a passing gondola, "Ho! Over here! Over here I said!" I was screaming, and I kept on crying out "Over here! Over here!" even after the gondolier had picked up speed. Other men were staring, but that no longer mattered. "Street of al-Mansur, and fast! Ten dirhams for your trouble, and I don't care how wet I get. A man's life is in danger." The gondola shuddered as the pole struck bottom; we lurched forward.

A few minutes later I shook the gates of my house. "Prince! Abulhassan! It's Abulhassan! Come, quick! Come!" I stopped speaking and froze: a strange man with a bright red beard had come into my courtyard.

"What's happened?" he cried as he opened the gates. "Where is she?"

I blinked: it was the prince. As well as dyeing his beard, he had added a large scar to his left cheek and a good deal of padding to his belly. In his plain turban and slightly dirty robe, he looked like an unprosperous merchant.

"She's meeting us on the ring road," I said, "just past the queen's estates. It's a change of plans, but we need to hurry. You have horses?"

"Yes! I'll get them."

He ran back to the stables; I followed him as fast as I could. He helped me mount without asking any questions.

X X

It was the end of the afternoon, and the streets were full of
merchants and peddlers, purchasers and porters, and dust from
the hooves of donkeys and horses. "I am a doctor! Make way!"
I called, and the prince cracked his whip, but we could not
avoid passing near one of the giant bazaars. People were
packed shoulder to shoulder; children seemed to want to
throw themselves under our horses. Guardsmen were on every
corner, passing through every alley, standing by the side of
religious men. Most didn't look at us; several recognized us
and bowed.

The crowd thinned. We sped up to a canter as the houses
thinned too; we passed serfs' huts on a giant estate, where
Queen Zubaidah's banner flew. Horsemen in her own brown
livery, different from the sultan's, stood guard by the gates.

We reached the ring road, so-called because it had been
built to circle the city's outskirts, but the City of Peace had
kept growing. The road now marked the boundary between
Zubaidah's estate and a new series of small villages; the bare,
whitewashed tower of a village mosque stood in the clear blue
sky. The afternoon was drawing to a close, and the plentiful
light was softening. On the right the ring road joined the
Damascus route and on the left the road to Persia. A herd of
camels was coming from the right. I turned towards them, but
the prince stopped his horse. "Where is she, Abulhassan? Are
we early?"

I looked at my horse's black mane and then at the gray
dust on the road. "No. Her servants told the sultan everything.

Mesrour came and took her to him. Mona managed to escape and tell me."

I looked up at the camels and at the cloud of dust surrounding them. Since Mona's appearance I had been rushing, hurrying where duty called me, but now all my duties had come to an end. Shemselnehar had been wise to pretend while she could that she was married, to imagine that she had a home with the young man beside me, to fantasize that she was safe.

I watched the camels plod towards us, on their way to the village slaughterhouse. As the sapphire sky deepened, I was calm. I knew that fear would return, that it would take all my self-control not to blubber for mercy when Mesrour approached with the Royal Sword of Justice. I had seen his face on one such occasion: the Chief of the Royal Eunuchs, His Majesty's Lord Executioner, the Blade Carrier of His Vengeance, had been smug. "I always knew he would come to this," said his cold, glittering eyes. "Good riddance. Perhaps now his majesty will understand that I am his only loyal servant, the only one who dreams at night of how best to serve his mighty hand." Mesrour had been disappointed: again and again, the sultan had chosen to trust other men and women, to look for solace greater than that which his elephant-sized executioner could provide.

In my head Shemselnehar was pleading, the same words over and over, amidst billowing white sheets; she wanted me to tell her that she could rely on the prince.

"Abulhassan!"

I blinked. The prince was speaking to me.

"So what happened next, Abulhassan?"

I stared. "What do you mean?"

"What happened, Abulhassan, after she went to the sultan?"

I frowned. The camels were getting closer; the air was filling with dust from their hooves. "I presume . . ." I paused, and a chill went through me.

"What exactly did you presume? And what do you know?"

"I presumed," I said slowly, "that he ordered her either killed or imprisoned, and that he also ordered your capture."

"You presumed," the prince said. "You don't know."

I nodded. But anything else was impossible, wasn't it?

"And then why," he continued, "did you bring me here, my lord?"

The camels were almost upon us; I could hear their tramping and out of the corner of my eye I saw their heads. To me, camels' thick, curved lips have always made them look as if they were grinning; at that moment they seemed to be mocking me.

"Because I wanted to save your life," I said, "and I was afraid that you would not leave if I told you the truth."

He looked away. "You were right."

The herd engulfed us: sweat, heat, and dust, camel grins drooling, flanks getting whipped, animal after animal trotting past, and then the camelherds' "Peace be upon you" in a desert accent as our horses shifted nervously; mine started and I had to pull sharply on the reins. He then began to rear, but when he came down he stayed still; the prince had jumped off his horse and grabbed my mount's bridle. He cooed into its ear for a moment, then led both horses towards the side of the road. The camels were taller than he was and almost as tall as I was on top of my horse; the prince had to weave his way through gaps in the yellow sea of camel hair. At the side I also dismounted and watched the herd flow by, kicking up dust which stung my eyes until they teared.

Shemselnehar had publicly forfeited the sultan's honor;

she could not be forgiven, and a moment before I had been certain of her death. But at the prince's question the thought had come to me: what if she denied everything? No one in his right mind would believe her, but the sultan might. She herself had been certain that the sultan would accept her word over that of anyone except Mesrour, and it hadn't been Mesrour who had seen her and the prince together. I blinked at the passing camels. Some of them were white like Azrael, but in the fading light they appeared the color of sand. I had always planned to return to the City of Peace. If on my arrival I was not arrested, then the sultan had chosen to believe her. Soon other witnesses would come forward, and the sultan would have to accept the truth and kill us both. Before that happened, I might be able to enter the Palace of Unending Pleasure. It had to be me; only I could possibly get past the eunuchs. Since my life would soon be taken in any case, I would not be risking anything by trying to save her.

The last camel passed; dust and silence remained; suddenly I was certain that she was alive and that I would be allowed to save her. I turned to the prince, who was watching me.

"I'm going back to the city," I said. "If she's alive, I'll bring her here."

"We are both going back. Or at least I am. You . . ."

"You know that I was always planning to return."

He looked at me, then bowed his head.

"You must wait outside the palace," I said. "If she's alive, it will be hard enough for me to get in; I could not possibly bring another man in with me."

He helped me mount my horse. This first flight, so panicked, had been for nothing. We were heading back into the City of Peace, to the palace that lay at its heart. As we rode the prince and I did not look at each other; I felt dwarfed by the empty space and the clear blue sky that surrounded me.

Only the white tower of the village mosque stood out, and it was behind me.

We rode past Queen Zubaidah's estates, past the scattered serfs' huts and the guardsmen in brown livery. We rode to where the houses became closer together and closer to the road, which filled with people coming to and from the evening markets. As houses and people began to surround me, cutting off the horizon and filling my ears with laughter, haggling, and curses, I felt as if the sky too were filling up, but it was only darkening. Poor men's hoods covered their faces in shadow; their silhouettes stretched out, tangled, crossed, and separated again. My fingers drummed my horse's neck, my knees pressed hard against his sides, and I stared straight ahead. Despite the level ground, I felt as if I were falling down into the city, as a man might slide down a grassy slope; and near the city proper, as houses pressed in from all sides, shoulders brushed my legs, and bursts of warm air fell on my face, I knew that I had reached the cliff at the slope's bottom, and was falling freely. I passed through the city gates without even a nod from the guards.

When we neared the palace grounds I looked at the prince; he nodded and drew his horse up.

"If I don't return within an hour . . ." I began to say.

"I'll be here," he said. "Or I'll join you." He smiled. "In one world or another, that is. But you know that I have always believed in the future. I still do. You'll return, Abulhassan, and you'll return with her. I know it."

I looked at him. Was he really so confident? Or was he just trying to call up my courage, as an old man might do for a younger one? His smile was warm, but his eyes showed fear.

"Yes," I said. "We will return. I know it too."

I continued on to the Palace of Eternal Pleasure.

The same eunuchs who before had not recognized me

stood outside Shemselnehar's palace. Now they stared as if I were a ghost; only after several heartbeats did they remember to bow. "I am here to see Shemselnehar," I announced. The eunuchs exchanged glances. They made no motion to open the gate. I glared. "Don't you recognize me?"

"Yes, my lord," said one, but still no one moved. Then the one who had spoken leaned over and whispered to another, who nodded. "One moment, my lord. I shall fetch Wasif."

I shook my head in annoyance. "Very well, but I hope he hurries. I'd like to be home for dinner." The man bowed and scurried off. As the others glanced at me and at each other, I looked away: at the palm trees swaying in columns on either side, then at the silver-plated gates that rose up into the sky. To my eye, the sky had shrunk: on the sides the tops of the tall palms gave it a jagged bottom, and in front of me the palace's white dome meant that I had to lean my head back to see the darkening blue. The sun, peeking through the palms, had turned orange.

"Abulhassan! What brings you here?" Wasif sat on his horse, staring. As always, he pulled on his mustache while his eyes darted, but now they darted all over me: at my turban and beard, dusty from riding; at my mud-splattered shoes and pants; at the prince's purebred stallion; and again and again at my eyes. Wasif had known me for years.

"I'm here to collect Shemselnehar."

Wasif's hand paused on his mustache. "What for, Abulhassan?"

"To take her to her parents. Open the gates, Wasif. I'd like to get her there and myself home before dinner."

Wasif pulled on his mustache; his eyes darted down to my boots and up to my eyes. "There have been strange stories

about you, Abulhassan, about you and Shemselnehar." So she
was alive still, certainly and truly.

"And the slave who spread such slander has been punished
severely. Wasif, if you wish to trouble his majesty, send for his
permission, but it will be you who requests it, not me."

Wasif's eyes stopped darting and rested on my own. Wasif
knew that it was incredible to say that I had betrayed the
sultan; to suggest that I had done so for a pair of lovers made
it ludicrous. He turned to his men. "Open the gates." He
made his horse step backwards; it shook its head and whinnied.
"His majesty is out inspecting the troops," he added curtly,
then turned to ride off through the palms.

"Don't bother to close the gates," I said as I rode in, "and
prepare a horse for my lady, as quickly as you can. Yes, she
will ride it. We'll be leaving in a moment."

I left my horse outside the circle of cypress trees that divided the outer and inner gardens. Once again I walked down
the pebble paths of red, gold, and white that matched the great
hall's carpet, and once again the great hall was dark. I stumbled
forward in the blackness, crouching down and reaching my
arms out to feel for couches or tables, but I still blundered
into objects that I could not even recognize; I tripped and
almost fell under a black dome so high that it could have been
the sky, but the skies in this mortal world are never so utterly
without stars or light. It was only a few minutes, but that
journey across the great hall felt longer than my ride into the
city.

At the far end the corridors' lanterns were lit. I went
down passages lined with tapestries, under upholstered ceil-
ings, up stairs whose rugs sank under my feet and tried to hold
them like mud; I reached Shemselnehar's door. I pushed it
open without knocking.

"Abulhassan! Oh, I knew you would come!" She rushed forward, took my hands, and held them in hers; they were cool and soft. "Where is the prince?"

"Just outside, waiting for you. He's disguised as a fat merchant with a red beard."

She squeezed my hands. "And how are we getting to him?"

"By horse. Are you ready to leave now?"

"Yes." She let go my hands and turned to put on a plain black veil and cloak. "We're going to make it, aren't we?"

I watched her wrap herself in the cloak until she was a flowing, shapeless black mass. "Yes," I said. "We will."

She led the way back down the stairs and corridors, taking my hand to lead me through the dark great hall; with her as my guide, the journey was swift. Only when we reached the cypress trees, where the eunuchs could see us, did she let go my hand and step back for me to lead. I stepped past the trees; the eunuchs bowed.

"Where is the horse for my lady?"

The eunuchs bowed again, and their leader gestured: next to my horse was a white mare, surrounded by half a dozen other eunuchs on horseback.

"I did not ask for guards."

"My lord, his majesty has commanded that she not leave the palace grounds unescorted."

"I am aware of that, and I am her escort. Help me onto my horse. My lady needs no assistance."

Once she was on her mare, Shemselnehar turned to the eunuchs. "What is your name?" she asked the first.

"Yakut, my lady."

"And your father?"

"Arslan, my lady."

She turned to the next. "And your name, with your father's?"

When she had all their names she turned away from them and faced forward, speaking to the road. "It is my wish and my command that you not follow me. You have all witnessed how his majesty treats those who dare disobey or slander me." She nodded at me. "Let us go, Abulhassan. If any are foolish enough to follow, tomorrow I will enjoy the opportunity to reassert my power." I bowed from horseback; none followed us as we began to ride. We passed the villas of those nobles who lived near the palace, and the prince joined us. He and Shemselnehar exchanged looks, and then he dropped back; he rode twenty or thirty paces behind as we passed another guardpost and entered the main road, crowded with people on foot and horseback.

"Left," I said quietly, "to the west gate."

She turned her horse. "That was too easy," she said after a moment.

I nodded. "Once he understood that you did not love him, he never meant to stop you." As she rode, she turned her head to look at me. Of all the men and women in this empire, the largest in the history of man, I was the only one who understood the sultan's heart. Did anyone understand mine? Yes, I thought: my wife. For all her silence and "husband"s, she understood me. I was luckier than the sultan. With Shemselnehar gone, and me dead, he would be alone.

"In his own way," I continued, "he loved you truly. He just did not know how to love you well." As in our very first chess game, he had not even tried to mount a defense; the choices had been all mine. "You will reach Spain," I concluded. "You should be discreet on your journey, but he will do nothing to hinder you. I am sure of it."

She looked at me a moment longer, but through her veil I could not see her expression. We continued to ride in silence. Shemselnehar had wrapped her cloak so that unless you were right in front of her and saw that her face was veiled, you would not guess that she was a woman; we rode through the streets without attracting attention. When an emir appeared with a train of attendants, we waited by the side with everyone else for him to pass. As we approached the city walls they rose higher and higher until they covered the sun; we rode through gray light, shadows, and the occasional lantern's burst of golden light, hanging down from an arch or bridge over our heads. We were simply one pair amidst the crowd as we passed through the gates, and the sun's orange disc reappeared, sinking into the horizon before us. We continued on for some time, until the crowd began to thin. I looked at her, and we stopped our horses. A moment later, the prince joined us.

"You'll go faster without me now," I said. "And remember, Shemselnehar, what I just said. You'll get to Spain. Please try not to hate him. For me, try." Through her thick veil, she looked at me. After a moment, she nodded.

"Now go," I said. "We've already said our good-byes many times."

The prince's face was too sad for me to look at; I turned back to Shemselnehar. Behind her cloak, behind her veil, even her eyes were invisible. Then she leaned over. For an instant she just held her face pressed against mine; then through the silk veil I felt her lips against my left cheek and then my right. "Good-bye, Abulhassan!" Without waiting for me to answer, she turned and whipped her horse. An instant later I felt a beard and rougher lips against my hand. "Good-bye, my lord," said the prince. "Our children will be told that you were their father's true father." Without saying another word, he too turned and whipped his horse.

I do not know how long I stared after them, but when I blinked, only the tip of the sun's orange disc still showed. Stars twinkled in the east, tiny torches flickered from on top of the city walls, and above my head the sky was darkest blue. As the sun slipped below the horizon, the call to prayer rang out from the city behind, but where I was the sound was faint. I gazed at the horizon until the last remnants of sun had faded. My horse had continued down the road on his own initiative, then drifted to the side to graze; I climbed down and let go of the reins. How many years was it since I had been outside the city at night? The sky was full of stars, vaster than my mind could comprehend; I smiled as I bent back my head to look at them. Down below, somewhere on earth, people were coming and going on a road, traveling in a stream that flowed and murmured next to me in the night. The cool, damp breeze felt solid against my cheeks, like a wet cloth; it saved me from vertigo as I stared at the stars and at the blackness, deeper than any pit, and without any bridge to cross over it. The stars were welcoming me home, I thought, home to the throne of God that extends all through the heavens and earth and down into the heart of man, even down into my own heart at that very moment. It was impossible that I could die.

I began to walk down the road, lit only by the stars. Occasional hooded figures galloped past; humble men leading donkeys stood aside for me, bowing their heads with respect. I walked firmly, striding through mud and not turning when galloping horses kicked dirt onto my face and clothes. My own horse followed even though I repeatedly told him not to bother, I would be fine on my own. Before I knew it I had reached the ring road, which went to Damascus and where earlier that day I had come with the prince. The village mosque's tower still stood straight, but now it was a dark silhouette against the starry sky. I turned towards it, passed through the courtyard, and entered the mosque proper.

It was empty, without even an attendant to take my shoes; I simply left them in the foyer before entering the hall. I walked to an edge far from the door and lay down on a rug which the high windows and hanging lamps left in shadow. The sultan was letting Shemselnehar escape; he would let me have this one extra night outside the city.

The mosque was small. Across the dusky dome, God's name, praise of His mercy, and threats of His vengeance on the Day of Judgment gleamed at me in silver. The lanterns' chains were invisible in the dim light; the flames appeared suspended, floating like djinn in the solid-seeming air. Idly, I read the verses. It would be a good time, I thought, to become religious. I had given up rationalist objections long before, so why did faith not come? It needed work, the sultan had said; but why did I not even want it to come?

"My lord, might a humble man be of service? If you are God-fearing, all of Yasin's meager means will be yours to dispose of." A young man had emerged from the shadows; he knelt in front of me, blocking the verses painted in silver upon the near wall. His black beard needed trimming, and the hems of his white robe were splattered with mud, but his hands were soft and his accent elegant. His nose was long and narrow like his face; his eyes and mouth radiated an eerie calm, like that of a corpse that has died an easy death.

I sat up and bowed my upper body. "My lord," I said, "I am grateful for your kindness, but I have need only of rest."

Yasin nodded. "But my lord, this mosque will soon become crowded, as the God-fearing come to pray. Much as it is a virtue to pray together, a man as weary as you appear, my lord, might prefer to rest in quiet. If you so desire, my home is open to you."

Why was he so eager to show me pity? I suddenly realized how filthy my beard had become, that my robe was not only muddy but that its hem had ripped. I looked up; his soft eyes returned my gaze with calm and kindness. Those eyes fascinated me; I had to blink a long moment before I could answer. "You are most kind, my lord. I fear only that I shall impose upon your hospitality."

The man bowed. "My hospitality is my duty, my lord, and I shall send for my palanquin. It will only be a moment."

A palanquin? Was the man mad? He couldn't possibly be wealthy enough to own a palanquin. A moment later he reappeared. "Do me the honor, my lord, of following me outside." Outside were two servants in neat, dark blue cloaks. They stood next to a palanquin of ivory, sandalwood, and silver, though the silver was tarnished and the ivory covered with dirt. I stooped down and stepped inside; its cushions were faded purple, but thick enough to envelop me as I sank into them. It had been years since I had ridden in a palanquin; I swallowed as the wood and silver box lurched up. The carriage had no curtains, so apart from the four poles that held the roof, I had an open view to all sides: I sailed amidst the stars and night; a cool breeze tickled my face as I drifted. Eventually I floated to a villa whose gates creaked as they opened. The garden was unlit, but by the stars I could see that the fountain was dry, the lawn mere dirt, and the orange trees barren of fruit or leaves; only the fig trees showed life. Suddenly the dead orange trees rose above me; the palanquin settled with a bump.

Yasin took me into a windowless room with bare walls and a pile of silk carpets. His servants pulled off several to make a bed on the floor, then left without bowing. We sat, I on the carpets, he on the floor, and his servants arrived with a jug of water and a bowl for us to wash our hands. They followed with a single bowl of cold lentils, a round loaf of bread, and a small bowl of dates. The bowls were silver, but so tarnished that only an alchemist could know it. "In the name of the Most High," Yasin said, and we ate. I scooped up lentils with bread and watched him. He looked up from his food only once, to smile at me. The room's walls were curved: they sloped in to make a dome at the top, where a gold lantern hung. The lamp was so bright that the brown walls seemed close.

When we finished eating, the servants brought in a jug of water for us to drink, then a bowl for us to wash our hands. After they left, again without bowing, Yasin looked up. "If you wish to sleep, my lord, I will leave you now."

I looked at his solemn face, his still eyes so unlike Wasif's; I glanced at the bare walls, warm in the bright light. "I am not tired."

Yasin nodded. We were quiet a moment. "If you wish," he said suddenly, "I would be honored to tell you my story."

I blinked. "Please."

He smiled and looked me straight in the eyes. When he began, it was in the tone of a man who has given the same speech many times, and now recites from memory.

"A little less than a year ago I, Yasin son of Shahriyar, was a wealthy merchant. Besides this house, I owned one in the city itself. Riding was my passion, and my stables contained purebred horses and camels from the Holy Land. One of my colleagues in Damascus had a pretty and virtuous daughter. I spoke to him when I was there on a trading journey, and we agreed on a dowry. I returned home, then prepared to spend several weeks with the family of my future wife. I sent several servants ahead with presents and provisions, but I chose to ride to Damascus by myself. What thrill is greater than riding alone in the desert at night, navigating by the stars? The threat of bandits only increases the thrill, especially when one has a mount capable of outrunning any other. Yet because of the danger I would have to give up this sport when I married. The trip was to be my last adventure.

"My fifth night out I saw a small patch of sand whirling. It looked too small and slow to be dangerous, but I chose to steer around it anyway. It moved with me and blocked my path. I slowed; it spoke. Its voice was soft and shivery, like the morning breeze, or running water. 'Man,' it said. 'Your camel is fast and reckless; he has heavy hooves. I have newborn sons, who are asleep not far from the path you are now taking. If you do not go another way, you may trample them.'

" 'Djinn,' I said. 'I will do as you ask.' I thought that she bowed. In any case, she drifted off down the wadi, no faster than the wind. I watched her disappear, then I looked about me. I was already most of the way through the wadi—I could see the end ahead of me. Have you ever been in a wadi? At night? Below you rocks and silt, to either side cliffs inaccessible to man or goat, and above a strip of stars, the Milky Way, clearer than you can ever see it outside the desert. To go another way, I would have to travel all the way back up the wadi. It was the season when it can rain, and a flash flood might sweep you down the wadi, drowning you. It was one of the dangers that added excitement, but I had already almost escaped it, and running the same risk twice is no adventure.

"I regretted having agreed so quickly. Surely the djinn had not understood my plight; she would have agreed to move her children if I had asked politely. After all, if my camel's hooves could harm them, a flood could too. I would continue down the wadi, I decided, slowly, cautiously keeping an eye out for the djinn or her children. I forgot that djinn are invisible to men unless they choose to reveal themselves.

"A few minutes later—I could see the end of the wadi—a huge mass of sand whirled in front of me and then solidified into thin legs, a giant chest, a fierce head, and huge arms wielding a saber as long as I am tall. It was all the color of sand except for the saber, which was steel. 'Man!' the voice boomed. 'Prepare to die! God is merciful, but I am not! Despite my wife's warning, you recklessly proceeded on your path. Your camel trampled upon my children, my beloved, my first born, and you have killed them! The Holy Book sets the penalty, and I choose the maximum! You have one minute to say your prayers, though I am confident that the Most Just will send your despicable soul to the pit where murderers of infants belong!'

"I jumped off my camel and begged for mercy. I explained how I had been afraid to go back up the wadi, that I had kept careful watch for them and had forgotten that I could not see them. The djinn was merciless. 'If you speak the truth, God may forgive you, but I must have justice. Say your prayers, man!' I told him that I was my widowed mother's only son, that my business was in a delicate stage and my partner was a scoundrel. If I died in the desert without making arrangements, my mother would be left without a copper. 'Grant me a year, O Djinn, and I will swear my most sacred oath to return and accept your sword. But grant me this year so that my mother may not die a poor woman, bereft of any fortune as well as her only son!'

"This moved him. His grandfather had been one of those djinn converted to the Faith by the Prophet himself. 'Man,' he said, 'will you swear upon your soul to return to this spot in one year's time?' 'I will.' 'Do so.' I did. The djinn set me free.

"I returned to the City of Peace. I wrote my friend that

I had been ruined and so could not marry his daughter. I sold my share of the business, provided for my mother, and retired to my old house, which you see around you. I had led an evil life, full of pride and vanity; much of my money had been made dishonestly. With one year to live before returning to God, I have been trying to do good to every man in need, and in this manner I hope to make up for my sins. I believe that God will be merciful, that the djinn was but His instrument, as are we all. That djinn was my salvation. He brought me away from a life of worldly vanity that would surely have ended in everlasting flames. God is truly the Most Merciful."

Yasin's gaze was deathly calm; the gold lantern shone on his ragged beard and dirty cloak. It was several moments before I managed to speak. "My lord," I said hoarsely, "when are you going back to the djinn?"

"In four weeks."

I could not tear my eyes away from his; they were the dull brown of dry earth. He blinked; I forced my head to turn. The wall was the same color as his eyes, it was breathing at me, flowing in and out . . . the walls were alive. I squeezed my eyes shut until the blackness swarmed with red patches. When I opened my eyes my head hurt for a moment, but the walls were walls again, their brown earth like that I used to play in as a child. Yasin's brow was furrowed with concern. "You are tired," he said. "I have spoken too long."

I swallowed. "My lord, your story is worth a month of sleeps, and I am honored that you have shared it. But now I indeed must rest."

Yasin nodded and stood up. "Good night, my lord."

Just after I had blown out the lantern and stretched out on the carpets, the call for the day's last prayer rang out from the village mosque.

XXI

The next morning Yasin himself brought in bread and a small bowl of milk, the same meal that I had had with Saleh: two exceptions in a lifetime of salt and dates for breakfast. I told him that I had to return to the city, but his hospitality had strengthened me. "May you transmit to the djinn, my lord, from a simple pharmacist in the city, a father's condolences on the loss of his children. And may you, my lord, enjoy the merciful death that you have merited." Yasin bowed and led me to my horse, which one of his servants had found the night before. I mounted and rode towards my home.

The day was sunny but without any wind: new dust was kicked up before the old had fallen, and the brown air tickled my throat. Old men and young boys led donkeys piled high with wood or grain; other men sold vegetables and fruit by the roadside, calling out the virtues of their produce as I passed. I thought that the men looked alone in the still, dusty air, tired even though the day had just begun. The city gates were manned by a lieutenant who knew me. He bowed deeply. "A good morning to your lordship." I pulled my horse to a stop and stared at him.

"Do you know me?"

The man stood up. "Why, your lordship is Abulhassan, the pharmacist. May I be of service to your lordship?"

"Have you received any orders concerning me?"

"No, but if your lordship desires any service, I shall be honored to oblige him."

"No, or rather yes, help me dismount." He did so. "Take

this horse to the stables of Prince Abulhassan of Persia—it belongs to his family. Do it at your convenience. You may wait till your watch is over, if you wish."

He bowed. "I myself shall take it to Prince Abulhassan's house at midday, the moment that my watch is over."

"Thank you. I am much obliged. A good morning to you."

"A good morning to you, your lordship."

Was this a dream? Or was it the prince and Shemselnehar who had been a dream?

I walked past smooth, whitewashed houses, then alongside the high walls of villas, their black gates topped with gold and adorned with banners. At this hour, just after the markets outside had opened, the inner city itself was relatively quiet; the people I saw were those privileged few who lived within its walls. Ivory and gold palanquins passed, gleaming in the morning sun while porters sweated beneath their handles. Several young lords who used to frequent my shop walked by, looking green, as if they'd drunk wine the night before; shamefaced, they quickly bowed and hurried on. Just before my house, Zaid, one of the empire's most esteemed clerics, unwrapped his deep black cloak and bowed. "How are you, Abulhassan?" I bowed back. "Well, and . . . and yourself, my dear Zaid?" He shook his head. "These are trying times. I just saw his majesty. He wants me to draw up a new statement of doctrine." I nodded, dumbly. "Well," he said, "I must hurry back to my wife. God keep you, Abulhassan." "God keep you too, Zaid." Dazed, I passed through the gates of my home.

Isaac approached as I was on my way to the laboratory. "Master, a messenger from his majesty came last night. He said you were to go to his majesty's palace as soon as you could, even if it was after curfew, though now I guess that doesn't matter. And mistress also told me to give you a message: 'Your daughter Zaynab asked about you. Please go see her this afternoon.' "

I looked at him closely. "Those were her exact words, Isaac?"

He nodded rapidly. "Yes, master. She made me recite them back to her."

"Thank you, Isaac. You may go."

Until a few weeks ago, my life had drifted from one year to the next without any change; now there were many new things I would do if I had one more year to live. Instead, I only had time to change the ashes. I would then wash my hands, face, and beard; I would put on clean clothes to face the sultan, my friend.

I went from the garden's daylight into my laboratory, which was dark: only a brown glow penetrated the leather window coverings. I made my way to the furnace, knelt down, and opened it. Red coals shone onto my face; there were a lot of ashes. I reached for the shovel. Still staring at the coals, I reached over my head to dig into the pot of ashes on the furnace's top, the pot that contained my flask of sulfur and mercury. I unloaded the cold ashes into a bucket, then thrust the shovel into the furnace for a load of fresh ones. Rather than risk scattering these on the floor, I stood up to deposit them. My eyes had been staring at the coals' red glow; in the gloom they saw only black for a moment, but I knew where to empty the shovel. I transferred several more loads. On the fourth or fifth shovelful of old ashes, a gleam caught my eye—a gleam that came from neither sulfur nor mercury. I put down the shovel. For a moment, I stood still; then I dug my hands into the pot. My left hand was in old, cold ashes; my right hand was amidst hot, fresh ones. I lifted out the flask. It was full of gold.

Even though I knew that gleam better than any miser, I

carried the flask over to my measuring table. I lit a lamp and measured the gold's level in the flask; from that I calculated its volume. Then I weighed it. One ratl of sulfur and one ratl of mercury had created nearly five ratls of gold. It was a miracle. Had my laboratory been entered? But what intruder would choose to give me a small fortune? The laboratory was already full of my own movements; it was too late to look for evidence of tampering, even if I had cared to. I rang for Isaac.

"Here," I said, handing him the flask. "Give this to my wife. Tell her it is for household expenses." I thought of going to see her myself, but I knew that if I did I would not be able to bear it. Besides, what could I say to her? When Isaac left I went to change clothes, to go to the sultan.

From my gates I walked through the morning air to a canal, then strode along the glistening water; I wanted to see some ducks. I was, I realized, more like my wife than I had thought: I had never enjoyed the nightingale's song as much as the duck's honest quack. That day the water was smooth, bright in the sunlight; I saw no ducks or even fish, just an occasional piece of wood floating gently. The still, silvery stream appeared solid, as if it might support my weight if I tried to walk across it.

I returned to the city streets, passing villas of lords I had known, and arrived at the Palace of the Golden Gate. I had not met a single guardsman.

"Ho! Who goes there?"

"Abulhassan the pharmacist."

The gates swung open; the guards bowed. "Enter, my lord. His majesty is expecting your lordship."

I walked down the outer garden's marble path; the silver-plated trees glimmered vaguely. I had gone perhaps halfway before I noticed the stillness. Usually peacocks strutted, swans drifted in pools, and turtledoves, parrots, and every known kind of songbird sang and fluttered about with their blue, red, and gold feathers. Now only the leaves of the trees rustled. The animals were all gone. At the palace proper the gates were open; the guards bowed to me.

"His majesty is awaiting your lordship in the throne room. His majesty desires your lordship to enter unaccompanied, if it please your lordship."

I walked into the great hall, its lamps dark for the first time in my memory. The sultan had never received me in the throne room, where he heard supplications from his subjects and ambassadors from abroad. In increasing darkness, I crossed the gigantic hall. I passed underneath its carved arches and painted ceiling, past the tile mosaics on the walls and the fountains that spouted musk and rose-scented water into the darkness; all was silent except for the sound of the water falling into basins. At the doors to the throne room I found Yazid. He did not bow; his tight lips and black eyes showed anger and also fear. "His majesty has changed his mind," he said curtly. "Go to the small garden. And hurry."

I walked through the Babylonian willows. He was sitting by the chessboard, looking out at the water. As I approached, I saw that the chessboard was bare.

"Is that you, Abulhassan?"

"Yes, sire."

"Stay where you are, please. I don't want to have to look at you."

We were quiet for a moment.

"Do you know what happened yesterday, Abulhassan?"

"I can guess, sire."

"I didn't ask if you could guess, I asked if you knew."

"No, sire."

Again, all was quiet for a moment. The willow trees swayed in the breeze.

"One of Shemselnehar's slaves was brought to me. She claimed that Shemselnehar and the Prince Abulhassan, the Persian, were in . . ." He paused. "She said that they were having an affair, and that you, my oldest and most trusted friend, were the intermediary—the procurer, if you will. She even said that you had introduced them. I called for Shemselnehar. I will not tell you what went through my head while I waited for her. In the past, I have found relief in telling you my thoughts and feelings, but now I know that they have never interested you particularly, except perhaps as amusement. For all these years you have simply been pretending friendship.

"Shemselnehar came. She was pale, but her eyes were fierce. I could see that Mesrour, that ox, had heard the slave's story and treated her roughly. I ordered Mesrour to leave, so that she and I were alone together. We were in the throne room, because that was where I was when her cursed slave came in. She didn't bow, and she didn't say anything to me. I came down from my throne and knelt at her feet and I took her hand, which was icy. Since my father's death, Abulhassan, it was the first time that I have knelt to any man or woman.

" 'My love,' I said, 'your slave came in with a tale of your infidelity. I am horrified that Mesrour and your other servants heard it, and I, your other slave, will punish Mesrour severely for his disrespect. My heart is sick but my head is clear, and you can cure my heart with a mere word. Tell me, my love, that the story is untrue, and I will believe you and torture anyone who dares disbelieve you until he will swear upon his soul that you tell the truth. Just say the word, Shemselnehar, say, "Harun, believe me, and not that slave." '

"I felt her hand warm a little, and I dared to look up. She was looking down at me, and only now, Abulhassan, only now that she is gone, only now can I admit to myself what I saw in her eyes. It was not gratitude or even relief. It was pity. 'Believe me,' she said after a moment. 'Believe me and let me go. I am still feeling ill.'

"I looked down again. 'Very well, Shemselnehar. I shall do as you ask.' I let go her hand. As for the rest, Abulhassan, you know it better than I do."

The willow trees were swaying; cold leaves brushed against my hand. The sultan looked down at his knees, then out at the water again.

"I will tell you that last night, after she left, I went into her room. There, on her bed, was the robe she had been wearing the last time I saw her. Inside the sleeve was a flask of poison."

He clenched his hands, then released them and pressed his palms together.

"Who sold her the poison? I tell you, Abulhassan, I thought of ordering all the pharmacists in the City of Peace killed. But then I realized that would mean your death, and so I was merciful."

The wind had died down. The only sound was the river, lapping against the wide stone steps that led from the sultan's chair into the water. I suddenly realized that I was going to live, that I would see my wife and visit my daughter that afternoon. I would see my grandson Abulhassan, who over time might know me as the prince had and my own sons had not; but I did not see any way to convince the sultan, who had been my last friend, of my love for him.

On the steps, the water lapped and splashed.

"Why . . ." I paused. "Why don't you kill me?"

"I planned to," he said. "I am ashamed to admit it, but I tried to give the order. Mesrour stood before me and waited." He shook his head. "I couldn't make the words come out. I could not order your death." He glanced at the bare chessboard for a moment, then, slowly, brought his hands down to rest on his knees. The river shone in the morning light. "Yazid too knows to leave you alone. He believes that it was all a plot between you and me to disgrace him, but it doesn't matter what he believes—he knows to obey me. And Nuraddin, needless to say, is delighted with what you've done." He shook his head. "But none of that concerns you, and really, none of it concerns me either. The Angel of Death shall wait his turn, Abulhassan. Now leave me. Leave me and let me never see your face again."

I looked at my feet but did not move. When I lifted my head, I saw Harun, all alone, staring out at the shining water. "Harun," I said. "Harun."

He said nothing.

I stood as long as I could bear it. Then I bowed, placing my hand on my head, as is customary when his majesty gives an order.

XXII

Once, several years ago, the prince told me a story from his childhood.

His family had a servant named Musa, who had grown old in their service. Never the quickest of men, Musa's mind had slowed further with age. One day, the prince cut a small hole in a bag of flour that he had to carry. Musa picked up the sack, slung it over his shoulder, and trudged off. The flour trickled down his back, inside his cloak, out of his pants, and onto the backs of his shoes. Old Musa kept plodding forward, one foot in front of the other. He did not even quicken his pace, though his burden was becoming lighter with each step. By the time he reached the kitchen, the bag was empty. Musa stared, then sat down on the floor. He looked straight ahead as the kitchen servants gathered around, saw the trail of flour, and began to laugh. The prince watched it all with delight; it was one of his most satisfying pranks.

Several hours later, the prince entered the warehouse on a whim. He saw Menaus, the steward, beating Musa. It was the first time the prince had seen a beating. Musa's face cringed with pain at each fall of the whip, then returned to a look of resignation. The whip left red marks on the old man's back. Menaus completed the punishment; the prince approached; and Musa shuffled off. He had the same plodding step as when he had been carrying the flour.

"Why was he beaten, Menaus?"

"For carelessness, most noble lord. He wasted a bag of good flour."

The prince ran out into the fields. Try as he might, he could not forget what he had seen. That evening, he told his mother what had happened.

The Lady Khadija shrugged. "That was wrong of you. But as for the slave, he still should have been more careful."

After evening prayer, the prince went to the servants' quarters. They were at the back of the estate, on the far side of the fields. Mud huts pressed one against the other; straw mats and cotton clothes lay on rocks and on roofs, drying. Several women were on top of the roofs, taking in clothes for the night; other women cooked and talked over copper cauldrons. Men were sitting around another fire, drinking and talking as night fell. Children played with pebbles in the dirt.

At the prince's appearance, the women stopped stirring their cauldrons; those gathering clothes let them drop; mothers hushed children and grabbed them by the hand. The men froze. After a moment, several tried to hide their cups in the folds of their robes; the one who held the jug looked vainly for a hiding place, then grasped the handles and stared at the prince, insolently. Only several days later, when talking to the steward, did the prince understand that they were drinking wine.

The prince felt a chill inside him that he had never known, but he still pushed on. "Where is Musa?" he asked. "Old Musa, who carries sacks of grain to the kitchen?"

A murmur ran through the crowd; a young woman disappeared into a hut. A moment later, Musa shuffled into the firelight, rubbing sleep out of his eyes. He bowed, too old and too tired to be fearful.

For the first time in his life, the prince's voice shook with nervousness. "I have come to apologize to Musa," he told the crowd. "Today I cut a hole in a bag of flour. He was punished for my mischief."

Musa stared at him.

"Today!" the prince said. "You were beaten for a bag of grain!"

Musa shook his head.

"I want to apologize and make amends!"

Musa still said nothing; the prince stepped forward. "Here." He pressed a gold dinar into the old man's hand. "And I am sorry." He turned and left.

Several weeks later, the prince came to the servants' quarters again. He had managed to acquire a jug of wine, and he brought it with him. He had hoped the men would let him sit around a fire and drink with them, but they were even more frightened than before. To drink wine with the young master! It was inconceivable, and not just because of the punishment his mother would inflict. The prince understood: there was at least one place in the world where he was not welcome. That place had seemed happy and warm until he entered it.

The prince began to treat his servants with respect and to question his mother's customs. He ceased to be satisfied with his life.

"If not for Musa, my lord," he told me, "I don't know if I ever would have sought you out."

If not for Musa then, I thought, my life too would have been different.

After my final meeting with the sultan, I left the Palace of the Golden Gate, to which I would never return. When I arrived home, my servants stared as if I had returned from the dead.

"Where is my wife?" I asked. "Where is Fatima?"

The servants murmured, then Isaac ran off into the harem. A moment later he returned, breathless. "She went to see your daughter Fatima, master. She said that she did not want to wait for you here alone."

I nodded. My eldest daughter was named after my wife. I had insisted on it, so many years before. "Run to my daughter's house, Isaac. Tell my wife that my life has been spared. The danger is past."

He blinked, then bowed and ran off. My servants still stood around me, in a circle. "His majesty has been merciful," I told them. "He is the most merciful of men, and I am deeply saddened that I shall no longer have the opportunity to serve him. I have been spared, but not pardoned." I looked at my servants, who continued to stare. "That is all," I said. "I have nothing more to tell you. Go back to work."

When they had gone, I stood alone in my courtyard. The morning sun shone hot upon my forehead. My daughter Fatima lived in the outer city; it would take an hour for Isaac to reach her house, another hour, at least, for my wife to come home. What was I to do? I had lived my entire life with one goal or another in front of me. After a moment, I left my house. I walked to the home of my daughter Zaynab and my grandson Abulhassan, whose birthday I had forgotten. People turned to stare as I walked, but what did I care for the eyes of others?

Fear returned at the gates of Zaynab's house. What would I tell her? What would I tell her husband Fadil? Their servants peered out at me. Only after a moment's hesitation did they open the gates.

"Announce me to my daughter, please."

Zaynab rushed out, all surprise and smiles. "My lord father!" She kissed my hand. "Why didn't you warn me you were coming? What's the occasion? And where's mother? Fadil's with a student right now, I'll get him when he's done with his lesson. We'll all have lunch together, if you like."

I looked at her. Of all the people that I knew, Zaynab and Fadil paid the least attention to what happened in the city. They were too involved in each other, in their children, and in Fadil's music. The servants knew, I realized, but no one had told her.

"I've just come for a visit, Zaynab. I am sorry that I didn't come on Abulhassan's birthday. I was so busy with, well . . ." I bowed my head. "You know me, Zaynab. I was far too busy, as I always am, or always was. I'd like to see him now, if I can. If he's not . . ." What did children do during the day? I had no idea, I realized. He wasn't old enough for lessons. "If he's not busy," I finished.

Zaynab smiled wider. "My lord father, of course he's not busy. What an idea!" She took my hand, continuing to talk as she led me to the nursery. "Busy! Wait till I tell mother you said that. Busy indeed! He could be napping, my lord father, but busy!"

I smiled with her. This visit was going to be easier than I had thought. How could it be that I had never thought to come as I was coming now, just to visit? As Zaynab brought me through the blue-and-red beads in the nursery doorway, I knew that I had been granted a second chance at life.

My grandson had been napping; he woke when we entered. He and I looked at each other for a long, serious moment. It was evident that he had no idea who I was, and I admired his caution.

"Hello, Abulhassan," I said to him.

He stood up, stepped to the side, and grabbed onto his mother's leg. I watched. He was adorable, yes, with the round face and pale skin of his father, the bright eyes of his mother and grandmother; but I had no idea what I was supposed to do.

Zaynab picked him up, hugged him, then put him down again. "Go on," she said, "Go and kiss the hand of your grandfather. He's to me what your father is to you. Go on, now, go over and say, 'my lord.' "

"No, Zaynab," I said. "Not my lord. Just grandfather."

She smiled. "Say, 'Hello, grandfather.' "

Abulhassan buried his head in her robe. From there, within the folds of cotton, I heard him murmur, "Hello, grandfather."

I smiled.

"Good!" she said. "Now walk to him."

Thinking it might help, I knelt down, just as I had so often done in front of a furnace, and stretched out my arms. My grandson kept his head buried in his mother's dress. I continued to kneel with my arms outstretched. I felt silly and was sure I looked it to Zaynab, but I didn't want to give up. I had spent a lifetime kneeling before furnaces; I could spend an afternoon kneeling for my grandson.

"Go on now," she said. "Have you forgotten how to walk? Do you want your grandfather to think you don't know how?"

He kept still a moment longer, then turned suddenly. He walked over to me, briefly touched my outstretched hands, then turned around. He wanted to run back to his mother, but he tripped on the way. After a moment's hesitation, he began to cry. Zaynab picked him up and cooed. He cried furiously for a little longer and then, without any transition, stopped and smiled at her.

I was amazed. I had never seen any of my children cry; Fatima would have forbidden it. Could all children do that, stop crying in an instant? It was, I suspected, something special about my grandson, a wonderful ability of his, that he could stop crying so quickly.

"What does he like to play with, Zaynab? He does like to play, doesn't he?"

She presented me with my choice of toys; I picked a pile of wooden blocks. They were painted different colors, and somehow reminded me of alchemy which, after all, is just a matter of combination. With great concentration on both sides, he and I settled down to play. It is harder than one might think to play with a young child: as he built walls and houses, called certain blocks sheep and others camels, I had to help him, but if I helped him too much he became angry.

We had scarcely finished the fold for sheep when Fadil arrived. He had a trim white sash tied around his blind eyes; he smiled as his son rushed to hug him, and then smiled wider when Zaynab told him that I was present. "Well, well, my lord father, this is an honor."

I stood up from our blocks and gave my hand to be kissed. This simple gesture was always a strange moment with Fadil: he had to grope for my hand and then feel it for an instant, gaining a grasp, before he brought it to his lips; his extra effort made the formality seem meaningful.

"So you are staying to lunch, my lord father?"

"Yes, Fadil."

"Very good, very good indeed. We are very much honored." He smiled again.

Every year, on the major feast days, Fadil came to our house, but for some reason, it was only that day that I noticed how he had changed. He was no longer the slim boy my daughter had fallen in love with; he was a prosperous, plump man, with a few gray hairs in his beard and an air of being pleased with the world. Yet he still smiled easily and sweetly, puzzled, as if he knew that happiness was all around him but he was not sure why.

Fadil groped for an instant and found his son's shoulders.

"So you've been playing with this little monkey then, eh?" He picked up his son and swung him through the air; my grandson squealed with delight. When he put him down, Zaynab took her son in her arms. "Come now, Abulhassan, your parents are going to eat with your grandfather now." From the look of surprise on his face, it was clear that he was accustomed to eating with his parents, but he said good-bye very properly. Fadil groped for my hand.

"Follow me, my lord father. We'll have lunch in another room."

Though blind, Fadil knew his home. He led me confidently through the garden to a small, pleasant room, with simple cushions and carpets.

"So, my lord, any news worthy of mention?"

I frowned. "Some, yes. But I'd like to wait until my daughter returns."

Fadil nodded and smiled. "Very well." He said nothing else; we sat in peaceful silence. Fadil and Zaynab liked me, I realized. They would continue to like me even after I told them what had happened. If, because he was my son-in-law, Fadil now performed less often, and never at court, he would not be angry; he would just spend more time playing music at home, for himself and his wife.

Zaynab entered with a water jug and a basin. As Fadil and I washed our hands, I noticed that my daughter too had grown up. She too was plump, and though her hair was long and dark, it was not as thick as it had once been. Happiness had kept her young, but she now had hints of lines at the corners of her mouth and eyes, though they only made her prettier. I dried my hands in the towel she handed me. I was amazed that I had fathered such a daughter, and I was stunned that I had put this—this opportunity to have lunch with them—at risk. I hadn't known what I had.

A servant brought in plates of food. Zaynab first served
me, then turned to help her husband. She took his hand and
placed it on all the different dishes, telling him what was what;
Fadil's fingers moved eagerly until he smiled with recognition.
She fed him several bites with her own hand before leaving
him to eat on his own. He ate with great pleasure, compli-
menting his wife after each dish. "This lamb is delicious, my
lord father, is it not? Would you ever have given her to me if
you knew what a wonderful cook she was? If I were still a
betting man, I would bet not."

When we finished, Zaynab wiped off his hands and
mouth with a cloth until he grasped her hand and kissed it.
She giggled and withdrew her hand, glancing at me.

I wished that Fatima had come. "Next time," I thought.
"And how wonderful, how lucky that I can say 'next time'
and know that it will be possible."

Zaynab stood to remove the plates, but Fadil put his hand
on her arm. "Our lord father has some news to tell us."

She sat back down.

"I don't know where to begin," I said. I bowed my head.
"I am surprised that you haven't heard any rumors."

I looked up. Their faces were attentive but blank. Fadil
had noticed the tone in my voice; his expression was unusually
solemn. It was just myself I was thinking about, I realized.
What about the sultan? I had lost a friend, but I still had
Fatima; I still had Zaynab and Fadil. Harun was alone, with
Nuraddin, Yazid, and a pair of sons who were preparing to
kill each other as soon as their father died.

Would he ever permit me to explain? I closed my eyes. I
had helped humiliate him in front of the empire. Even if some
day he wished to, which was far from certain, he could not
forgive such an insult. I would wear white, I decided, white

until the end of my days. Sooner or later, he would hear of it. He would know what it meant.

"I have betrayed his majesty."

Zaynab's eyes widened. Fadil pursed his lips and was still.

"He has chosen to spare my life, but I am never again to enter his presence."

We were quiet.

"How," Fadil finally said, "did you betray him, my lord father?"

"I helped Shemselnehar run away with Abulhassan Ali, the Prince of Persia. They left last night. Merciful as he is, the sultan permitted them to escape."

Zaynab stared. Fadil was nodding slowly. What had happened, exactly? I had no idea how to explain it.

"Why, my lord?" asked Fadil.

"I'm not sure. It's as if I were drunk. I did what I had to." I paused. "It's still very confusing to me. I just saw his majesty this morning, right before I came to you. I had expected to die."

"We are honored, my lord father," said Fadil after a pause, "deeply honored that you chose to come here, to us, at this moment. We hope that you will come here often."

Zaynab looked at Fadil, then reached over and squeezed his hand. After a moment's hesitation, she leaned across the lunch plates, touched my hand, and then squeezed it too.

I smiled. "Thank you, my daughter. Thank you, my son." I stood up. "I think I had better go. Fatima may have returned home by now. But I'll come back soon. Next time, perhaps, I'll be better able to explain."

Fadil stood up too. "Come for dinner tonight, my lord father. Come and bring my beautiful mother-in-law with you. You are never here often enough."

"Well," I said. "Well. Perhaps I will."

I walked home, ignoring the stares from passersby.

My wife had not yet returned; I entered my library, which was cool and dark. What had happened? I wanted to tell Fadil, Zaynab, and my wife. One day my grandson Abulhassan would want to know too. He ought not to hear only the rumors, the stories that would grow distorted with the years. Yet more than my grandson, I thought suddenly, more than my wife and more than my children, the person whom I wanted to tell this story to was Harun. If I could make him understand how much, even in my betrayal, I cared for him—how much I loved him—then after my death I would face the bridge to the afterlife, if not with confidence, then certainly with hope. There just might be a spot, before the golden gates of Paradise, where I could wait along with the other sinners who had still done a little good in their lives.

"I could not order your death," he had told me. If I wrote my story, I thought he would read it. He could never forgive me, at least not publicly, but who knew? Perhaps one day a mysterious merchant would enter my villa, his face covered by a hood. He might ask for medicines or simply hospitality, but without a doubt, at some point in our conversation, he would ask if I liked to play chess. It was something to hope for.

There was one thing I had to do before I started writing. I stood up and went into my laboratory. I stood amidst the dark furnaces and stills, the glimmering scales and flasks, and I called for Isaac. "Come," I said. "Bring me wood and coal." I fired up my largest furnace. The coals turned red and my face turned red with them; the edges of my beard began to smoke.

"Bring me the beakers, all of them, and the glass cups," I told Isaac. He brought them. One by one, I fed them into the flames. "Now the cloths," I told him, "the filters of hair and of silk. The scales, both the brass and the silver, the sets of two and the sets of five." My precious scales melted into slag. "Bring the stills, bring the brazier, tongs, shears, and hammer." He brought them and then my powders and liquids, the jars of sulfur and mercury, the flasks of verdigris, cinnabar, sal ammoniac, arsenic, pigeon dung, vitriol, camel bone marrow . . . I fed in jars and pots, mortars and pestles, mirrors and weights, salt and silver. I stared into the flames as the instruments melted, as mercury ran and then vaporized in the incredible heat. Behind me others besides Isaac were gathering, but I did not turn from the flames. "More jars," I called out. "More metals and tools and powders. Bring whatever will fit, and break what can be broken so that it will fit." I no longer knew what was placed in my hands; I pressed everything into the furnace and stared at the flames. My head was light and my eyes, full of fire, began to tear.

Although I had not turned from the flames, I suddenly knew that my wife had entered. I closed my eyes. Without the prince, without the sultan, and without my alchemy, what did I have in my life, except her and the children?

I stepped back from the furnace and opened my eyes. From a few steps back, the flames weren't quite so blinding.

"Isaac," I said. "You and Tarik will hire porters, and this afternoon carry all of this equipment, everything that I could not burn, and cast it into the river." I turned around. All of my servants had gathered, even those that worked in the kitchen. My wife stood among them.

She looked at me with her clear bright eyes. Her face was blank, but after fifty years, I knew her well. She understood what had happened; she was grateful that I was alive; and a sob of happiness welled up inside me. All my life, I had been selfish and distracted. What had I done that she should be happy that I lived? What had I done to earn her love? Yet there she was, standing in my laboratory. If there was a God, He surely was the Most Merciful.

I wiped the sweat from my brow.

"Fatima," I said. "I went to see Zaynab and Fadil this morning, when you were out. They invited me to come back for dinner this evening. Will you come?"

Her eyes held mine. Although her lips were serious, I knew that I saw a twinkle in her bright, bright eyes. "Go yourself," she said finally. "Go see your daughter and your grandson. Another time I shall come with you, but this evening I shall stay here . . ." Her eyes twinkled brighter and now even her lips gave a hint of a smile. "I shall stay here, Abulhassan."

Abulhassan. After half a century, she had called me by name again. I bowed my head, unable to stop a smile, silly like a child's, from spreading across my face. "Thank you, Fatima. Thank you." I looked up, still smiling. "But, Fatima, my other name, the one my mother gave me?"

Her smile turned into a grin, mischievous as only she could be. "Maybe later, Abulhassan, maybe later. But Abulhassan is the man I married."

She was right, as she always was. She held my gaze for a moment longer, then turned to leave, beckoning for the servants to follow. After a moment I left too. I left my laboratory to walk the way I had just come, through the streets of the City of Peace to the home of my daughter and her son, who was named Abulhassan, after me.

AUTHOR'S NOTE

The sultan Harun al-Rashid ("the righteous") ruled from 786 to 809 AD (164 to 187 in the Islamic calendar.) My story is set towards the end of his reign, some years after he executed Jafar al-Barmaki. Harun's sister once asked him why he had killed his most trusted friend and advisor. "My child, my life, my greatest happiness," he answered, "why should you wish to know the reason? If my right arm knew the reason, I would cut off my right arm."

The poem attributed to "Abu Nuwas" really is by Abu Nuwas, the great poet, drinker, lover, and favorite of Harun's court. The "old song" Abulhassan quotes in the novel's fifth paragraph is from a poem by al-Shirazi. The other quote I give to Abu Nuwas, "only drunkards understand the language of the rose," is actually by Omar Khayyam, who lived several centuries later. The reader will forgive this anachronism. It is very much the sort of thing that Abu Nuwas would have said.

The pharmaceutical and alchemical recipes were all available in the medieval Arab world, and Abulhassan's attributions (to Jabir, al-Siddaq, etc.) are as accurate as the murky world of alchemy permits. The "Holy Book" is, of course, the Holy Koran. My quotes are from George Sale's English version. The religious controversies presented in this novel are also historical, though some of them happened slightly after Harun's death.

Abulhassan, the prince, and Shemselnehar are my own inventions. My original inspiration was a story in the *Arabian Nights,* "L'histoire des amours d'Aboulhassan," in Antoine

Galland's translation. The similarities between the fairy tale and my novel are limited to the names of the characters and fragments of the plot. Jafar's imaginary feast and certain details about Queen Zubaidah are also not historical, but inspired by different tales in the *Arabian Nights*.

The City of Peace was founded in 758 AD, soon after the end of the civil war that caused Abulhassan so much suffering. By the ninth century, when the largest cities in Europe had at most forty thousand people, the City of Peace had over a million inhabitants. Many people had already begun to call it by its present name, Baghdad.

I have recreated the city as accurately as historical documents permit, but I have taken some liberties. The palace in the city's center, for example, sometimes called the Palace of the Green Dome and sometimes called the Palace of the Golden Gate, was standing in Harun's day, but he chose to live in another palace, outside the city walls. There are other, similarly minor details that I have altered, but I believe that I have remained true to the spirit of the times, at least as they were for the privileged classes.

Harun's empire stretched from Afghanistan to the edge of Spain, where a rival Muslim dynasty ruled. After his death, his sons plunged the empire into civil war. Baghdad never regained the glory of Harun's day. His city thus became the place of legend, where storytellers set djinn and flying carpets, magic lanterns, underground treasures, and star-crossed lovers. Like the prince and Shemselnehar, Abulhassan and Fatima, these lovers usually end up together, more or less happy, and more or less forever.